A Male Doberman

Named Esther:

A Mordecai Glass Mystery

Howard Rogers

A Male Doberman Named Esther:
A Mordecai Glass Mystery

ISBN-13: 978-1546518556
ISBN-10: 154651855X

I am very grateful to Casey for being my friend and mentor, and to Diana for creating the perfect book cover. I appreciate all the efforts of those who critiqued my work, especially Barry, my writing partner. And thanks to Ruth who put up with me and my writing for twenty years, and, of course, to China, the Doberman who was the model for Esther.

Cover Art & Design by Diana Huang
dianahuang.com

ONE

Uncle Julius, owner of the Stein Detective Agency, tightened his grip on the steering wheel, his hands turning ghost-white as he drove into the turf of the South Side Dragons, a motorcycle gang that favored using and selling drugs and blowtorching rival gangs. Glancing at Mordecai in the passenger seat, he wondered if he'd made the right decision to put his nephew on the streets on such a bitter cold night.

Mordecai was watching a Great Dane prancing along Jefferson Avenue when the dog turned its head to look at him. He shivered. No denying, dogs terrified him. The teeth marks of Fritz, his stepmother's German Shepherd, were still visible on the back of his hand. If he stared at the scars too long, they throbbed.

"Don't do anything foolish again," Julius said.

"I ain't gonna do anything crazy, I promise."

"You got into a heated confrontation over a parking space when you weren't even driving a car."

"How did I know the shit bag was a big shot Clayton lawyer? All I wanted to do was help that kid stand up to a bully."

Julius shook his head. The dispute was none of your business. Russell Parker is badmouthing you all over Clayton and our detective agency is losing clients. For God's sake, didn't you ever hear of walking away?"

Mordecai clamped his mouth shut.

Julius steered his Cadillac onto garbage-strewn Juanita Street, and nodded toward the San Remo Bar.

"That's the hangout of the South Side Dragons and across the street is a deserted grocery store. The alcove is your stake out."

Mordecai's heart beat faster. As a lookout, he'd finally be in the middle of the action. He was dressed for the cold, wearing ragged trousers, a wool scarf bleached of its color, a wool cap, a Salvation Army overcoat obscuring a ripped wool sweater and red sneakers with black tape wrapped around the toes. Beads of sweat dripped from his forehead spattering BB spots on the overcoat. What a great disguise. If the Dragons spotted him, they'd take him for a homeless bum, no threat to them.

"Who are we snatching?" Mordecai asked.

"Rescuing, not that cheap street talk. The client hired us to rescue his runaway teenage daughter from the Dragons. Her father's money is keeping our agency afloat."

Mordecai held up a photo of his mother. "Esther, wish me luck." His voice was reverential. He kissed the picture and returned it to his wallet.

Frowning his uncle said, "Don't call her Esther. She's your mother."

Julius cruised to the far end of Juanita, parked and handed him a photo of a blond teenage girl. "That's our target, Elizabeth." The picture captured her rosy cheeks, her unblemished skin and her look of innocence.

"Do you think she would date a private detective?"

"This is serious business. Mordecai, if the Dragons spot you, they'll roast you."

"Don't worry. I'm wearing asbestos underwear."

Julius twisted to face Mordecai and held out his hand. "Give me your cellphone. I don't want you anywhere near this place when rescue begins."

He slapped his cellphone into his uncle's palm.

"Once you spot Elizabeth, call me from the Circle K, three blocks north on Jefferson. After the call, go home." Uncle Julius handed him a roll of quarters for the phone and the bus.

Mordecai kept the hurt out of his voice. "Crap, I'm not in the rescue?"

"For once have patience. I can't afford another Russell Parker. If you weren't family . . ." Julius's jaw was set. He kissed Mordecai on the forehead. "No buts - please - nothing impulsive. My heart couldn't take it."

TWO

Mordecai huddled in the boarded-up alcove, waiting. Ratty cars were parked bumper-to-bumper along the narrow side street except in front of the San Remo. The empty space was the Dragons' imperial turf.

As the cold crept through the holes in his sneakers, he stomped his feet to keep his toes from freezing. For the next two hours, his only company was the traffic noise of Jefferson Avenue drifting to his stakeout.

He pulled out the photo of his dead mother from his wallet. "Esther, Uncle Julius' nagging is driving me crazy. Sorry, mom, I didn't mean to bitch. I gotta break free, start my own agency. This time I'm serious."

A motorcycle roar ended his conversation. He whispered he loved her and kissed the photo before putting it back in his wallet.

A tall helmetless biker on a Harley pulled into the South Side Dragons' parking space. In the late morning his gaunt face looked like it hadn't seen the sun in years, a sign of too much booze and meth. The biker gave him a hard stare.

Adopting the stone face of a boxer, Mordecai held the biker's stare and watched him swagger toward the alcove, no doubt looking for trouble. Mordecai raised his hand hiding his grin. He'd show the biker why two years ago he won his three matches as a Golden Gloves welterweight. He clenched his fists, hunched his shoulders and tucked in his chin. Keep walking, punk.

A barking dog halted the biker in the middle of the street. His gaze turned toward the mutt. Then the gaunt-faced punk glared at Mordecai and spat in his direction a brownish glob, the color of chewing tobacco.

The biker yelled, "You old hag, your fucking mutt betta not shit near my bike, understand?" The punk whirled and slithered into the San Remo.

Mordecai stared at the dog and his heart froze. Holy shit, it was coming toward him. It could be a Pit Bull, maybe a Doberman, or German Shepherd. Whatever it was, it was too damn close. There was no escape. He retreated deep into the alcove, pressing his back against the boarded-up entrance.

The scars on the back of his hand throbbed. Quickly, he pulled off his ragged jacket and spread it wide in front of him like a matador cape.

The boxy head of the mongrel with its pointed devil ears popped into the opening of the alcove. The mongrel was dragging an old lady who struggled to restrain the beast.

"He's friendly," she said.

Mordecai imagined the flashing white teeth about to crush his hand, completing the mangling that Nazi Fritz had started. His heart pounding, he sucked in his breath and held it.

When the beast was within two feet, Mordecai threw the coat. It collapsed like a windless sail over the dog's head and trunk, and blindfolded the animal. The dog froze and a second later shook off the coat.

The old lady screamed, "What are you doing to my baby?"

As the mongrel attempted to pull away from its owner, Mordecai scampered out of the alcove and dashed toward Jefferson Avenue.

He waited by the Circle K until he couldn't see the woman and her dog anymore. He walked slowly back toward the alcove. The old woman and the mongrel were gone, thank God. He saw his coat in the middle of the street. Obviously, the old lady had thrown it into the road where a car had run over it. The torn sleeve had spilled lining. He put it on. It coordinated with the rest of his disguise.

* * *

An hour later a motorcycle bumped against the curb. The biker revved the engine loud before he kicked down the stand and dismounted. He was short, no taller than Mordecai. The biker, along with his passenger, wore black leather jackets emblazoned with a Dragon. His passenger didn't move.

The biker shouted, "Move your fat ass, you lazy bitch."

The passenger removed her helmet. It might be Elizabeth, but Mordecai was unsure if her hair was blonde enough.

She held out her hand to the biker and he shoved it away. Then he slapped her across the face, snapping back her head. "I ain't your maid."

"Don't be mad at me, Torch," she pleaded.

He pushed her down and stared at her lying on the street.

She extended her hand. "Torch, help me up."

Torch strode around the bike, grabbed her between her legs and squeezed.

"It hurts." She screamed, tears rolling down her face.

"You're wearing the jacket of the Dragons, stop acting like a rich bitch."

Rich bitch, Mordecai repeated to himself. It must be Elizabeth.

She squirmed on the ground, moaning.

Torch turned, stared at Mordecai and marched across the street to the alcove.

"What are you looking at? You smelly piece of shit."

"I ...I ...I ... no ... smell," Mordecai stuttered.

Torch spat hitting Mordecai's ragged winter coat. "Ain't no answer. What you doing here? You a narc?"

"No nic."

"You betta be gone by the time I reach the bar, you retard." Then he threw a punch.

Mordecai pulled back his head. The blow glanced off his nose, but stung.

"Dog shit, you heard me. You betta be gone." He strode back to his bike.

Mordecai gingerly wiggled the bridge of his nose with his gloved fingers. Nothing broken, but he boiled over the sneak punch.

He watched Elizabeth pull herself upright by the passenger seat. She stumbled toward the bar, like she was wigged out. Near the bar entrance, Torch kicked her in the leg, and she toppled to the ground. Lying there, she let out a long moan and Torch stepped over her. Rising to her feet moments later she stumbled into the San Remo.

Mordecai took a few steps toward Jefferson Avenue but halted. By the time he'd get to the telephone, who knew what sadistic torture Torch would do to Elizabeth?

Two motorcycles in front of the bar meant only two riders had gone into the San Remo. He strode across the street and kicked over Torch's bike. Then he burst into the San Remo.

The wooden door slammed against the wall, its frosted glass pane shaking.

He scanned the room. The aisle leading to the back dining room was narrow, squeezed by the bar counter and stools, hardly wide enough for two bikers to attack him at the same time. Slumped at the nearest table were Elizabeth and the punk, Torch, shoulder to shoulder like two love birds. Thank God, only two bikers. He smiled. These jack offs would learn whom they were messing with. He would let them attack him in the aisle, where each one in turn would be his punching bag.

A shadowy figure rose from a rear table next to the back wall and moved out of the dark toward him. The bar lights began to reveal a guy with flaming red hair and a scruffy red beard. The third biker must have entered through a back door.

Shit, the odds against him had grown.

The tall, gaunt-faced biker, who had started across the street toward Mordecai, leaped from a bar stool and blocked his way. He wore a silver cross hanging from his ear.

"Haul ass, Shorty."

The bartender asked, "What are ya doing here?"

"I'm taking her home," Mordecai said loudly.

The bartender picked up the phone and quickly dialed.

Elizabeth and Torch banged their beer bottles on a metal table. "Stomp him, Clyde, stomp him . . ."

"Kill the fag," Red yelled.

Clyde cocked his arm. "I'm going to cut off your nuts and eat them for breakfast."

Mordecai lunged and ripped off his earring. Splattered blood painted the sleeve of Mordecai's tattered coat a bright red. He quickly palmed the roll of quarters his uncle had given him and hooked a punch into Clyde's bloody ear and a short right to his mouth.

His eyes wide, Clyde stood frozen and then collapsed without a sound. His right hand stung from hitting Clyde's buckteeth. "Let's go, Elizabeth."

She and Torch remained sitting.

Red, walking over to Clyde, lifted him under his shoulders and dragged him back to a rear table.

Torch whispered in Elizabeth's ear. She grabbed the beer bottle and laughed wildly.

When a distant police siren sounded, Elizabeth sauntered toward the front door.

"I'm outta here," she yelled.

"Torch ain't going to punch you anymore," Mordecai whispered.

Her walk was unsteady. Elizabeth belonged in the blazer of Saint Agnes, not in the leather jacket of the South Side Dragons. How in God's name did she hook up with Torch?

As she squeezed by him, she slammed the bottle against Mordecai's jaw, beer poured over him.

The room spinning, Mordecai leaned his hip on the bar stool to stay upright. His nostrils flared with the noxious smell of beer. Suddenly he saw a smiling Torch. The scumbag, waving a beer bottle, weaved from the wall to the bar counter and back again as if he were drunk, but it was Mordecai's vision that was inebriated.

When feeling groggy in the Golden Gloves, he'd dance away from his opponent, while throwing continuous left jabs, praying for the bell to end the round. This time, no bell was going to save him.

Torch shouted, "You're gonna crawl back to your sewer with a busted head. Your ass is mine."

Mordecai was unsure where Torch's head was. How was he going to throw a punch? He could throw one punch before he was stomped. He raised his arms to protect his face.

Torch laughed. "Her rich daddy should have sent a man to save her instead of a pussy."

Mordecai could hear him snorting as he approached.

Torch raised the bottle above his head -- a poor fighting position. Bikers didn't belong to a gang to fight one-on-one. Torch shuffled forward, his beer breath violating Mordecai's face.

As the bottle swung down toward Mordecai's skull, he blocked it with his right forearm and then gripped the back of Torch's neck with his left hand. With the roll of quarters in his palm, he threw a straight right punch, landing squarely on Torch's nose. His nasal cartilage splintered and blood squirted freely. Quarters fell to the floor, so did Torch.

As the police siren suddenly died, he stepped on Torch's arm, heading for the rear entrance.

"You belong in an insane asylum," the bartender yelled. "The Dragons are going to blowtorch you."

Mordecai staggered out the back door. In his gloved hand he squeezed the quarters he had left. Thank God, he had bus fare. With his other hand, he ran his fingers along his throbbing jaw line. Lowering his hand, he saw tiny glass flakes embedded in his blood smeared fingertips. Better haul ass out of south St. Louis before the gang blowtorched him. But where the hell could he hide?

THREE

Mordecai hesitated in front of Rita Cohen's apartment. He was exhausted and his back ached from the bumpy city bus ride escaping to Clayton. He ran his fingers through his unruly hair trying to civilize it. The way he looked wouldn't invite an open-armed greeting.

Rita, a former college classmate and now a graduate student at Washington University, demanded Mordecai keep an unforgiving schedule of Tuesday afternoons of oral sex. She refused to go all the way, wanting to be a virgin on her wedding day when she married a physician, a lawyer or, in desperation, a dentist.

It was Monday, the wrong day of the week. He knocked gently on her door. No answer. Without a hiding place, his uncle would track him down. Finally, he banged on the door.

There were clicks of three locks as she unbolted the door, fearing that muggers and rapists lurked in the halls of her suburban Clayton apartment building. The door flew open five inches until a metal chain jerked it to a rattling halt and a blue eye peered out. Saying nothing, she slammed the door shut.

His jaw dropped and his heart skipped a beat. She probably didn't recognize him in his disguise.

"It's me, Mordecai. Please open the door."

The door shot open, and she pulled him into the living room. He almost stumbled over her, surprised by her strength. She was a pencil stub, no bigger than five feet, two inches tall and 100 pounds. She wore a reddish gym suit. Her forehead glistened, her top was damp, and she gave off an aroma that excited him.

Her face, usually soft and inviting, was unfriendly. Her eyes locked on his bruised jaw, then his blood-splattered taped sneakers.

She exploded. "My God, what will my neighbors say? I date a homeless man."

He collapsed on a chair as if all the energy was squeezed out of him. He wanted to forget the fiasco at the San Remo.

"You smell of beer. What happened?"

He cleared his throat and told his story. He omitted Elizabeth smashing a beer bottle against his jaw. Rita murmured sympathetic words until he let slip the 'South Side Dragons'.

She asked, "What's that?"

"A motorcycle club."

Her eyes widened as if she were watching a horror movie. She rushed to the front window and peered out. She quickly closed the shutters. "It's a biker gang. My God, what if they followed you here?"

Walking over to the shutters and opening a wooden slat, he peeked out. There were no bikers on the street. "Don't worry. It's all clear."

Her voice was shrill. "You're always screwing up. Remember the demonstration against the CIA recruiting on campus and you're the only student expelled."

"I wasn't expelled but quit to show the asshole administration I was serious about the cause."

She eyed him fiercely. "Don't lie. You didn't care that much about the cause. Today's hero, tomorrow's fool; that's what my father said."

He tapped his chest. "Me! I was the only student who didn't run from the cops."

"Big deal. Look at you now. You're smart. You could have been a doctor. Instead, you decided to be a hero and drop out." She sighed loudly. "You're only twenty-three, young enough to get a degree."

"School was boring."

"Now your antics are the talk of the Jewish community. They're saying you're 'meshuggana' like your mother."

"Them lying shits." He took a deep breath to hold down his anger.

"I don't like your cursing."

His breathing became rapid. "They spread rumors that she hung herself from a chandelier - a damn fucking lie. She accidentally overdosed."

"Calm down, you're making me nervous. What are you going to do 'bout the motorcycle thugs?"

He bellowed, "Calm down? Should I forget the lies about my mother?"

The telephone rang. She gasped. "What if it's the bikers?"

"Neah. They don't know I'm here."

She lifted the receiver, her hand shaking and listened for a moment. "It's for you."

He mouthed, "Who?"

She didn't answer, handing him the phone.

"When were you going to call me?" Uncle Julius asked. "I returned to relieve you, there were three squad cars. You promised me not to act crazy."

"I was saving Elizabeth." It was a weak apology, having violated his uncle's orders.

"Whatever you do, don't go home."

"The Dragons?" asked Mordecai.

"They're gunning for you."

He wiped the sweat off his brow, worried he had left a trail that the gang could follow as easily as his uncle had. "How did you find me?"

"Mordecai, she's in your cell and the reverse telephone index gave me the address."

Mordecai gulped as he watched Rita peel off her sweatshirt. She was braless.

Julius coughed. "You need to hunker down for the next three months."

His eyes were fixated on her swollen nipples. "Where do I hunker down?" Mordecai asked.

"Meet me downstairs now," his uncle said abruptly and hung up.

"I know," she said, "it isn't Tuesday, but . . ."

"I can't."

Rita sauntered to his chair and knelt. She ran her finger up his leg. She stopped at his zipper.

"Please don't," he whispered.

Her manicured fingers unzipped his fly. "Maybe we could try something new after we take a shower."

He shook his head. "Uncle Julius would neuter me if I kept him waiting."

"Telephone him," she smiled, "and tell him that you had a gastrointestinal problem. Only ten minutes."

"He wouldn't believe me." He stood and pulled away.

She grabbed his arm. "Mordecai, you can't leave."

At the door, he turned, "Sorry."

As he closed the door, his balls ached. Crap, with his luck going from bad to worse, his chance of Rita ever showering with him was evaporating as quickly as his chance of Julius forgiving him for the San Remo fiasco.

Outside was his uncle's Cadillac. Mordecai slid into the passenger seat and steeled himself for his uncle's wrath. Julius didn't even glance at him but shot into the traffic going ten miles over the speed limit, which he never did.

Mordecai coughed to clear his throat. He wanted his uncle to have faith in him, to believe he'd done the right thing trying to rescue Elizabeth.

"Her father will be grateful to get his daughter back in one piece."

His uncle remained silent. His face frozen, he blasted his horn at a slow moving sedan. Finally he spoke, his voice dripping with disgust. "How could a guy so bright, be so stupid? It was the dumbest, the most dangerous thing you've ever done. My God, a motorcycle gang. Where's your brain?"

"It'd be just as bad if you went into the bar to rescue Elizabeth."

"No!" he replied, his face turning bright red. "I paid off the city police to arrest these bikers for outstanding warrants and Elizabeth for underage drinking. The cops would have called her father to come get her. No one would suspect I was involved. Just the usual police hassle of the gang."

Mordecai knew his uncle's plan was smart. He just nodded.

His uncle turned right on a yellow traffic signal and parked in front of Mordecai's apartment.

"We have to get you out of town, so throw some clothes in a suitcase fast. A lady called yesterday wanting you to investigate a dog research place in Shakespeare, Arizona."

"Forget it. I hate dogs."

"She asked for you."

Mordecai watched Julius pull a Glock from his waistband. "I didn't know you packed a gun."

"I borrowed it. We could be in big trouble if they spot us."

"Have you ever shot anybody?" Mordecai asked.

He studied Mordecai's face. "You're going to Arizona," he insisted. "Perhaps you have too much of your mother in you."

"Don't worry. I don't take pills."

His uncle sighed. "When you get back, you might be better off at your father's shoe store."

"No!"

"Don't be silly."

"I'd rather die." Mordecai paused. "You untie a shoe, you're inches away from a smelly foot in your face. The smell can asphyxiate you."

His uncle shook his head. "We'll talk about it when you get back."

FOUR

Mordecai stood frozen before the dog lady's suite at the St. Louis Ritz-Carlton. His fate was sealed; he'd end up in a jerkwater town in Arizona. It could be worse: the South Side Dragons blowtorching him or Julius lecturing him to death.

His last meal had been two bagels at breakfast. His stomach rumbled. Two doors away, lying on the thick carpet, was a room-service tray with a half-eaten sandwich in one of the dishes. Mordecai imagined wolfing it down but worried he might regurgitate in the middle of the interview.

He pulled his mom's photo from his wallet, kissed it, and whispered, "Esther, wish me luck."

When he knocked, the door swung open to expose a woman looking every inch a cowgirl. Her outfit, fringed knee-length dress and fringed leather vest, startled him. Not the kind of clothing you see in St. Louis in the middle of winter or at any other time.

She was pleasant looking, a tall woman with a narrow nose and big, wide-set eyes, maybe pretty to some people. But her face was too symmetrical for his taste, too bland to have character. A bump on the bridge of her nose would do wonders for her looks. Then he noticed her eyes: one had a bluish tint and the other green.

"Ms. Santa Johnson?" he asked.

Her long fingers clasped his arm and steered him into the suite and onto a couch. "My friends call me Ana, only one N. I was named after my mother's prized Doberman." She grinned, a wide grin, as if it was an honor to be named after a dog.

He nodded with a slight smile to appear approving of her name. If he had a child, he'd never name his kid after a dog.

Ana strode across the sitting room to a wet bar and returned with a cup of coffee and tray of finger sandwiches. Although thirsty, he didn't drink because of his unsteady hand.

"I sat with Russell Parker at the annual Animal Protection League dinner. Asked him who was the most fearless detective in St Louis? He picked you without hesitation."

There was a long uncomfortable pause. Why would the asshole lawyer recommend him?

"Do you want to know how we work? Maybe our last case, a rescue?"

She patted the back of his hand.

"No thank you. Do you have a dog?"

"I was raised with a German Shepherd."

"Let me fill you in," she said. "The Army is funding a heinous secret project at the Animal Research Center in Shakespeare, Arizona, called Sight and Kill. These ARC butchers drill holes deep into the brains of Dobies and insert antennas - electrodes that stick up from the skull. They call themselves animal behaviorists but are nothing more than butchers."

Even with holes in its head, a Doberman would scare the shit out of Mordecai. Turning down the job wasn't an option. He had to get out of town, pronto. "Aren't they called killer dogs?"

She blanched. "Dobies are charming, loyal – your best friend for life." She sniffled, and her voice turned shrill. "ARC devils call it research; I call it genocide."

With her blue-green eyes growing teary, she leaped to her feet and bolted to the bathroom.

His mouth feeling dry, Mordecai walked to the wet bar for a glass of water. He stood over a foul smelling ash tray with two crushed, half-smoked cigarillos. He suspected she'd interviewed another PI.

When Ana returned, her face was freshly scrubbed and she apologized for leaving abruptly.

"We must save the Dobermans," she said calmly.

"So what exactly do I hafta do?" he asked.

"I'll pay top dollar for this mission – five thousand."

Five thousand was enough dough to break free of his uncle, to start his own agency. To be his own boss swelled him with a warm feeling. If he screwed up, it was his screw up. You couldn't beat that.

Ana went behind the bar, retrieved an accordion folder and a bottle of Jack Daniel's. She sauntered to the chair.

"Like some?"

He shook his head. The bourbon would muddle his brain and put him over the edge.

She placed the accordion folder on the table and poured Jack Daniel's into her coffee cup. She pulled out a paper from the folder and handed it to him, saying that it came anonymously:

Army wants test of SIGHT AND KILL

Life for SAK or death

General Nguyen shouting Killer

Dogs of Nam

Rumor of sale to pharmaceutical consortium very secretive

No talk in front of me

He spying on me

Looking for human prey to field test killer dogs

?me? the prey

When safe write again

A Dog Hugger

Sunny Begay

"Do you have the envelope?" he asked.

She handed him the envelope sent to the Dorothea Doberman Sanctuary in Apache Junction, postmarked Tucson. The address was written in block letters with a red crayon. No handwriting clues here.

"Who's Dorothea," he asked.

"My mother. She died of a broken heart." Her voice broke. "She selectively bred Dobies for ARC because Sam Houston told her they would be trained as therapy dogs. When she discovered the truth, the shame killed her."

He nodded vigorously, then paused for a respectful minute. "Any idea what the note means?" he asked.

She took a gulp of bourbon and wiped her mouth with the back of her hand. "General Nguyen is an ex-Vietnamese general. He helped fund ARC by smuggling drugs into the United States. The senile old general thinks the conflict in Nam isn't over. The one spying is Hans, the Afrikaner head of security. There's a rumor the Army might rescind the funding. I want to make sure that happens."

She tilted the accordion folder. A cell phone, a business credit card and a bundle of cash spilled out.

"If you need to contact me, press recall and hit the number 47."

His gaze was locked on the money.

She pushed the bundle towards him. "Count it."

There were fifty one-hundred dollar bills in the bundle. She was paying him top dollar, which showed respect for his talent.

"Go to the Apache Bar in Shakespeare, the ARC staff drink there. Tell them you're looking for your lost stepsister, Sunny Begay. Using that name will alert the person who wrote the letter. That's your informant."

"Any guess who Sunny Begay is?"

She furrowed her brow. "She's probably dead."

His heart rate bumped up a few notches. This case was the action he wanted.

She banged on the coffee table. "Those bastards! Animals deserve the same respect as humans. We are supposed to take care of those who can't speak for themselves. They call us Dog Huggers because we cry for our beloved animals. We've got to speak for those who can't speak for themselves."

Her body trembled. A torrent of tears flowed down her cheeks, most of them spilling on the frilly collar of her blouse. Her voice was hysterical. "Collect damaging evidence about ARC or burn it to the ground."

"I'm a detective, not an arsonist." Mordecai fingered the envelope. How could anyone feel that bad about a stinking dog?

Calm came over her as if the emotional outburst never happened, her voice mellowing to soft and fluffy. "Sometimes I get carried away. I'd never ask you to do something criminal."

She had rollercoaster emotions, he thought. A hysterical client was his escape from the Dragons.

A minute later he stepped into the hallway, as the door closed with a whoosh. At the end of the long hallway the red, green and blue carpet melded into a rainbow, and the half-eaten sandwich was still there.

Rubbing his fingers across the outside of the manila envelope, he felt the edges of a brick of hundred dollar bills. This money was the beginning of his Cadillac ride to the future Mordecai Glass Detective Agency. No more grubby meals. He was going to celebrate tonight.

Holy Moses, the waters had parted for him.

FIVE

Driving to Lambert Airport, Uncle Julius asked about the interview.

When Mordecai finished his tale, Julius shook his head, muttering, "Why so large a retainer. Why doesn't she know who Sunny Begay is?" He exhaled loudly. "Her story doesn't sound kosher."

"She isn't Jewish."

Julius snorted. "You're a detective, not a comedian." His uncle glanced at him. "If it's dangerous, you should walk away."

"Will you put me back in field operations?" Mordecai asked. Julius had sentenced him to office work.

"Maybe."

"If I smell or see killer Dobermans, I'm on the next flight back to St. Louis. They're Nazi dogs like Fritz."

His uncle scowled. "Give your complaining a rest."

"All I said was Fritz is a Nazi."

He glared at Mordecai. "Don't act cute. You put down your stepmother every chance you get."

"I'll stop badmouthing her when Witch stops calling Esther crazy." His mother insisted he call her Esther, not mom, evidence to his father and Uncle Julius she suffered from emotional problems.

"Your problem, Mordecai: you wallow in ancient grievances."

Mordecai curled his lips. "I can't have amnesia about what she says about Esther."

Uncle Julius frowned but said nothing.

***

They arrived at the deserted departure area at midnight. His red-eye American Airline flight to Phoenix didn't leave until 3 a.m. Julius kissed him on the forehead and said, "Don't forget to call your father."

"Don't forget to feed the cat."

"It's the fifth time you asked me."

"She's pregnant."

"I'm going to be the proud uncle of another cat," Julius muttered.

"What was I supposed to do? Let her starve?"

He shook his head as if exasperated. "You're worse than your mother - taking in street cats."

Opening the car door, Mordecai announced, "I'm going to ace this one."

Grabbing his arm, his uncle said, "Don't talk to your mother while waiting for your flight."

"I'll talk where no one can hear me." He watched the Cadillac slide out of the departure area and head back to highway 70. As the tail light faded from view, he felt free, as if pardoned from his office prison.

***

Quiet engulfed Mordecai as he entered the cavernous terminal, and headed to the chapel, the best sleeping benches, according to Uncle Julius. He saw a few stranded passengers, dozing, curled in plastic chairs. At least, he'd have a better bed. His glance wandered over the wooden benches and the painting behind the altar, an abstract of Moses holding clay tablets. He pulled out an alarm clock and a small pillow from his carryon.

He pulled out the photo of Esther which he held carefully by its edge. He related an edited version of why he took an Arizona case and added, "Esther, I can't figure out why a lawyer, Russell Parker, who despises me, recommended me for the case."

He heard rustling behind him and swiveled to see a tall black security guard striding through the chapel entrance. He motioned for Mordecai to stand. The guard's eyes strip searched him. "We got a complaint," the guard said. "Who were you talking to?"

"No one." He locked his innocent gaze on the guard's eyes. "I like to pray aloud. A condemned-to-hell atheist must have heard me." He smiled.

The guard didn't return his smile. "Why are you here so early?"

He gulped, thinking fast. He handed his ticket to the guard. When the guard examined the ticket, Mordecai said, "I couldn't sleep and didn't want to miss the flight." He paused and then added a tremor to his voice. "My mom is very sick."

"Keep it silent. Voices carry here." The guard handed back the ticket and left.

He kissed Esther's forehead on the photo. He stretched out on the bench, resting his head on his pillow.

He was pleased that his mind was as quick as his left jab had been in the Golden Gloves.

SIX

Mordecai, leaving terminal 3, entered the balmy weather of Phoenix, so different from the freezing cold of St. Louis. He pulled the cell phone from his carryon bag, having promised Uncle Julius he'd call his father as soon as he landed. He might as well get the unpleasantness over with.

"Who's this?" asked his stepmother.

"Mordecai. I need to speak to Dad."

Her voice sounded like the shrieking of bad brakes. "Mortimer, that's your name. You were named after Mortimer Adler, the philosopher."

"It's my mom's name for me." He'd changed it to show he was loyal to his dead mother. This change annoyed his stepmother but not his dad.

"Why couldn't you inherit your father's good genes, instead of your mother's curse?"

The phone went silent followed by, "Ben, it's your son, Mortimer."

He heard Fritz barking and Witch trying to calm the dog by speaking caressingly to the hundred pounds of Nazi fury. There was muttering and his father's heavy breathing came on the phone.

"I'm in Arizona," Mordecai said.

"Julius told me. It's a cock-a-mammy case."

"No, no. It's a chance to convince Uncle Julius I can handle a case on my own."

"There's no future in being a detective. Give it up and the shoe store will be yours one day."

"Uncle Julius will need someone to manage the detective agency when he retires."

"Julius thinks you're too impetuous."

"Did he tell you that?"

"No. He's too protective of you."

"He can tell me. I'm not a teenager."

"The job sounds dangerous," his father said.

"If I smell a whiff of violence, I'll get on the plane back to St. Louis."

"You decide to leave, I'll send you the plane ticket." Pausing, his father asked, "Why didn't you visit me before you left?"

"That Nazi dog hates me."

"Mort, Fritz is too old and arthritic to do anything to you."

"Once a Nazi, always a Nazi. I have Fritz's teeth marks on the back of my hand to prove it."

"Mort, stop being dramatic. That Fritz died years ago."

Dramatic! What bullshit. Every German Shepherd that Witch owned was named Fritz. "You're always making excuses for her dog."

"Son, those incidents were long ago."

Mordecai exhaled loudly, tired of his dad defending his stepmother. "Next time I'll come over."

"What's the weather like there?"

He looked at the blue sky. "Overcast."

"Julius and I have never been to Arizona. We could come and see how you're doing."

His heart skipped a beat. He'd never break free, but arguing would make them more resolute to visit him. "Good idea. If I can't wrap it up in two weeks, you and Uncle Julius could help me."

His father's voice was tense. "What's wrong? You're so agreeable."

SEVEN

Mordecai drove east on Highway 60 toward Shakespeare, Arizona, in a rented Pontiac Trans Am with the windows down and a strong breeze massaging his face. He passed mile after mile of barren landscape. Seeing no humans or animals, the empty surroundings gave him the creeps.

Suddenly out of nowhere, a strange looking mutt started crossing the road in front of him carrying a bloody rabbit in its mouth. Even in the slums of St. Louis he'd never seen a stranger looking dog. It looked a little like a husky, but it was tan colored and smaller. Its ears pointed upward and its tail hung down. Mordecai slowed but didn't stop. The dumb beast better haul ass or it was road kill. The dog raised its head, staring at Mordecai. He swerved onto the shoulder.

The car jerked to a halt. Damn it. He was stuck. The ground was sand, not dirt. Better off hitting the beast than spending time waiting for a tow truck. He shifted into reverse, stalled several times, and then rolled free with a sigh of relief. When he looked up, the dog was gone.

* * *

It was miles before he saw the sign announcing Gonzalez Pass. The road narrowed to two lanes and began to climb. On his left was a steeply pitched rocky slope, about ten feet high. On his right the ground dropped off into a deep canyon. Just ahead were four two-foot high wooden crosses, decorated with red and blue plastic flowers. A memorial of some kind, but to what?

Mordecai slowly pulled the Pontiac off the road and stopped. On one of the crosses he could see an oval photo of a black-and-tan Doberman with two wires sticking straight up from its skull and an inscription that read: 'We weep for Experimental Doberman 106, 8 month old female, murdered by the Animal Research Center.'

He wasn't one of the "Weeping WE" -- for damn sure. Ana Johnson hired him to close down the ARC. Crying wasn't included in his contract.

Just then a black Hummer sped over the hill toward him and swerved onto the shoulder knocking down one of the crosses. The driver slammed on the brakes coming abruptly to a halt in front of the Trans Am, blocking its path. Was the driver on a suicide mission?

The side panel read 'Security Patrol, Animal Research Center'. A twentyish-looking man stepped out. He wore Army fatigues and a sleeveless t-shirt, revealing his meaty arms. He walked to the car, placed one hand on the roof and dangled a bat in the other. His upper right arm was tattooed in red with the name 'Dutch'.

"Are you a Dog Hugger?"

"Huh! What are you talking 'bout? I hate dogs."

"So why did you stop next to the cross, wise guy? You think I can't smell a Dog Hugger?"

"Didn't you hear me?" Mordecai asked.

"Where are you going?"

"Shakespeare."

"To the protest." Dutch's voice was triumphal. He tapped his metal bat against the Pontiac's door.

Mordecai shoved open the car door, forcing Dutch back, and stepped out.

"What the hell are you doing to the car? I gotta pay for the damage."

"I catch you protesting, your ass is mine, Shrimp."

"Shrimp!" Mordecai's facial muscles tightened.

Dutch whacked the bat against his palm.

"What are you like without a bat?" Mordecai asked.

Smirking, Dutch said, "I'm never without it." He walked over to a cross and adopted a golfer's stance as if he were hitting off a tee. He swung and split the cross in half, a big grin on his face.

"Why the hell did you do that?" Mordecai yelled.

"Tell your friends I'll be back to finish the job." Dutch laughed, got into the Hummer, and drove off with a squeal from the tires.

If Mordecai ever had a choice between saving this shit bag or a mutt, the dog would win hands down.

As he watched the security vehicle pull away, kicking up dirt, his eyes locked on the license plate, MAI 07. When he couldn't read the plate anymore, he retrieved the cross and wiggled it into the ground. This dirt was hard as a rock. "Shit," he muttered. "I need a mallet."

Mordecai stared at the cross in his hand and then at the slope sliding down to the dry creek at the bottom of the canyon. Why was he trying to plant the cross? So the fat slob could have it for batting practice? So a dog breed known as killers could have a memorial plaque like a soldier buried in Arlington?

Even the Doberman's sad eyes in the photo didn't evoke any pity. Mordecai Glass, a savior of these killers. What a joke. There was time to turn around the Pontiac, drive to Sky Harbor and fly back to St. Louis. What a ball busting dilemma: killer Dobermans or South Side Dragons. He heaved the cross and watched it tumble down the slope and plop into the creek bed.

EIGHT

Travis Cardwell cruised around Phoenix in his father's Mercedes convertible with the top down. He enjoyed the stares from pedestrians who noticed his striking image, the breeze ruffling his long, wavy blond hair. He'd been typecast in five off-Broadway plays as a tall, handsome boyfriend with wide shoulders, smiling lips, sculpted nose and smooth skin, features so attractive that young women waited at the stage door for his autograph and a moment of flirtation. But no matter how many times he auditioned, he never got the part of the rugged guy.

His cell phone played 'Maria' from 'West Side Story'. He hoped the call was from one of his Broadway acting buddies, or maybe Kelly. But her calls were more infrequent since he left the Big Apple. He missed her, but she'd never give up New York for Shakespeare, Arizona, not that he blamed her.

The caller said matter-of-factly, "Travis - Sarah Riley of Levine, Levine and Waxman Law Firm. We have a client who is interested in the Animal Research Center. Can we talk?"

He wanted to correct her: Everyone familiar with the center called it ARC.

"I'm sorry but I can't sell it."

"We know. We studied Sam Houston Cardwell's Trust." Her reply was sharp as if correcting an idiot. "We can talk if you're interested. You'll find the offer tantalizing."

He pulled to the curb. What harm could it do to meet? It could be a pleasant diversion. If she was unmarried and between twenty-five and forty, he could charm her, find out what she was up to. "When can we meet?"

She gave him her address, adding, "I can squeeze you in the next half-hour. Please don't be late."

She talked to him like he was in kindergarten. Still she wasn't half as abrasive as a Broadway producer. Travis spun the car around and headed for the I-10 ramp toward downtown Phoenix. As he neared his exit, the highway turned to gridlock. Time ticked away. He pounded the horn, knowing it didn't do any good. Should he call her? Neah. She was the one who called him. Finally, traffic began to creep forward.

Forty minutes after they talked, Travis pulled into the Arizona Center. There were a few empty spaces at the far end of the lot and one near the entrance for handicap drivers. He hung Sam Houston's disability tag on the rear view mirror. He was just late enough to make a glamorous entrance.

Travis rode the elevator to the seventeenth floor. Stepping into the lobby, he whistled softly. The area was surrounded by picture windows that framed fantastic views of Camelback Mountain to the northeast and the Diamondback Stadium to the south. The place was high-priced talent. Still, even if the offer was for real, could the Trust be broken?

A young, attractive secretary escorted him to Sarah Riley's office. The hallway ended at mahogany doors flanked by portraits of sour-faced men with narrow ties. If he ever played a stodgy lawyer, he'd model these constipated old farts.

The secretary knocked on the door and opened it. Sarah Riley sat bolt upright in a leather chair behind a desk. Travis suspected she was short, real short. She had the narrow face of a sparrow with acne pits. Her skin was the color of sauerkraut. Her makeup had been carefully applied to hide her defects; it wasn't artful enough to fool an actor's eye.

It was hard to believe that this pubescent-looking woman with teenage acne was the hard-ass on the phone. Probably acting tough was her way of making her mark in this dog pit of male lawyers. He doubted a young person wanted to have her portrait stuck on the wall next to those old farts. Maybe he and Sara had something in common. Both were trying to get ahead.

There were two plush velvet-covered armchairs in the far corner near the picture window, but Sara pointed him to a plain wooden chair on the left side of the desk. He slipped himself gracefully into the chair.

She said, "Need a few minutes to finish up my previous client." Her gaze never left the folder on her desk.

After glancing at Sarah's profile and her diplomas from the University of Chicago and Yale, Travis stared at the blank beige wall. He began to tap his foot.

"Would you mind if I moved my chair?"

She hesitated a few moments and then nodded.

He stood and lifted the chair to the desk's right side. Now he had a view of downtown Phoenix, not beige paint. "Thanks."

Travis relaxed and yawned. "How did you know I'd get here in time?" he asked.

She looked at her note book. "Our condolences on your father's death."

"Sam Houston. He insisted everyone call him that." In fact, Travis was never allowed to call him dad or father, only Sam Houston.

"Interesting." She sounded dismissive. "We learned quite a lot about you."

"I dislike people spying on me," Travis said.

"Spying isn't a word we use," Sarah replied. "Lawyers call it due diligence. We expect you to do the same."

He smiled as if unafraid of any revelation. "So what do you know?"

She lifted a file from the side of the desk. "Target was raised in Shakespeare, Arizona. At thirteen, Target was sent to Lawrenceville, a prep school in New Jersey. A so-so academic record, but he was active in theater." She licked her lips. "He went to the New School in Manhattan, majored in theater arts. His academic record was so-so, but he was active in student productions - good reviews."

He smiled. "If you'd asked me, I would have told you."

"Been a marginal actor."

Travis bolted upright. "An actor has to pay his dues."

She kept staring at the file.

"His friends are actors, at least connected to the theater. They live in roach-infested apartments and work as waiters and waitresses to survive. Target lived in an expensive studio on Amsterdam and 79th Street."

"Roaches make my skin crawl."

She continued. "Besides an occasional off-Broadway role and going to cattle calls, time was spent taking acting lessons. Has a girlfriend - doesn't seem to be a serious relationship."

"I'm a dedicated actor."

Sarah flipped over a page.

"Target now lives in Shakespeare, Arizona, but spends most of his time in Phoenix driving to art museums, movies and theater productions or just meandering around the city."

"You could have saved your money by asking me."

She closed the file.

"Friends said your father, excuse me, Sam Houston, pampered you. A nice allowance so you never had to struggle."

"They told the investigator what the investigator wanted to hear. They're actors. You learned some petty details. So what?"

Sarah shook her head. "When Sam Houston died, you came back to Shakespeare, for what? To save the center or your allowance?"

"Think you can buy it cheaply?" Travis replied.

"No, the opposite is true. The Pharmaceutical Consortium will make a generous offer of five million, two hundred thousand dollars, because they know you won't interfere with the new management."

"But I can't sell it."

"You sign an agreement with the Consortium, turning over control of the day-to-day operations and work out of the Consortium's New York office. Technically, you're still the CEO. The Trust isn't violated and as far as the Defense Department is concerned, nothing has changed."

She just might be his Moses showing him the way to the Promise Land. His acting buddies had advised him if he wanted to break a theatrical contract, get a Jew lawyer. A contract meant nothing to those people. He looked out the picture window. In the last fifteen minutes his life had changed. Now he could buy a SoHo condo and ask Kelly to move in with him.

He leaned back and took two deep breaths. "Why does the Pharmaceutical Consortium want ARC?"

"What I can tell you now," Sarah answered, "is that ARC is well situated for the development and testing of new drugs. Its location and the Army's oversight position it well for certain confidential operations."

"The drugs the Consortium is working on must be controversial?" Travis inquired.

"That's confidential."

Score one for Sara. "Are you telling me, it's none of my business?"

She smiled.

Travis smiled back. Let her think she won the negotiation. Soon he'd be back in New York, and Sara Riley, like ARC, would be a distant memory.

"About the money, I want half now and the rest in six months."

"You receive $200,000 when we sign the agreement and then approximately $83,000 every month for the next 60 months, with mutual renewal."

"No deal. They could cancel after a few months and where would I be? Half now and the rest in six months. Can't they afford the whole amount?"

"I'd have to clear it with the Consortium, but it could be acceptable. The agreement is void if the center loses its Top Secret classification," Sara answered.

"When can we sign the agreement? Of course, I'll have my lawyer go over it."

He didn't have a lawyer, but finding one was no problem: there were plenty of sewers.

She put the file in a drawer, signaling his dismissal. "In two weeks, but before we sign anything, you must deal with the registered letter sent to you from the Department of Defense. By this time it's probably on your desk."

"How do you know DoD sent me a letter?"

"We have DoD friends." She took a deep breath. "They want you to get rid of the head of security."

Hans! Was she out of her mind? Hans would have to be carried out feet first before he'd leave.

"Done," he said.

Her hand snaked under the desk, and the door clicked open.

Travis stood and offered to shake, but kept his hand far enough away so she had to stand. He towered over her. He stepped back and said, "You're awful short." This was a great drama and he was the lead character.

NINE

Finally the road descended into Copper City where many storefronts on the right were boarded up with 'For Rent' signs plastered on discolored wood. Behind the fence on the left was a billboard proclaiming the land was the property of BJB Copper. A dump truck sitting on a hillside belched a stream of hot lava on the lifeless earth that quickly turned to black sludge heaps and looked like Mordecai's idea of hell. He felt like he was driving into a bad dream.

A few men and women shuffled along the street, their heads bowed, as if in a funeral. He'd driven into a dying town. The city just needed grave stones to become a cemetery.

His stomach grumbled. In the last eight hours he'd eaten only airline peanuts. At the end of the town he spotted a big sign that read Rudy's Restaurant. It turned out to be a rickety luncheon stand. He jammed on his brakes, U-turned and pulled into a gravel parking lot. He slipped onto a revolving stool under a warm afternoon sun.

The cook, a wizened man with a drooping left eye, was grilling slices of beef. The grill was located against the side wall so the lone cook could gaze at Mordecai, the parking lot and the road. He nodded at Mordecai and said in a thick Mexican accent, "Senor, I'll be soon with you."

"Take your time, Rudy."

The fat droplets sizzled and Rudy cooked furiously as if there was a line of salivating customers. His forehead was covered with sweat. After precisely wrapping the burritos in wax paper with gnarled fingers, he dumped them in a large plastic container on the counter.

Mordecai didn't see even a lone customer. Did the old man expect a luncheon rush of apparitions?

A factory horn bellowed in the distance, and a red truck pulled into the parking area of dirt and shrubs and stopped next to Mordecai's rental, kicking up a dust cloud. Embossed on the front door was BJB COPPER. Exiting the truck was a muscular man with light brown skin, wearing a hard hat smudged with red earth. He gave Mordecai a hard look, his gaze focusing on his loafers. He said something in Spanish and Rudy laughed.

The miner handed Rudy a check and hauled away the container.

Rudy said, "You a lucky hombre. Lopez thought you a college boy going to the ARC protest. He was goin' to beat you to a pulp. Then he saw your tasseled loafers. Dog Huggers wear work boots. Those rich, snot-nosed college kids believe they have callused hands from turning book pages."

Mordecai's gut tightened. Why did Lopez think he could kick his ass? Because the asshole was taller? "I'll be forever grateful for my loafers."

"Good you ain't lookin' for trouble," Rudy said.

Mordecai nodded as if agreeing with Rudy. "What the hell is ARC?"

"Animal Research Center."

Mordecai wrinkled his forehead as if confused.

"Why does a miner care 'bout animals?"

"The ARC's jobs, good paying ones. BJB laid off most miners before Christmas – not even sorry. The bastards did it to open a bigger mine in South America. All that's left is a skeleton crew. Do you believe that?" He made the sign of the cross. "Without ARC, no good paying jobs. The whole area would be decay without it, and now these punks are trying to shut it down. A picnic for them; for us, it's about feeding our kids." He paused to wipe his forehead with the back of his hand. "Killing a town is no good," he sputtered. "Worse than killing a man."

"How about cattle?" Mordecai asked. "Isn't this the west?"

"Look at the land. No good grass, no good cattle."

The smell of grease wafted to Mordecai. As his stomach grumbled, he felt light headed. He had to eat before he fainted.

"How about a cheeseburger?"

"A beef burrito, okay?" He picked up a tortilla as if Mordecai agreed.

Mordecai shook his head, refusing to eat any food that was his stepmother's favorite treat. "Do you have anything else?"

"A pork burrito, that's it."

"My people don't eat pork." He was about to ask if there was another restaurant in town, but Rudy's sad eye stopped him.

"There are no people of the Hebrew faith in Copper City. It's the shredded pork burrito for you."

Mordecai said nothing, not wanting to disrespect an old man by leaving. He winced watching Rudy dump goop on the tortilla. Could he eat the meal without gagging?

A minute later a paper plate appeared in front of Mordecai, who closed his eyes and took a small bite, then a big one. It tasted damn good. As he was swallowing, there was a continuous honking, and a battered school bus lumbered into view, covered in psychedelic designs, with young riders hanging out the window, their long hair flowing wildly like seaweed in a strong ocean current.

The bus slowed, and more heads popped out of the windows. The driver stroked an uneven rhythm on the bus horn. Some beats were long, some were short; some were repeated, some were not. It sounded like the bus driver was playing a musical instrument.

Leaning on the counter, Rudy bolted upright like a sprinter from a starting block. His eyes were as angry as a thunderstorm and he grabbed his cell phone and pressed automatic dial.

Mordecai heard only parts of Rudy's conversation because of the noise from the bus.

The old man yelled, "Dirty hippie bastards . . . A bus full of Dog Huggers . . . college punks."

Mordecai narrowed his eyes, hopefully looking serious. "They're just a bunch of weirdoes."

Rudy shook his head. "These Dog Huggers want to shut down ARC because a few mangy mutts are sacrificed. The invasion of ARC for them is nothing more than an excuse to have a party."

"Rudy, to me, one less vicious dog is no more upsetting than one less mosquito."

"Uh-huh." Rudy said.

As Mordecai chomped on a mouthful of his sandwich, his cellphone buzzed.

"Thanks for calling your father," said Uncle Julius, always the family peacemaker. "Your dad said you're coming back in two weeks."

"It depends. Maybe sooner."

"What's Shakespeare like?"

Mordecai took a sip of his soda, wetting his sudden dry mouth. "I'm in Copper City, having a delicious lunch at Rudy's luncheon stand."

Rudy, who heard his compliment, beamed.

"What are you going to do when you get there?"

"Get the lay of the land."

"Mordecai, stay away from trouble." He paused. "You don't want another 'South Side Dragons'."

"Christ, don't you guys ever forget?"

"Mordecai, we're Jews, not Goyum."

"I have ta go. Love you." Glancing at his watch, he saw he was running late. Ana wanted him to get to the Apache Bar no later than 4:30 p.m. before the ARC shift ended. He had no idea why the time was crucial. He began to wolf down his food. At the rate he was eating, he'd have indigestion.

Rudy asked, "Always eat fast or in a hurry to go someplace?"

He pushed away his paper plate, paid his bill, hesitated and then dropped three dollars, watching them float onto the counter. Maybe too generous, but the right tip for an ancient man with a drooping lupus eye, sweating over a grill.

"I'm going to Shakespeare - searching for my missing stepsister - Sunny Begay."

"I'd look someplace else," said Rudy. "Your story could get you in trouble."

"Why do you say that?"

"Wrong tribe of Indians."

He looked at a stone-faced Rudy, puzzled. "I hate dogs. Isn't that enough?"

Abruptly, Rudy looked skyward and pointed at big black birds with colored wing tips, floating in the thermals. "Watch yourself, or the turkey buzzards will be circling your corpse."

"It can't be that bad."

"Troublemakers have deadly accidents in Shakespeare: they fall down mining pits or get eaten by coyotes in the hills. In the old days, you were accused, then hung and finally had a trial. Nothing has changed."

"Do they ever say 'sorry' if the wrong man is hung?" asked Mordecai sarcastically.

"I'd look someplace else."

"Are you threatening me?"

Rudy wiped his hand with a cloth. "I thought your people were smart."

Mordecai looked down at the three dollars lying on the counter. Letting someone think he could be intimidated rubbed him raw. He stood and, without hesitating, picked up his tip.

TEN

Late Monday afternoon Travis was pacing the office like a guard dog. A few hours earlier his life was an easy trip to Broadway. Now the DoD letter was ripping his insides apart. He halted at the roll top desk at the rear of the office and grabbed the letter addressed to him and signed by Brigadier General Jack Jensen. He read it again, which roiled his stomach:

To: Travis Cardwell, CEO

From: General Jack Jensen

Be advised that a field test of the Sight and Kill project is planned for the immediate future. The test will begin with implanting an electrode in the subcortical brain of Doberman 143. After the test, the Sight and Kill contract with the Animal Research Center will be under discussion.

Travis was savvy enough to be wary of the phrase 'under discussion.' It was a bureaucratic phrase that could mean many things -- some of them disastrous. If the Army contract was cancelled, the pharmaceutical sale was down the toilet. He tossed the letter onto his desk.

A knock on the door halted his pacing. At the door was Harley Fuller, the Chief Animal Behaviorist, who went by the name Slinger, short for gun slinger. His thick handle-bar mustache hid his upper lip. He wore a blue denim shirt with silver metal buttons and a clasped turquoise bolo tie, brown corduroy pants, a silver belt buckle as big as a fist and pointy black cowboy boots. He coughed, breaking the silence. "I haven't been in the office since Sam Houston's death."

Travis added a hesitation to his voice. "I've been meaning to invite you sooner to discuss the status of the project, but financial stuff . . . I'm trying to get up to speed." He paused.

"Sam Houston had one wish before he died. His vision can't die, but must be brought to fruition. There are rumors I'm more interested in my acting career than his vision. What kind of son would I be if I walked away from my father's dying wish? The Sight and Kill project is Sam Houston's memorial. I swore to him it wouldn't fail."

Slinger's face brightened.

Travis said, "I need a briefing on Sight and Kill."

"ARC is an armament company," Slinger said dryly. "We manufacture killer Dobermans. We implant an electrode in the Doberman's brain and a minuscule electrical charge in its subcortical reward center makes the dog like a drug addict. Believe it or not, the Dobie will turn down sex or food for an electrical pulse." His eyes brightened. "You should see the implanted dog dance, even on its hind legs, for a hot spot buzz."

Slinger sounded like a proud father, Travis thought.

The Animal Behaviorist continued. "But there are complications. If your implant misses the hot spot by more than a millimeter, you have a Doberman who will convulse within a week. The hot spot is smaller than a pea and in the medial hypothalamus but hard to locate."

"What the hell is the hypothalamus?"

"It's deep in the subcortical brain, but don't worry. I know where it's located. Your father implanted in the wrong area, insisting a sturdier line of Dobermans wouldn't suffer seizures. Sam Houston wouldn't listen. We had to sacrifice more than a hundred Dobermans at our lab and the fifty-three Dobermans we shipped to Fort Huachuca convulsed after they arrived. Special Ops isn't happy and Doberman breeders are boycotting us. Now the convulsions are managed, but our DoD informant has let us know a group in the Pentagon wants to replace the Dobermans with a Remote-Controlled Killer Robotic Vehicle.

"Why would the Army do that?"

"Because robots don't have seizures."

Travis picked up General Jensen's letter and handed it to the Chief Animal Behaviorist.

Slinger read it, nodding as if he already knew what it said. "Our DoD informant left me the bad news on my cell." He shook his head. "Because of the breeders' boycott, we have only one Doberman not implanted."

"Can our inside man postpone the site visit?"

Slinger shook his head. "Just an unknown Army guy Sam Houston bribed."

A tightness gripped Travis' chest. "We got to protect that dog. Twenty-four hour protection, right now."

"No," Slinger said. "That will alert Dog Huggers to how crucial Doberman 143 is. They'll attempt to kidnap him. Better to keep everything looking normal. Let me handle it."

Travis crumpled the letter and threw it into the wastepaper basket. "I'm pleased that we're going to make a great team."

Slinger stood at the door and gave him a wide smile.

Travis watched the door close behind Slinger. He sighed deeply. His future as an actor depended on the renewal of the contract.

ELEVEN

Soon after Slinger left his office, Travis emailed General Jensen requesting that Harley Fuller conduct Sight and Kill test trials instead of him. The small alteration would avoid the reviewer asking Travis questions about brain function, hot spots and any other bullshit.

Instead of General Jack Jensen, the reply was signed by Samuel Watkins, Consultant to General Jensen. The consulting lowlife declared Travis alone, no one else, not the Chief Animal Behaviorist, would conduct the field trial. Travis had no authority to change one word, one period, of the Sight and Kill contract. Countermanding the agreement would cancel the contract.

* * *

The guard house phone buzzed and a squeaky voice warned Travis that Sam Watkins had arrived. Travis' chest tightened and his breathing grew shallow. He scuttled to the office liquor cabinet, pulled out a bottle of Grey Goose and filled the shot glass to the brim. It took two swallows to empty the glass. It was enough liquor to lift the tension in his chest.

He moved the visitor chair to the corner and grabbed one with a padded seat and back, the most comfortable looking chair in the office. Sam Houston had crowned this chair 'the tilt'. An almost imperceptible short leg made the sitting person concentrate on keeping the chair balanced and not on the matter being discussed. A devious ploy but brilliant, Sam Houston had bragged.

He heard footsteps. Opening the door, Travis' jaw dropped. There stood a guy whose only military apparel was a tattered army belt. Short and stocky, carrying a battered brief case, he wore a cotton shirt with a button down collar, no tie and jeans that were frayed around his ankles.

"I thought you'd be in uniform."

Without offering his hand, he mumbled, "Sam Watkins."

Travis looked at Watkins' gray hair with his sides shaved so close that the dark liver spots dotted his scalp like ink spots. Maybe the Pentagon didn't take this review seriously?

Watkins walked with an awkward gait toward the front of the office and halted at the relief map of Vietnam above the cabinet. Scrawled in the map's lower left-hand corner in Sam Houston's hand writing was the inscription:

We didn't lose Nam, we quit.

The war had been a ghost haunting Sam Houston, but his father had been too young to have served in Nam.

Sam Watkins muttered: "Quit . . . we stopped banging our head against the wall."

A military man badmouthing the war must be an opening negotiating ploy. "Sam Houston didn't take defeat easily," Travis said.

"Your father - what a phony name. His birth certificate says Lamar Albert Cardwell."

The put down of Sam Houston hardly bothered Travis. His father was distant, caring only about his crazy Sight and Kill.

Gently grasping Watkins' elbow, Travis tried to steer him away from the relief map. "You look tired." He pointed at the tilted chair.

Watkins didn't budge.

"Sam Houston is dead," Travis said.

A sharp laugh escaped from Watkins' twisted lips. "It's more personal. The Army sent me into the jungle to shadow that ghoul, Hans Botha, to see how the dogs performed against a drug gang. Hans and your asshole father made a deal with the local dealers to stop me from snooping. Guess what? A poison stick buried in the ground punctured my left foot and part of it was amputated, finishing my Army career. Now I'm the civilian manager of Sight and Kill."

Stomach acid was burning a path in Travis' throat. His dream was deteriorating by the second. He looked at the red-faced site reviewer. Damn, getting an inspector with a grudge was bad luck. He'd hoped for one who just wanted money.

"Like a drink?"

Watkins mumbled as if he were answering an impertinent question.

Travis pulled his armchair away from the roll top desk and set it across from his standing visitor and lowered his six feet, three inch frame into the chair gracefully.

Picking up the tilt chair, Watkins studied it as if he were choosing a seat for a Broadway play. Finally he shoved away the tilt chair and dragged over a different armchair, its legs scraping on the floor. He sat ramrod straight. His craggy face was as expressive as a jagged rock.

"That's the famous tilt chair that site reviewers have been talking about. Nice try."

Travis shrugged, not sure what to answer.

"We have a problem," Watkins said. "The understanding has been broken."

His chest felt constricted. "What understanding?"

"Those on the outside can never see what's on the inside."

"What are you talking about?" Travis asked.

"Do you know Theresa McCracken, a breeder of Dobermans and silly small dogs?"

He shook his head, his blond hair brushing his neck.

"Mrs. McCracken received an anonymous letter accusing ARC of torturing animals."

"Animal lovers are always upset over animal research." He paused to see Watkins' reaction. None. He continued, "There are always rumors when you have tight security."

"Mrs. McCracken gave the letter to her husband. Do you know her husband, the Honorable Thomas McCracken on the Defense Appropriations Subcommittee?"

Like a skilled prosecutor, Watkins had led him into a trap. If the questioning continued, Watkins could make him look like an incompetent jerk, unaware of a security breech.

When Travis hesitated, Watkins opened his briefcase and handed him a memo. It was from Brigadier General Jack Jensen, Special Projects Directorate to Samuel Watkins, Pentagon Consultant, to investigate an inquiry from Representative McCracken.

With the vodka taking hold, Travis felt light-headed. Make the bastard pay for his arrogance. Less money.

Watkins continued: "Listen, McCracken isn't a bleeding heart. He indulges his wife so he can spend more private time with his secretary. He's dollar-and-cents." He exhaled loudly. "He's well versed in using animals as weapons. Told me a Harvard shrink - B.F. Skinner - taught pigeons to dive bomb into the rising sun painted on Japanese warships. Do you know what happened to that brilliant idea?"

Travis shook his head.

"The bomb was too heavy for the bird. After the war, the Defense Department admitted its decision was a mistake. The Russians trained dogs to attack German tanks, carrying Molotov cocktails. Do you know what happened?"

Knowing Watkins had prepared his speech and was going to deliver it, no matter what Travis said, he said nothing.

"The starving Russians ate the dogs." His lips twisted into what could be considered a smile.

"What's your point?" Travis asked.

"McCracken liked Sam Houston's idea of using the dogs for jungle fighting." He shook his head. "But so little success."

"A technical difficulty, that's all."

"Still convulsing and dying, after God knows how many years?"

"Sam Houston mistook where the hot spot was located," Travis confessed. "But after his death, our Chief Animal Behaviorist corrected his error."

Watkins sneered. "You had to wait until he died to discover this."

Travis repeated what Slinger had told him, unsure of its meaning. "A thin wire probe has to hit exactly the pleasure center, the size of a pea, somewhere subcortical in the medial hypothalamus. No brain atlas shows exactly where it is."

"Yeah, sure," Watkins said sarcastically.

"We've increased our accuracy to 90%," said Travis. It was a percentage he made up.

His mouth twisted, Watkins replied, "In the middle of Fort Huachuca field tests, the dogs convulsed and died, worse than your M-16 jamming."

Travis held out Slinger's report. "This explains the problems and the solutions. We need more time. We're ready to go big: a squad of killer Dobermans, maybe two squads."

Taking Slinger's report as if it might burn his hand, Watkins said, "The Pentagon has let out a contract to develop a robot to replace the dogs. And McCracken wants to know if the ARC contract should be terminated - immediately. I thought I'd tell you the good news first."

"The premature death problem is over," Travis repeated. There was desperation in his voice.

"That's what you've been telling site reviewers for years." Watkins glanced at his watch. "Let's move this along. I've a meeting in Shakespeare."

Travis felt his forehead muscles knotting. Reducing the usual bribe was now out of the question. He handed an envelope to Watkins.

"Will that take care of the problem?"

Watkins counted the money quickly. "Five thousand, not enough for my foot."

"How much more?"

Watkins grinned. "You're pulling a fast one. I know about the sale."

Travis gulped. "Who told you?"

"Me. The Consortium came to me for advice because they heard I've been involved in secret animal research. Dog Huggers have been causing them trouble and they want a government cover. When I heard Sam Houston died, I recommended ARC."

"Fifteen thousand?" asked Travis.

Watkins pulled a cigarillo from his shirt pocket. The ARC was a non-smoking building. His ash would drip on the floor. Travis refused to find him an ashtray.

He flared a wooden match with a flick of his thumb nail and inhaled deeply. "Hans offered me $300,000."

"How could he do that?" Travis asked.

"He said he'd take care of you. Buy you out or..." Watkins shrugged. "I told him I needed to think about it. But that wasn't enough money. My ex-wife and kids couldn't live with my bitterness over the loss of my career. That injury is going to cost you." There was a speck of spittle on the corner of his mouth. "A third of the sale price, one point nine million."

"That's robbery."

"Of course it is. I plan to live comfortably in my retirement and buy my way into my daughters' heart through my grandchild."

"What do I get for my money?" Travis asked.

"Things you can't do. I'll tell Mrs. McCracken the rumors were false. My buddy General Jack will take care of Representative McCracken."

Staring at this disheveled man, it was obvious Watkins had set him up. If this was a chess match, Watkins was a master and he was a beginner. Now he was defenseless, but he wasn't going to let Watkins piggyback on his inheritance. No way would he give him 1.9 million. He'd wiggle out of the deal, somehow. Immediately he thought of one way. Could he kill someone?

Travis said, "We still have two more problems: The Pharmaceutical Consortium wants Hans gone, and there's my stepsister."

"Don't worry about your stepsister. I'll take care of her, but it'll cost you. You have to do something about Hans." Watkins asked, "do we have an understanding?"

Travis nodded.

He inhaled deeply on the cigarillo, letting out the smoke slowly. "I forgot to tell you another complication: General Jensen is going to pay a surprise visit to see Sight and Kill, from the implant to the field trial at Fort Huachuca."

Travis gulped. "We've only three dogs, only one not implanted."

"You betta make sure nothing happens to that mongrel."

"What else have you forgot to mention?" His heart beats felt like hammer strokes.

Watkins' face softened into a smile. "Don't get any idea of reneging. I don't feel any qualms about killing a drug dealer," he paused, "or an actor."

TWELVE

Mordecai drove under a railroad trestle into downtown Shakespeare. He parked at the bottom of Derringer Street, next to ARC MOTORS proudly displaying Mercedes and BMWs.

He followed Ana's instructions to a T. She was as controlling as Uncle Julius, telling him to go straight to the Apache Bar and say he was searching for long-lost stepsister Sunny Begay. At least, Ana didn't tell him when to piss.

He walked toward the Apache Bar thinking about Ana's plan. The setup stirred an uneasy feeling. Begay was a strange name he'd never heard before, too conspicuous for undercover work. Something like Alice Smith would attract far less attention. Changing his stepsister's name was enticing but it could screw the deal and Ana's sweet money.

A leathery-faced man limped into his path. He was dressed similarly to everyone else Mordecai had seen in Arizona except for a tattered army belt holding up his frayed pants. A dark leaf cigarillo dangled precariously from his mouth.

"I'm your handler," the stranger said.

He tried to sidestep the stranger who moved to block his way and ended up close enough so Mordecai could smell the stench of the cigarillo.

"I don't have any spare change. Buzz off."

The stranger smirked and exhaled cigarillo breath into Mordecai's face.

"Don't blow that shit in my face."

"You don't understand who I am, Mr. Glass."

Mordecai furrowed his brow. "How the hell do you know my name?"

"Ana hired me to be your guide." He extended his hand. "Sam Watkins."

Ignoring the offer of a handshake and remembering the disgusting smell of cigarillos, he wondered how Ana could hire this little shit, and why she didn't tell him.

"Get out of my way."

Watkins looked around. "You're going to walk slowly as if we're old friends and I'm telling you 'bout the town." Grabbing Mordecai's elbow, he tried to steer him.

"I don't need a guide."

"Are you kidding?" Watson asked sharply. Stepping back but still holding his elbow, he studied Mordecai as if doing an appraisal. His gaze locked on Mordecai's shoes.

Mordecai shook off Watkins' grasp. "Back off or else."

"If you're going to last in Shakespeare, you need some free advice. Tassel loafers will get you an ass whipping at the Apache Bar."

Mordecai knew that being too noticeable was not healthy for an undercover detective. This Watkins guy could be right – his shoes might give him away. He glanced at his watch. "I gotta be at the Bar," he said forcefully.

"Drink at the Aperitif. That's where the professional people go." Watkins exhaled a puff of smoke.

It smelled exactly like the putrid odor of the three crushed cigarillos in the ashtray at Ana's Ritz-Carlton Suite. Watkins and Ana going behind his back ticked him off. He felt his chest tighten. Was Watkins trying to take over his case and cheat him out of his promised bonus?

"I don't need advice on where to drink."

"Look," Watkins stepped closer to Mordecai, "Ana wants us to work together. I'm a Consultant to the Pentagon. It's my job to make sure an upcoming field trial at the ARC is successful. After that's over, everybody gets paid and you can finish your job for Ana – or just leave town."

"I work alone," Mordecai told him.

"If people discover you're a Dog Hugger, you'll be killed," Watkins said. "Where would that leave me?"

"I don't give a shit that my getting killed ruins your day. It certainly messes up mine."

Watkins grinned. He chewed the cigar end vigorously, picked tobacco flakes from his tongue and spat.

"Mordecai," he said, "nobody in Shakespeare is on your side - nobody, not even me. That's what you're up against. All you have to do is stay out of my way. When the field test is over, do whatever you want. And we all get rich."

Mordecai raised his eyebrows. "Yeah sure, you'll make me a millionaire."

Trekking toward the Apache Bar, he noticed even at this slow pace, Watkins, who was limping, had to stop, bend over and rub his right leg vigorously. A few moments later he had to double time to catch up.

"We need to be vigilant," Watkins said in a muted voice. "Town folk suspect you're plotting to shut down the ARC, they'll get rid of you. And maybe the Army will do the job for them."

He rolled his eyes. "The Army - hard to believe."

Watkins cleared his throat and said, "the Army has a big investment in the dogs." He laughed.

Mordecai didn't join in Watkins' laughter. "Why the hell would the Army be interested?"

"Ana didn't tell you?" Watkins asked suspiciously.

"No." Mordecai shook his head for emphasis. He needed to know what Watkins knew. "So what's the big deal?"

"The surgical procedure done at ARC on the brains gives the handler complete control over these dogs from a distance. It's an Army strategist's dream."

Mordecai shook his head to show disbelief. "How in God's name does drilling holes in the dog's brain make the killer more obedient? Hadn't the Army heard of police dogs?"

Watkins shrugged. "The bitch left you in the dark."

"So what's your deal?" Mordecai asked.

He whispered, "She hired you to shut down ARC anyway you can. But I'm going to keep you from being fed to the coyotes and also make you rich." He paused to wipe sweat from his forehead with his sleeve. "The ARC is being sold to a Pharmaceutical Consortium for millions, and your share could be big, real big."

"What makes ARC so valuable?"

"The Consortium can test any drug it wants any way it wants to without the FDA interfering," Watkins said, "because the site is classified top secret. And the Army won't interfere as long as the Sight and Kill field test is successful."

"How do I make money?"

"I identify you as a Dog Hugger about to mess up the sale and then I contract with the Consortium for big bucks to neutralize you."

Mordecai gulped. Playing along with this guy could be his funeral. "Do I get an open or closed casket?"

Grinning, Watkins tapped his ash off with his forefinger and watched it scatter in a slight breeze.

"What's my share?" Mordecai asked.

"Sixty thousand."

This offer was big money. He could start the Mordecai Glass Detective Agency, hire a secretary and place ads in the Clayton phonebook. But Watkins could be full of shit.

"How do you know so much?" Mordecai asked.

"I'm the Pharmaceutical Consortium consultant. I suggested to the Consortium to buy the ARC when I heard Sam Houston had kicked the bucket. I'm offering you a good deal. All you have to do is keep me informed about what the Dog Huggers are planning."

Mordecai asked. "Didn't Ana hire you to help her protect the dogs?"

"Maybe she thought that's what I would do. But I see that as your job. I report to the army."

"You play both sides," Mordecai said.

"That's how you survive in Shakespeare."

As they got closer to the Apache Bar, the buildings abruptly looked grubby. A Mexican restaurant had black tape meandering across a narrow diagonal crack in the window.

"If ARC leaves town," Watkins said, "all of Shakespeare will look like this joint."

Peering through the window, Mordecai saw it was crowded. "It's popular."

"It has the best Mexican food in town and cheap, too. That's where the real folk eat, not those places where uppity customers wear ties."

They reached a dirt-encrusted window, a flickering Budweiser sign on its last leg. Watkins said, "This is the Apache. I have to know where you stand."

When Mordecai hesitated, Watkins added in a whisper, "I'll give you another ten thousand. Are you with me?"

"For killing me? Not a great deal."

The crevices in Watkins' leathery face turned red. "I don't have all goddam day for your decision."

"I gotta think it over."

"Are you stringing me along?"

Mordecai smiled broadly.

Stepping closer, Watkins grabbed Mordecai's leather jacket. "No more stalling. You could end up in a mining pit. I want an answer now."

"Let go of my jacket." He smiled again. "And don't ever threaten me."

Watkins tightened his grip.

Mordecai chopped down with his elbow as hard as he could.

A short cry of pain escaped Watkins' lips. His eyes widened. He looked bewildered and started backing up into traffic. A van was bearing down on him.

"Watch out," Mordecai yelled.

"You son of a . . ." Watkins never finished. He made an awkward move, resembling something between a stumble and a belly flop, landing on the hood of a parked Ford as the passing van blared its horn, narrowly missing him.

Mordecai leaned over the prostrate Watkins. "You got my answer."

"You're a dead bastard," said Watkins and limped off.

THIRTEEN

Mordecai took a deep breath and strode up to the Apache Bar. The dark stained panels of the heavy wooden door displayed a carving of spear-carrying Indians and a crudely chiseled: KILL DOG HUGGERS. Maybe Watkins was right about his being in danger. But from whom? And why didn't Ana tell him about Watkins?

He pulled open the heavy door and went inside. The Bar was shadowy and smelled of stale beer, and the floor was streaked with dirt. The bartender, a gigantic Indian with a moon face, eyed him. He must have been six-four and two hundred seventy pounds. His dark, mistrustful eyes tracked Mordecai's every step.

Mordecai dropped his gaze to the wide-plank floor, avoiding a staring contest.

A hush hung over the place, except for the clanking in the back room of pool balls echoing off the tin ceiling. Sitting alone at a corner table was a gloomy woman with rolls of fat cascading off her face and arms like a waterfall. Raising high her Bud toward the hanging fluorescent light, she shouted, "Chief, another Bud, on the tab."

"I ain't your credit union," he answered.

Already he liked the bar. It was grubby like an authentic bar of the old west with cowboys, dirty, riding in from the range to have a beer and smelling like cattle.

The heavy-set woman in her tent dress lumbered to the bar, grabbed the beer bottle and took a swig, then asked Mordecai, "What the hell are you doing in Shakespeare?"

The bartender frowned. "Bertha, go back to your table. Odell will be in soon."

She weaved back to her table.

Mordecai said to the barkeep, "How are ya doing?"

"What will you have?"

Mordecai hesitated, thinking that beer was his ticking time bomb. The first few beers tasted acrid, usually moderating his imbibing. By the fourth one, the bitter taste disappeared and, presto, the next beer turned him into an earsplitting belligerent asshole. Saying the wrong thing to the bartender could lead to an explosion. Ordering a diet coke in this working class bar would announce 'Dog Hugger'.

The bartender continued to wipe the counter with a dishrag. "I don't have all day."

"All right, make it a beer."

Mordecai took a sip and winced. Then he smacked his lips together as if enjoying the drink. How could anybody drink this foul stuff? If the beer touched his lips without a big swallow, there was no danger of getting drunk.

He handed the bartender a photo. "I'm looking for my stepsister. This is a picture of my mother, but my stepsister looks just like her." It was a brilliant cover story, building a lie on a truth.

The bartender didn't look at the photo and shook his head. "Don't know her."

"I heard she hung out here - Sunny Begay."

The bartender straightened up as if a loud noise startled him. Crow's feet sprouted at the outer corners of his eyes. "What's your game, partner?"

He shrugged. "No game."

The bartender inhaled deeply. "Begay is an Indian name. Your blond sister ain't no Native American. What tribe are you from?"

"Ashkenazi." The bartender wouldn't understand his joke. Maybe it would piss the guy off, but he couldn't stop himself.

"Never heard of them," the bartender answered, his menacing voice came from deep in his throat.

"We're a tribe from eastern Europe," Mordecai replied.

"Look in the mirror. You're a white man."

"Chief, I'm not a white man. I'm a Jew."

The bartender didn't laugh. Instead he grabbed Mordecai's arm digging his fingers into his muscle.

Mordecai flinched from the sharp pain.

"Don't call me Chief," he said. "It ain't good manners."

"But she called you Chief."

"You ain't her."

As soon as he relaxed his grip, Mordecai pulled his arm away.

"You don't have a sister named Sunny Begay." The bartender's mouth burst into a shit-eating grin.

For a few moments, Mordecai rubbed the sore spot. "If she ain't my sister, why would I be interested in her?"

"You're a bounty hunter." He picked up the beer glass and wiped away the wet ring on the counter. "You're the third one this year looking for Sunny Begay. The other two were bumbling. They left town suddenly in the middle of the night. One so quick, the rental company had to tow the car to Phoenix. I bet you don't last either."

Unsure what to say, Mordecai shook his head.

The bartender added, "Cut me in for 20% and I'll help you find her."

Mordecai had to think about the offer.

"I don't have all day."

"Partner," Mordecai nodded. He'd charge the bartender's services to Ana.

The bartender stuck out his big hand, which swallowed Mordecai's. "How much are we getting for this job?"

"Twelve thousand dollars."

"Twenty percent for me." He licked his lips. "Twenty-four hundred. I wasn't any good at math in school, but I could do my percentages. The name is Wesley Titla, Wes, but call me Chief."

After introducing himself, Mordecai casually dropped a hundred dollars on the counter, feeling like Humphrey Bogart tipping an informant, he said. "Keep the change."

* * *

After picking up the beer, he settled at a scarred back table.

The fat woman collided against his table and dropped, like a boulder, into a seat. Her eyes were hazy, and the smell of beer oozed from her big pores.

"You're not from around here."

He smiled to appear friendly.

"How could you tell?" Mordecai asked.

"Your shoes don't smell of cow shit." She gulped some air. "Have you heard the one about the two cowboys, Ted and Ned?"

He shook his head. "It isn't about an eastern dude who didn't know a cow from a bull, is it?" Mordecai asked.

"Ted and Ned are in an outhouse on the range, pissing, when Ted accidentally drops a quarter down the hole. Ted reaches into his pocket and pulls out a dollar and throws it down the hole. Puzzled, Ned says, 'Why did you do that?' Ted replies, 'I ain't going to reach down there for a quarter.' "

Laughing, Mordecai pushed the photo across the table and asked if she knew someone who looked like the woman in the picture. "Her name is Sunny Begay."

"I wear a size eighteen dress and proud of it. I'm a big woman and it takes two names to describe me: Big Bertha. I don't know any girls less than size sixteen."

"Sunny Begay, do you know her?" he inquired again.

"I don't know any blond Indians."

She gulped her beer and wiped the back of her hand across her mouth. "Do you know how to mop?"

"Yeah."

"If Odell doesn't show up, we'll be short staffed . Would you like a job at the ARC?"

He refused to work mopping floors, even though it was a great undercover job.

"You've never seen her?"

She stretched her arms out, like the wings of a gigantic bird and two large mounds of flesh sagged from the upper half. "She told you she lived in Shakespeare?"

He gulped - a dangerous question. "I never met her."

The haze in her eyes lifted as if a light had gone on behind them. She leaned forward and rested her chin on her palms, asking, "How can that be?"

He took a deep breath. "Three weeks ago my mother committed suicide. Just before she died she confessed she had another child, a daughter named Sunny Begay."

"You poor baby, City Boy."

"My mom wanted to tell her daughter she loved her. That's why I'm here. Want another beer?" he asked.

"Let's arm wrestle for it," Big Bertha offered.

They plopped their elbows on the table. Her pork-chop mitt shadowed his hand. "Small man, small hand, small weenie." She laughed.

He wiggled his fingers free and hid his hand in his lap. "The beer is on me."

"Afraid you'll lose?"

FOURTEEN

The fluorescent lights hanging from the ceiling flickered, casting pale patches on the wooden floor. Big Bertha gulped swallows of beer, belching. She mumbled to Chief - would crazy-ass Odell be sober enough to show up for the ARC cleaning crew? She inquired three times. She didn't seem to care that Chief ignored her.

Two hours later Mordecai was imbibing by the bottle instead of the glass. Although drops of beer dribbled down his chin from the bottle neck, none of the patrons looked at him for more than a moment. Chance had given him a great disguise. He was the sloppy drinking buddy of Big Bertha, indistinguishable from the other half-bagged customers.

The door opened and the three grizzled drinkers at the counter turned to see a thin man with broad-shoulders lurch into the bar. His clothes looked rumpled and unwashed. He looked around as if searching for someone.

Bertha pulled her beer bottle away from her chapped lips. Her eyes widened. She sighed and excitedly waved the newcomer over to the table. "Son of a bitch!"

The ashen-faced man wobbled across the dirt-streaked floor.

"Odell, where the hell have you been?" She stood, engulfed him in her arms, then stepped back and looked him over, patting him on the top of the head. "I almost hired City Boy to replace you."

"I ain't going back." Odell paused. "They'll kill me for talking too much."

She punched him lightly on his arm as if Odell was joking. "Don't be crazy. Your heavy drinking is getting the better of you. You talk like that, you gonna lose your job."

Odell collapsed into a chair, letting out an exhausted breath.

Without being asked, Chief placed a beer and whiskey on the table.

Odell's voice quivered. "I stumbled across the Devil who was exercising his dogs. Growing on their skulls were silver-colored twigs, like Christmas ornaments, that shined in the moonlight." He crossed himself.

Big Bertha, raising her eyebrows, turned to Mordecai. "Odell believes the Devil, along with his dogs, prowls Round Mountain to guard a secret gold mine. He sees a loony-tunes tree worshipper and calls him the Devil. Can you believe that, City Boy?"

Using two hands Odell poured his whiskey into the beer glass. He picked up his drink, his hand shaking like a hanging traffic light in a hurricane, the liquor splashing over the rim.

"I saw the Devil as plain as my shakes."

"Don't be a fool, Odell. Scaring people with that bunk puts ARC on edge. Say you saw a bunch of Apache kids in tribal customs honoring the Wind Warrior. Save your job." She belched, wiped the back of her hand across her mouth.

Gulping his boilermaker, he averted his gaze away from Bertha.

She glanced at her watch. "Time for work. I could have lost my job covering for you." She snorted. "How 'bout you, City Boy, want a job?"

Odell tugged the sleeve of Mordecai's leather jacket. "Don't work there."

"I don't mop. I'm a . . ." He stopped himself from saying private detective.

She pushed herself up using the table and lumbered out of the Apache. "The hell with all of you."

His hand shaking, Odell took a swallow of his boilermaker, a few drops falling from his lips. After closing his eyes for a moment, wiping sweat off his forehead, he spoke as if he'd been interrupted in the middle of telling his tale. "There I was searching in the brush for the hidden mine entrance, twenty yards below the ARC, when the Devil spotted my flashlight. With a full moon I saw him on the hill top, waving his two guns. Worse, those two horned dogs were snarling like I was their next meal.

"I zigzagged down the hill. I ran right, they ran right. I ran left, they ran left. They had my scent. All the time the Devil was yelling, nothing I understood. If he didn't shoot me, the demon dogs would eat me alive.

"I tripped and rolled into a gulley. Thank God. I was hidden from the Devil but not the dogs. The dogs stopped at the gulley's edge, foaming. If they attacked, I prayed for a quick death. They prowled above me. I was sure the dogs could see me, hear me and smell me, but no attack. Then the Devil wailed what sounded like, 'Where's the mountain goat?' And finally they moved off, disappearing. Do I look like a goat?" he asked.

"I don't see the family resemblance," said Mordecai, thinking Odell must really be sloshed.

"How much did you drink tonight?"

"I had a little to drink."

Mordecai looked at his watery eyes. What did a little mean for this disturbed guy? Enough liquor to have a hallucination?

"Do you think I'd quit the best-paying job in town for no reason, no way?"

Mordecai didn't reply.

His gaze locked on Mordecai. "Do you think I'm crazy?"

How could he answer that question without riling Odell? "Beer for me and a boilermaker for my friend," Mordecai yelled to Chief. He felt a chill as someone held the door open for quite a while. "Holy shit," Odell whispered, "it's Hans, the Nazi."

Swiveling in his chair, Mordecai saw a small, wiry man with short dyed black hair, who marched straight to their table. Hans leaned over the table, smiling and shot out his hand. "I'm Hans Botha, head of security for the ARC."

Instinctively, Mordecai shook it. He was surprised that Hans' hand was as big as his hand.

The security head said, "Me and Odell have something private to discuss."

When Mordecai remained sitting, Hans tightened his grip. His nails dug into the back of Mordecai's hand. The pain made him wince. He stared at Hans' confident smile. No one had bullied him since he was the shortest kid in the sixth grade and the intimidation wasn't going to work now. Leaning back in the chair, he jerked Hans forward.

Startled, Hans loosened his grip.

Mordecai pulled his hand free. "You forgot to eat your Wheaties this morning."

"City Boy ain't leaving," Odell said. "And I didn't invite you to join us."

Still standing, Hans looked at Odell, "You're drinking like a street bum - shooting off your mouth. ARC will pay for your alcohol rehab."

"You can't tell me what to do. I quit."

Hans balled his hand into a fist. "You're saying crazy things. That shit ain't good for ARC. We want you to stop or else . . ."

"Are you a bleeding-heart preacher?" Mordecai asked in a challenging tone. His body felt like a coiled spring.

"Asshole, you betta leave before your mouth gets you in trouble," Hans said.

"You ain't big enough to run me out of town," Mordecai replied.

"In the jungle," Hans said, "it's the small things you don't see that are dangerous. Hans turned away. Resembling a soldier on parade with his shiny black shirt and his chin jutting out, he strutted across the bar and slammed the door behind him.

"What are you grinning about, City Boy?"

"I was looking forward to a showdown."

"Maybe it ain't safe being near you," Odell said.

Well beyond his two glass limit, Mordecai took a large swallow. There was disbelief in his voice. "Is there really gold in Round Mountain?"

Odell replied emphatically, "The gold is there."

"How can you be so sure?"

A wide smile rushed across his pale face. He looked around. Satisfied no one was listening, he whispered, "An old prospector told me before he died that The Lost Dutchman Mine was in Round Mountain, not the Superstitions."

He looked at the glassy-eyed Odell. Why would his weird tale about the Devil that nobody believed be so threatening to the ARC, and Hans?

"So why is Hans pissed you're talking about the Devil?"

Odell took a gulp of his boilermaker, his Adam's apple bobbing like a fishing float.

"It's my big mouth. Because ARC doesn't want people to know it breeds horned dogs."

"Are you sure you didn't see something else?"

"Do you believe in the Devil?" Odell asked. Without waiting for an answer, he added, "I do, and I believe in the dogs of the Devil."

"People see things in the middle of the night that ain't there." Odell couldn't convince him of the supernatural, no matter how hard he tried.

"You're like Bertha. To her, what I saw was just a nature-worshipping nut."

"Maybe Bertha is right," Mordecai said dryly.

"Last Sunday I saw the disciples of the Devil dressed in flowing white robes, and wearing thick, blue rubber gloves, lugging a wooden casket to a black funeral van and driving off, without turning on its headlights. You think that was my imagination?"

Mordecai shrugged. "I wasn't there."

"Am I a liar?" Odell asked sharply.

"You said you saw it, you saw it."

His voice quivered. "There was never a gun shot, and I ain't deaf. When the dogs shuffled away, I peered over the edge of the gulley and the Devil was aiming his guns at the dogs. He was about to shoot them for not killing me. I hauled ass and never looked back." Odell shuddered. "It wasn't the boilermakers making me see the Devil."

Mordecai broke out in a wide-mouth grin.

"City Boy, this ain't a joke."

"I believe you saw the dogs." But Mordecai knew his assurance was too late.

Odell stood. "Big Bertha offered you my job, take it, smart guy, and you'll learn I ain't lying."

Mordecai watched him slam the door as he staggered out, so drunk he left a half-consumed boilermaker on the table. He might know something important, but he was a hallucinating drunk - and sensitive, too.

FIFTEEN

At two-thirty in the morning, beer oozing from his pores, Mordecai walked out of the Apache Bar into the silence of a deserted street. The scattered street lamps barely lit his way. He staggered down Derringer toward his rental car. The illumination was crapping out the farther he walked. There were dark patches where he almost tripped. He looked up at the few night lights in the apartment windows above the shops that provided most of the illumination.

Tonight, because of the booze, he'd made amateur mistakes: he'd been nasty to poor Odell, had rejected Bertha's offer of a job at the ARC, and had told Hans to piss off.

His Pontiac was hidden in the darkness. He pressed the panic button on the remote transmitter, breaking the silence with a sharp beeping, which he quickly killed. He hit the open button and dropped the car ring into his pants pocket. The metallic click unlocking the car door marked the end of an evening of blunders. At least, no one knew why he'd come to Shakespeare except the asshole Sam Watkins.

A voice said, "In the jungle . . ."

He whirled to face Hans, barely recognizing him in the darkness. He stepped backwards, jamming his back against a nearby car handle.

Hans unbuttoned his camouflage jacket, his hand slipping inside. A moment later, he waved a six-inch long, silver object. "Need a shave?" Hans asked, a cruel grin on his face.

As the knife flicked toward Mordecai's cheek, he pulled back his head. He felt a breeze - the bastard missed. "Thanks for the offer. I shaved this morning."

"Too bad." Hans' streaking hand was too fast to avoid the tip of the blade. It pricked his cheek.

He pressed his finger against the stinging spot. It was wet but the cut was no worse than a nick. His hands tightened into fists as he calculated the striking distance. One or two punches would drop the taunting asshole.

Hans began to dance around him, first to his right, then to his left, but never close enough for Mordecai to land a punch.

Hans said, "This is the way I like to do it."

Taking a deep breath, Mordecai felt like a sitting duck. Groveling was out. It would only excite the sadistic prick. He had to do something, but what?

"What are you doing here?" Hans stroked the blade.

"I'm looking for my missing stepsister." He patted his pants pocket. "I've her picture in my wallet. Maybe you have seen her," he said, stalling for time.

"Let me see it," Hans demanded, "unless you want another shave." He flipped the knife from his right hand to his left and back again.

Mordecai retrieved his wallet, looking for an opening to throw a punch.

Hans stepped back, forcing Mordecai to completely extend his arm to hand over the photo. Hans clasped the edge of the picture as if it were fragile. "What's her name, Dog Hugger?"

"I hate dogs."

Hans ripped the photo in half and tossed it on the ground.

Quickly, Mordecai bent over and picked up the pieces, returning them to his pants pocket. The key ring pressed against the back of his hand. The key was a weapon, just not much of one. With it between his index and middle fingers he could puncture an eye, but only if he got close enough.

Using the sole of his heavy boot, Hans pushed a crouching Mordecai against the Pontiac. "I ain't done with you yet. Do you have a last word?"

Mordecai's beer haze had lifted. Hans had a knife and knew how to wield it. But Mordecai had an advantage. The bastard had probably never faced a boxer in a street fight.

"A key ain't goin' to save you." Hans chuckled, his mouth stretching wide.

He moved in closer, without bobbing or weaving, expecting Mordecai to throw a straight right hand.

Mordecai slid ever so slightly and threw a right cross at Hans' eye. The edge of the key grazed Hans' nose. Shit! The miss was the curse of his short arms.

"You're a dead man." Hans' tone was gleeful.

"I've three kids," Mordecai pleaded.

"You're a lying chicken shit." He held the knife waist high, pointing at Mordecai's belly.

Mordecai's fingers twitched wildly, roaming over the key ring. He was pinned against the car. He hit the panic button. A shrieking horn and flashing headlights came alive. It felt like New Year's Eve. Residents raised their shades to see what the commotion was about.

Hans looked up at the faces in the windows. "Next time there'll be no next time," he said and sauntered away.

Mordecai slouched against the car. He'd barely arrived in Shakespeare and already two people wanted to kill him.

SIXTEEN

In the Sanctuary Hotel luxury suite (paid for by Ana), he wiped down the dining room table with a wet towel and then washed his hands four times. Taking a deep breath, he began the operation. He had to be as careful as a plastic surgeon reconstructing a face. He laid his precious photo face down on the table. Slowly, he lined up the two jagged photo pieces, and then with his razor blade, he cut the scotch tape, which he'd borrowed from the desk clerk, into a minuscule square and attached the photo edges together. He stopped to scrutinize his handiwork, assuring himself the edges were aligned. Wiping the sweat off his brow, he repeated the process with shaky fingers until he'd patched the entire rip. It took a half hour to complete the job.

He turned the photo face up. The photo's color camouflaged the thin line across her chest, making it barely noticeable.

Exhausted he trudged by the bathroom, peering at an inviting Jacuzzi, and into the bedroom. He collapsed onto a king bed, his head sinking into the pillow.

He held up her photo to the ceiling light. Her peasant blouse blended with her glowing blue eyes and cascading dark hair. Her beatific face shone bright without depression or mania. This photo was his only memorial of her. She had been cremated and Witch had buried his mom's photos, knickknacks - everything Esther - in a storage bin. He would never let her memory die.

He whispered to the picture: "Esther, I betrayed you. I used your photo in my undercover work. Hans befouled your memorial because I put my career above your memory. Never again will I do that."

He kissed the photo three times, each time saying, "Forgive me."

His nose began to run. He rolled across the bed to the night table and grabbed a box of Kleenex. He blew his nose and wiped his chin. Sniffling, he carefully placed her picture back in his wallet to be locked away as if in a tomb.

He looked at his duffel bag, unsure if he should unpack. The desire to leave town blazed hot. His client dumped him in Shakespeare without giving a shit about his survival. Ana should have warned him about the knife-wielding Hans who could have slashed his face to ribbons. If she had alerted him, he wouldn't have mouthed off to Hans at the Apache Bar. Furthermore, she should have been more cautious when naming his fictitious sister Sunny Begay. The last name was Native American and, certainly, Mordecai wasn't a member of her tribe. As soon as he uttered Sunny Begay, Chief and Big Bertha suspected he was up to something devious. And then there was Watkins. Did Ana really hire Watkins, too?

After the crap Ana had pulled, there was no reason to hang around Shakespeare. He had the money Ana had given him and her credit card - it was enough dough to vacation in Las Vegas.

Again he looked at the duffel bag and sniffled. Rolling out of bed, he unzipped the bag and grabbed a pair of sweat pants and a sweat shirt. He put the rest of his stuff in a dresser.

He couldn't walk away from the desecration of his mom's memorial without making Hans pay.

SEVENTEEN

Last night he was ticked off. Now in the late morning, Mordecai felt like a man of leisure, enjoying the amenities of the suite. The cupboard and the refrigerator overflowed with food. Tempted but not pigging out, he limited himself to a breakfast of fresh orange juice, yogurt and oatmeal and topped it off with a coffee latte.

He sipped his drink while he soaked in the Jacuzzi. There was no hurry to dump the case. It was unlikely that he'd get another case as lucrative as this one again. He slipped on a plush bathrobe from the closet and dried off using a thick cotton towel.

The good life was making his decision to see the case through easier. It was Uncle Julius' rigid rule, not his, to dump an untrustworthy client. It was stupid to give up the big money. Also, the case could be a test of his detective skills.

He dressed quickly. A better idea than leaving Shakespeare was to investigate what Ana was up to.

It took ten minutes to leave town and reach the winding mountain road toward the Dorothea Doberman Sanctuary. There was hardly any traffic on this shrub-covered stretch of Highway 60. When his Trans Am drifted over the highway markers, the tires pinged. He glanced in the mirror to see if a cop car was behind him. Instead, he saw a blurry vehicle that looked miles away, coming fast.

A horn blared, startling Mordecai. Where did the asshole think he should go? This was a two-lane road with a no-passing line. A steep dirt embankment hugged the road on the right. A narrow shoulder dropped off sharply to a white-water river on the left. He glanced at a camouflage-colored Hummer in his review mirror. His pursuer was an ARC security vehicle, not good news. The driver, trying to intimidate him, was a small guy, who stuck his hand out the window and gave him the middle finger.

No doubt, the driver was the little prick.

Mordecai straddled the no-passing line, forcing the Hummer, if it wanted to pass, to ride the left-hand shoulder of a long, steep hill. "Top this, you dumb shit," he muttered.

Suddenly the Hummer disappeared from his rearview mirror and popped up in his side view mirror. Hans tried to pass him on the left by riding partially on the shoulder, but Mordecai frustrated his attempt by speeding up.

A long haul truck topped the ridge and barreled down the slope toward them. By playing chicken in the trucker's lane, Hans was about to create a three-vehicle pileup. Mordecai hit the brakes to let Hans cut into the right lane, but the crazy bastard continued in the left lane as if oblivious to the danger.

The truck was closing fast on the Hummer. The cab swerved into Mordecai's lane. Its trailer wiggled for a second and then jackknifed.

Holy shit! He'd kept his foot on the brake and veered into the dirt embankment, hoping he was far enough back.

He dove to the matted floor and slammed his eyes shut. The truck was screeching and its pitch, like an approaching high-speed train, was climbing higher. It was his funeral dirge. A deep breath stuck in his throat. Maybe his last. Abruptly, the pitch began to drop. The truck had stopped.

His breath escaped, propelled out like a high-pressure water hose. He spit out the dust inhaled from the mat and sat up. The cab was upright but the trailer was on its side. The accident blocked two lanes and the Hummer had escaped over the crest of the hill. Mordecai's heart was racing. When it slowed, he got out and walked toward the truck. The driver waved he was okay.

The insane Hans had almost killed him and the truck driver. It was a warning he would kill without a second thought.

The truck driver called the police. Mordecai said he had an emergency and asked the driver to tell the police he was staying at Sanctuary Hotel in Shakespeare and would fill out his accident report in a couple of hours. He heard the driver repeat this information and then tell the police that he couldn't identify the person who ran him off the road. That suited Mordecai just fine. He'd settle this matter himself.

Mordecai drove around the trailer on the shoulder and continued toward Apache Junction, trying to relax. Suddenly, he saw Hans tailgating two eighteen-wheelers. He hung back the length of a football field. Hans exited at Apache Junction and Mordecai behind him.

Hans parked in the back row of Sanctuary Plaza and Mordecai chose a spot ten cars away. Mordecai saw the storefront he was looking for. Dorothea Doberman Sanctuary was plastered on its glass front. This was Ana's joint. He grabbed the tire iron. It was payback time.

Hans' eye was up against a video camera with a telescopic lens. Who was the dummy spying on? No one was in front of the Doberman shelter.

Mordecai waited. Peering over the cars, he had a decent view of the top half of Hans in a black military shirt. His hair was black and cut in a pageboy, instead of last night's salt-and-pepper buzz cut. The crazy bastard must be wearing a wig, a half-ass disguise.

A bunch of college age kids exited the Dorothea Doberman Sanctuary, talking excitedly to each other, their voices loud and their hands in perpetual motion. Some carried signs which read, 'Stop the Holocaust of the Dobermans' and others had placards which showed a photo of a killer Doberman with a noticeable growth on its skull. Hans was busy taping the protesters.

Being too far away, Mordecai couldn't hear what the kids were saying. He squeezed the tire iron so tightly his hand began to cramp, but he'd wait to see what the asshole was up to. He was going to enjoy beating the crazy bastard. The fight would be a knife versus a tire iron and his advantage would be the speed of his hands.

The protesters left, but Hans continued to tape an overweight man with a crop of fuzzy hair, who slapped the others on their backs and hugged the pretty women. When the fuzzy-haired target went back into the shelter, Hans lowered his camera. Still standing in the middle of the lane, a convertible honked at him, wanting to pass. He swiveled around and kicked the convertible's front fender, "You dumb prick!"

Mordecai raised the tire iron shoulder high and moved closer, hoping that Hans would draw his knife. That way he could tell the police it was self-defense. Hans looked shorter than he did last night. Darkness must add inches to the height of an assailant. Mordecai coughed. Hans glanced at him and back at the shelter. Mordecai had a full-length view of his adversary. Hans' black military shirt drew his attention. He lowered his tire iron. His adversary had boobs.

EIGHTEEN

Mordecai walked back to his car and put the tire iron away. He wasn't going to beat up a woman, even if she did just run some poor truck driver off the road. He wasn't going into the Dorothea Sanctuary either because he didn't know who might be inside. He needed more information before he confronted anyone. He got back in the Pontiac and headed toward Shakespeare.

Mordecai parked the car in front of the Apache Bar. He pulled his mother's photo from his jacket and rubbed his finger across the scotch tape where Hans had torn it. He thought about all the times he'd put his life at risk in just the last couple of days by being impulsive and by not using good judgment. Then he thought about the picture.

"Esther, he can't rip you in two and get away with it."

He wondered if anyone in the bar had heard about the accident. He pressed the car horn long and hard, yelling, "I'm back." He felt a little better.

When he stepped into the Apache Bar, the ammonia invaded his nose and throat, sending him into a coughing fit. "Your cleanser is lethal," he shouted at Chief.

The bartender was calmly washing beer glasses. "You're pissed because I didn't tell you about Hans. I thought he would just threaten you."

"Pissed! He made me look like an amateur, but it wasn't that bad."

"I heard it was an old fashioned ass whipping."

"An exaggeration."

"Don't feel so bad. Hans did the same thing to Pedro."

"Who? The bounty hunter you told me about?"

He laughed. With his full-moon face, wide-open mouth and gapped teeth, he looked like a Halloween pumpkin. "He was as much a bounty hunter as you are."

"Last night you told me he was one."

Nodding, Chief said, "Last night you told me you were one."

"You asked me if I was a bounty hunter. What did you expect me to say?"

He smiled and wiped away the wet glass ring from the counter.

"You took my money. Is that honorable?"

"It's the White Man's way," Chief replied.

It was useless to argue. "So what do you know?"

Chief extended his hand. "How much is it worth?"

He slapped a fifty-dollar bill into his palm.

"The woman who hired him . . . Amanda, Anita . . . "

"Ana," he corrected Chief.

"Yeah, Ana hired him because he advertised himself as a detective, but it was a cover for being a fixer."

"A fixer, what the hell is that?" It sounded like a plumber.

"A gringo's arrested in Nogales, Pedro can get him out of jail for a price." He fell silent, his lips locked shut.

"That isn't all?" Mordecai asked.

Chief said nothing.

Mordecai crumpled another fifty and let it drop to the counter.

Chief leaned closer to him, resting his massive arms on the counter and smoothed out the bill.

"Pedro and me became friends. Ana telling him he was the straw that stirred the drink – he knew it was bullshit – and that made him suspicious."

"So what happened?"

"He disappeared, a third-rate detective in over his head." He glanced at the front door. "What are you going to do?"

"I'm going to finish what Pedro started."

Chief locked his gaze on him while wiping the counter for almost a minute, even though it was clean. "You could disappear, too."

"I'm too good of an investigator to disappear."

Chief grabbed his arm. "Play it smart."

"I ain't a third-rate detective."

NINETEEN

Travis didn't hear the footsteps. He was hunkered down at his roll top desk, his back to the door, when Hans snuck up behind him, moving with deadly silence as if his combat boots were ballet slippers. Hearing Han's phony cough, he swiveled to face the sneaky bastard.

"Don't you knock?"

"What did the blood sucker Watkins want?"

"He's the site reviewer for the field test."

"Really, the Army must be desperate."

Travis told him about the Pharmaceutical Consortium's offer, but nothing about Sara Riley wanting Hans dumped.

"The Consortium wants ARC's security clearance and is willing to pay big bucks for it." Then he fished the crumpled DoD letter from the waste paper basket and attempted to smooth it out. Satisfied with his effort, he handed Brigadier General Jack Jensen's crinkled letter to Hans.

Hans read it slowly, his lips moving. Finally he let it flutter to the floor. His face was expressionless. "So?"

"Watkins wants you to resign. If you don't, he'll tell General Jensen the field trial was a failure. Poof, the money is gone. It's his pay-back. Blames you and Sam Houston for the loss of his foot, his Army career, his marriage."

Hans sneered. "You can't sell ARC."

"The Consortium will make me a figurehead. Took a Jew law firm to figure out that one." Travis ambled over to the liquor cabinet and poured himself a double shot of Vodka.

Hans refused the offer of a drink. Suddenly he flipped a stiletto back-and-forth between his hands. "What are we going to do?"

"You resign and after the Consortium takes over, I hire you back."

"What happens if they say 'no'?"

"I'll take care of you." Once Travis had his money, Hans was on his own.

"I've a better idea. I cut off Watkins' balls if has any and feed him to the dogs." The stiletto blade shot out.

"We can't afford any trouble before the deal is done," Travis insisted.

Hans just smirked.

Travis loudly cleared his throat. "There's a rumor you nearly beat a protester to death."

"So?" Hans' dark eyes never blinked.

"A police investigation could kill the deal."

"Do you want me to kiss a Dog Hugger's ass?"

Travis said softly, "Apologize and offer him money, a job, something that cools him."

He wiped the blade on his sleeve. "Haven't used this beauty in a long time."

"Maybe later after we sign, you can use it," Travis said. He finished his Vodka. Watkins would have to wait to die. And he'd have to do something about Hans. He was certain Hans would never resign.

TWENTY

The bar patrons stopped bellowing at each other and yelling at Chief for another round. Mordecai turned to the entrance and saw Hans striding toward them, a smile plastered across his narrow mouth as if seeing an old friend after a long absence.

Mordecai felt the patrons' eyes questioning his courage. This was a chance to show last night's ass-whipping was an aberration. He gulped down his beer.

"Let the bastard try something. I'll tattoo his face with a smashed mug."

Chief hustled over and cautioned Hans, "I don't want trouble."

"No trouble, Chief."

"I told you, my name is Wesley."

Hans leaned across the table. Chief tensed. Mordecai lifted the beer glass, ready to break it. Hans patted Mordecai on the shoulder, saying, "Whatever my friend has is on my tab. Okay, Chief Wesley? Bring us two more beers."

"I don't want your money." Mordecai pushed back his chair so he had room to spring up to defend himself.

Chief moved away but kept watching Mordecai.

"You okay?" Hans asked, sounding genuinely concerned.

"Why you asking?" His voice was harsh, loud enough for Chief to hear. Chief wasn't going to think he was sucking up to this guy.

"The other night things got out of hand."

Mordecai glared. "You feel bad about shaving me."

"Someone called me saying you were a Dog Hugger."

"Who was that?"

"An anonymous woman. Somebody who doesn't like you."

"Maybe because I ain't one of them."

"But who knows you? You're a stranger here."

Chief brought over two beers. "I see you guys kissed and made up."

Looking at Chief, Hans said, "This is one tough man." Turning back to Mordecai, "I could tell the way you took the beating, you weren't one of them - never pleading like the other Dog Huggers. You're a soldier. When I was in combat, I could have used a man like you."

"You trying to recruit me?" asked Mordecai, his voice dripping with sarcasm.

Hans didn't seem to notice.

"Those days are over. It's good you weren't killed. That would have brought back too many bad memories."

"I wouldn't want to give you bad memories."

Hans pulled up his shirt and pointed to his bullet and shrapnel wounds. "When I was wounded, I never whimpered - never. That would have compromised the mission. I sucked it up like you did last night. Some mercenaries under my command screamed, pleaded, cried for their mothers. I couldn't stand that. Lately, I can still hear them in my sleep."

Mordecai remained silent. Why was he telling him this crap.

"If you need anything - a job, a loan, whatever - let me know." Standing, Hans held out his hand.

Mordecai shifted the beer glass to his left hand, ready for combat.

Hans shook Mordecai's right hand gently. "You're a good soldier."

"How about a job?"

Hans nodded. "Telephone the ARC and say I recommended you."

Hans turned and walked away. Mordecai was sure no person could change that quickly. Hans was going to try something nasty. It was crazy to take the job, but it would impress Ana and get him more money.

TWENTY ONE

Hans headed for the exit, but looked back every few steps as if expecting a sneak attack. The door swung open. Big Bertha stepped in and Hans grabbed her arm. He leaned in close, the top of his head reaching her chin. He whispered rapidly to her and she nodded.
As he left, he turned to smile at Mordecai.

The smile of a viper, Mordecai thought. He finished his beer and took a deep breath now that the Jungle Fighter was gone. Big Bertha slid into the chair across from him. She was dressed in overalls with a denim work shirt underneath. She was the perfect picture of a driver of an 18-wheeler. She smiled. "What happened with Hans?"

"We kissed and made up," Mordecai said.

"Really?" She waved at Chief, held up two fingers and mouthed, "two beers."

"He sort of offered me a job but never closed the deal. So what did he say to you?" Mordecai asked.

"He was worried you'd turn down the offer," Bertha said. "You must be a charmer."

"Why didn't he tell me himself?"

"It ain't his way." She paused. "You have an interview at 9 a.m. with the boss man. Just act like a super patriotic American who hates trees and animal lovers, and the job is yours. By the way, when Travis Cardwell interviews you, he'll ask where you're staying."

"The Sanctuary Hotel."

"Bad choice. That's where Dog Huggers stay. Move to the Alamo Hotel."

Mordecai's chest tightened. Ana had chosen the wrong hotel, not her first dreadful choice. He was now questioning everything Ana told him.

Chief brought over two beers. "You and Hans smoked the peace pipe, but the white man always forgets the treaty."

"Should I take the ARC job?" Mordecai asked Bertha.

Chief answered instead, "He could kill you."

She contorted the corners of her mouth. "Because he's an Afrikaner and brags he's a killer? Only a simpleton believes his bullshit. Take the job."

Chief's piercing voice shot back. "Who are you calling a dummy?"

They snapped at each other, which had nothing to do with him. His ears were ringing from the name-calling. Mordecai looked around the room, his gaze settling on the banner behind the bar:

ARM WRESTLING –MEN AND WOMEN

Was there a woman that could challenge Big Bertha in arm wrestling?

After a while, he said, "You guys are as useful as used toilet paper."

Chief whispered, "Shit, it's Mai."

The door flew open and a petite young woman dressed in military fatigues bolted into the bar. There was a momentary hush throughout the room, as if a fierce wind had suddenly stopped blowing.

Mordecai was about to ask who she was, but it was obvious. She had Hans' triangular face, except her black hair was cut in a page boy that softened her features. She was actually fairly attractive in the dim light of the Apache Bar. She was also the woman who tried to force him off the road.

"Watch out," Chief whispered. "She's as nasty as her father."

The customers watched her every step, carrying a video camera and an envelope.

He was sure the envelope contained the Sanctuary Plaza tape.

"My Dad left?" she asked.

"He left 'bout ten minutes ago," Big Bertha said.

"Thank God he didn't see the Hummer." Then her hostile black eyes studied Mordecai. "You look familiar."

"I have a classic Semitic face."

She pulled a chair to sit across from him for a closer look. "What kind of car do you drive?"

"A purple Cadillac."

Her face brightened. "A pimp's car. Are you a pimp?"

"Mai," Big Bertha interjected, "he's interviewing for an ARC job."

"He ain't the one who tried to run me off the road. The guy who smashed up Dad's Hummer drove a Pontiac. I catch the bastard, I cut off his balls."

Chief put a hand on Mordecai's shoulder. "White man here all day."

Her eyes narrowed. "I didn't say when it happened."

Sitting up straight, with her shoulder pulled back, Mai turned to Big Bertha. She held out the envelope.

"Take this to my Dad," Mai commanded. "He's going to be pissed if he sees the damage to the car."

"I'm off the next two days," Big Bertha replied dryly and flattened her hands on the table.

Mai pouted. "I'll arm wrestle you for it. Give you some practice. If I last a minute, you have to deliver it."

Big Bertha's arm darted across the table, her huge hand swallowing Mai's. She threw Mai off balance, slamming her hand into the wooden table, making a loud thump.

"You're no competition." Big Bertha yawned. "Let Mordecai take the package out to ARC tomorrow."

"I ain't UPS."

"What are you smirking about, Pimp Man? I don't forget people who cross me."

Big Bertha took a gulp of beer and wiped the foam from her lips. "Arm wrestle him for it?"

"No way," said Mordecai. "I don't do hand-to-hand combat with a girl." He said girl with emphasis.

"What kind of creature gave birth to a chicken shit like you?" Mai thrust out her jaw.

He retaliated, "Bitch, watch your tongue or I'll pull it out."

Mai smiled.

"Okay, I'll arm wrestle." He was going to wipe away her smile.

All four walked to the butcher table. While Mordecai sat silent, Mai and Big Bertha negotiated. If Mai lasted three minutes, she'd win against Mordecai and he'd deliver the package. Chief placed a timer on the table. Mordecai and Mai sat, grabbed the metal rod with their left hands and clasped each other's right hands.

Big Bertha said, "Mordecai, you know shit. Brace your elbow against the padded wooden block."

Although Mai's hand was smaller than his, she wiggled her fingers until her hand was over his.

"Mai, that's cheating," Chief said and called for a reset.

"The strap," Big Bertha said, and Chief walked over to the bar. Big Bertha held their hands together, and Chief wrapped a leather strap around them. Mai's long nails dug into Mordecai's skin. He gritted his teeth.

Abruptly Big Bertha released her grip surprising Mordecai. Mai pushed his hand downward. His wrist buckled and his hand was halfway to the table before he was able to resist her thrust. Struggling, he broke out in a sweat. Although his back was to the customers, he heard snorts and groans. A drop of sweat plopped on the table, evidence he was straining to defeat this petite young woman. Would they think he was a nebbish?

"Mordecai, slow down," Big Bertha said.

Chief added, "You got plenty of time, Mordecai."

He moved her hand upward an inch or two. But his wrist was still bent backwards. He was breathing heavily while she was breathing evenly.

"She's trying to tire you," Chief said.

Finally, he maneuvered his hand to an upright position and straightened his wrist. He heard sighs of relief from the audience. He caught stray remarks: "She's tricky like Hans." "He doesn't look like much." "Twenty bucks Mai lasts two minutes."

Mordecai grinned. "You had your chance, little girl."

"Don't be a chauvinistic pig," Mai replied.

Taking a deep breath, he began to push her arm downward until her hand almost touched the table. Her jaw muscles were twitching.

He said, "This is fun."

The murmuring behind him grew louder. Big Bertha said, "They're rooting you on, Mordecai."

Chief announced, "Two minutes, twenty-nine seconds."

He turned his head to acknowledge the support. In that instant his grip relaxed. He was still grinning at the audience, when Mai hammered his arm back toward the table and locked her wrist. He was still certain he could beat her, because he was stronger than her. He pushed against her hand, barely moving it. He had lost some of his strength.

The pain struck suddenly, his fingers cramping. He wiggled his fingers to relieve the pain. Wiggling caused him to give up three or four inches and there were very few to spare.

"Ten seconds," Chief said.

"Now, Mordecai," Big Bertha yelled.

The timer buzzed.

"You're a twit." Mai pushed the envelope toward him. "You lose this, you'll piss sitting down." She raised her arm in victory, picked up her camera, and strutted out of the Apache Bar, with no one clapping or cheering.

"You blew it," Chief said with disgust in his voice and returned to the bar.

The murmuring started as soon as the door closed behind Mai and grew in intensity until it drowned the clicking of billiard balls. They were gossiping about his loss.

A stocky man with blacksmith's arms stomped to the table and leaned close, casting a shadow over a sitting Mordecai. "What the hell's wrong with you? You let a tiny girl kick your ass."

Mordecai wanted to explain his defeat, but he was too proud to do that. His hand had cramped, that was all. That could happen to anyone.

"It wasn't the Super Bowl."

"Not the Super Bowl." The stocky man hit his fist on the table. "It was worse. I lost seventy-five bucks, my wife's food money, because you're afraid if you won, Hans would do a number on you again."

Who was this big jerk looming over him, rapidly exhaling breaths of beer, whiskey and cigarettes, making him feel shitty like his stepmother used to do? Mordecai dug into his pocket and pulled out his roll. "Here's a hundred and keep the change."

The jerk looked puzzled, but took the money and left without saying 'thank you.'

Big Bertha frowned. "You lost to Mai because you were showing off. Now you let a drunk manipulate you into giving him money so you can feel better."

He shrugged. She was right, which made him feel worse.

Feeling sorry for himself, Mordecai remembered where he'd seen her name – crazy Dutch's license plate. He wondered if they'd all be after him soon.

"Now you're Mai's errand boy," Bertha said slamming her beer bottle on the table for emphasis.

TWENTY TWO

At the hotel, Mordecai parked his car in the rear lot, where the security light barely reached it. He squeezed into a tight space surrounded by battered cars, whose bumper stickers read, "KILLING ANIMALS IS GENOCIDE." Why did protesters need to say everything in capital letters?

While slowly opening the back door with his key card, he heard laughter and shouting, protesters partying. Well, he was going to enjoy himself too, lounging in his suite, soaking in the Jacuzzi, rather than sleeping in an ordinary room at the Alamo Hotel like Big Bertha had advised him. Of course, if Hans discovered him at the Sanctuary, that could be trouble.

Mordecai decided to stop by the front desk to check for messages. Sure enough, someone had left a police report for him to fill out. He filled in most of the lines and handed it back to the clerk.

"I saw a bad accident. Could you send this back to the police department?"

He decided to take the stairs. Half way to the second floor, the distinctive odor of marijuana wafted in the stairwell. Leaning over the bannister, he saw above him a pair of hiking boots and thick hairy legs. The shoes were clod hoppers, not Hans' small feet.

As Mordecai climbed higher, a pudgy guy with fuzzy hair whispered, "Mordecai?"

When Mordecai nodded, fuzzy-hair pinched out his joint and placed it inside a pill box.

"Who are you?" Mordecai asked.

"Lennie Tarr."

"Why are you here? What do you want?"

"Special delivery." He tossed an envelope to Mordecai.

Mordecai caught it. "Okay, you made your delivery." He tried to squeeze by Tarr, but he blocked his way.

"Ana said you're to lead the protest."

"I don't know you." Another jerk that Ana sprung on him.

Tarr continued, "We're supposed to check out the ARC tonight and map out our sit-in."

"I don't know what you're talking about." A sit-in was crazy, putting Hans on high alert, not what he wanted. "If I were you, I'd be careful."

"I got a chance for a big bonus, so don't get in my way."

He felt like hitting Tarr in the mouth. How many more Tarrs had Ana hired? Would these amateurs Benedict Arnold him?

"Don't be a chicken shit." Tarr called after him.

* * *

Inside, Mordecai ripped open the envelope which held a cashier's check for three thousand dollars. Despite the cash, he was ticked off. Ana never told him what she was doing, and kept screwing up his investigation. The sit-in could make Travis suspicious and Mordecai could be fed to the killer Dobermans.

Mordecai dragged the table with the VCR on top of it into the bathroom and turned on the Jacuzzi's faucet to lukewarm. The tape had been rewound. He put it in the VCR and slid into the tub. The jets of water pulsated against his body, which didn't relieve his tension. He reset the faucet to hot, hoping it'd help him relax.

The phone rang. He pushed the off button on the Jacuzzi and the VCR. "Hello." He tried to disguise his voice by deepening it.

"Just listen." The voice said. "No name. I heard what you're planning. I have something to tell you."

"Like what?"

"I'll show you and then you can haul ass out of town."

"Can't you tell me over the phone?" Mordecai asked. Was the phone bugged?

Mordecai heard the background bar noise. The voice said, "At two-fifteen in the morning come to my place. When you see the signal, drive to the back."

"Why am I doing this?" Mordecai asked.

"When the game is chess, you can't survive playing checkers," the voice said.

"I don't speak metaphor."

The voice cleared his throat. "Three investigators came to Shakespeare and disappeared. They're probably rotting in an abandoned mining pit."

"Enough of the scary stuff. It ain't Halloween, Chief."

"I told you, no names," Chief bellowed and Mordecai heard the phone click off.

The mist was rising as he stepped back into the Jacuzzi; his relaxed mood gone. He turned on the video. So far, Mai had shot nothing interesting, just a bunch of college kids walking out of a store front, carrying picket signs and laughing. Why would a protest, which was mostly harmless students, threaten the ARC? The camera swung up for a moment, revealing the name plastered over the door - the Dorothea Doberman Sanctuary. The hotel and the rescue center and the plaza were all called sanctuary. Was that a coincidence?

He sat upright to get a better look at the VCR. It was Lennie Tarr waving the protesters over to his side. When they crowded around him, he gestured and pointed. All the faces were focused on him. When he stopped talking, the protesters walked away, but the camera stayed focused on him. Obviously Lennie was the target of the interest.

Tarr returned to the entrance. A woman, leaning out of the doorway, with a Doberman at her side, said something to him. He could swear the woman, although not in focus, was Ana. He rewound the tape and paused it. The woman's image was too shadowed to tell even if her hair was blond, much less if it was Ana. Why had Mai focused her camera on Lennie, or the woman?

Mordecai, putting on his robe, picked up his cell phone. It was too dangerous to be seen with Tarr. He asked the front desk to page Lennie Tarr.

"Who is this?" Tarr slurred his words.

"Don't go tonight."

"I'm not." His voice was loud. "Tomorrow morning I'm hiking Round Mountain."

"They've targeted you."

"Afraid I'll also collect your bonus - you chicken shit."

"You fat ass prick," Mordecai yelled into his cell, but Tarr had already hung up.

TWENTY THREE

Mordecai parked his car in front of Apache Bar. He arrived at 2:05 a.m., ten minutes early, because he was afraid to miss the signal. But he had no idea what the signal was. For the next twenty-five minutes he saw a few customers stagger out and then watched Chief lock the front door from the inside.

Sighing he looked at the blinking Budweiser sign in the front window, cracked his knuckles and picked at a cuticle until it was raw. He wanted to bang on the bar's door and when it opened, he'd barge in and demand Chief tell him the big secret and it better not waste his time since he had a 9 a.m. interview with the ARC director.

Why had he agreed to meet at this hour? A lone man sitting in a car was sure to draw police attention. He glanced at the apartments above the nearby shops. Was there an ARC employee, hiding behind a darkened window, telephoning Hans? By keeping Mordecai waiting, Chief might as well announce over a bullhorn that he was here.

A flashing light painted the windshield yellow and blue. Shit, it was the police. What should he say? That he was a tourist admiring the Budweiser sign or that he was too sleepy to drive? He turned to face the cop who nodded and drove off as Mordecai nodded back.

Inside the car, the air was pungent, reeking of nervous energy. Lowering the window, he inhaled the cool night air carrying the scent of mountain pine. The beer sign flickered off, then on and then off. This must be the signal.

Following instructions, Mordecai pulled away from the front of the bar and started down Derringer Street, and hung a right at the first side street. Within a hundred feet of turning into the side street, he cut into an alley, bouncing on a speed bump. The dimly lit alley was a perfect spot for an ambush. He slowed to a crawl. Broken shards of glass glimmered in the headlights and pieces of paper fluttered away, like birds, from his bumper. He stopped by the back door of the Apache Bar and peered into the darkness.

The passenger door flew open and a gym bag was thrown into the back. A gigantic figure, dressed in a black outfit and wearing a hood, jammed itself into the front passenger seat. Chief fiddled with the lever under the seat, pushed it back and slumped down, seemingly blanketing every available inch.

"Was the last guy sitting in the seat a midget?"

"What is this about? It better be good. I've an interview in the morning."

Chief straightened up in the seat, his head almost touching the top and stared at Mordecai. "An education, that's what you get. Drive to Round Mountain."

"I don't need an education."

"I wanta show you that you know nothing."

"You took your sweet time, keeping me waiting until three, almost blowing my cover."

Chief pulled off his hood. "A customer got sick. Had to clean up."

"Did you see the damn squad car?"

"I called the cops."

His stomach acid burned his throat. Was Chief an idiot? He slammed his palm against the steering wheel. "You did what?"

"I told them you were waiting for me, so they wouldn't wonder what you were doing."

"Okay, what's the information going to cost me?" The money-hungry bastard was going to rob him.

"Nothing."

"What's the catch?"

"Go back to St Louis. You don't know this land." He paused. "Look at you. You're wearing loafers, a leather jacket and khaki pants. You might as well have Dog Hugger tattooed on your forehead."

"I know what I'm doing. Ana hired me to find out why Sight and Kill is torturing animals. I'm going to do it."

Chief shook his head. "You're here two days and people are talking about the Pimp Man and his pimp mobile. You couldn't go to the bathroom without half the town noticing. Is that what a detective is supposed to do?"

"I showed everyone Hans couldn't run me off."

Chief snorted. "I'm going to show you what this is about." Then he fell silent.

Mordecai drove slowly along a sparsely traveled Highway 60, seeing only one set of oncoming lights in the distance. He looked off the road into the darkness. Brush and cactus were mere shadows. In this God forsaken desert, there were no houses or streetlights. Unlike a city boy who liked the wilderness, he felt alien here. He glanced at Chief slumped in the seat.

Finally Chief said, "Leave Shakespeare before you get hurt." He dug into his pocket, pulled out a wad of bills wrapped in a rubber band, removed the rubber band and fanned the money. "This is all the money you gave me. It's yours."

Mordecai held his palm straight up, refusing the offer.

"Don't take the job at the ARC. I don't want to ship you home in a coffin."

"If I can't handle this case, I should go back to selling shoes at my old man's shoe store. Maybe go back to college and become an accountant."

"If you are killed, an investigation could close ARC. Where would we work? Who would fund the Apache Health Service in Shakespeare? Everything would be ruined. Because of a crazy lady saving Dobermans. Forget the damn dogs." Chief opened the window and threw out the money. "It's blood money."

Mordecai watched the wind toss the bills around and glanced in the car mirror to make sure the scattered cash wasn't a signal. "Whose blood?"

"Pedro," Chief said.

"He's the third-rate detective from Nogales you told me about." He paused. "You said he vanished."

Chief smiled. "I lied. He's dead."

TWENTY FOUR

Chief was grinning, his mouth as wide as a canyon, revealing his chipped front tooth.

Mordecai glared. "Praise the Lord, you told the truth for once. All you've done is bullshit me."

"And you. What about Sunny Begay?"

"I was undercover," replied Mordecai.

Suddenly Chief bellowed, "You missed the road."

He jammed on his brakes, skidded and made a horseshoe turn, his tires squealing. "Where the hell is the road?"

Chief yelled, "Here."

Mordecai peered into the desert, spotting a brownish stretch surrounded by hellish darkness. He yanked the steering wheel hard onto a brown patch and ended on dirt, a poor excuse for a road.

"I told you, the path is across from Al's All Night Diner, recessed back on the parking lot."

"I didn't see any lights," Mordecai protested.

"It closes at two."

"What kind of game is this?"

"My game," Chief replied.

Mordecai heard Chief chuckle. Piss on him - the irritating Apache with high-school humor.

The tires churned up a cloud of dust obscuring his vision. When his headlights picked up a gravel pull over, Chief told him to park.

Chief swiveled, his massive shoulders banging against Mordecai. "What you see, what you hear, you tell no one, not the Dog Huggers, not the cops." He squeezed Mordecai's collar bone. "You shut your mouth."

Mordecai winced. "You don't have to break a bone to make your point. So where's Pedro?"

"In a cave." He unzipped his gym bag and handed him a black tunic, a black hood, Maglite and pruning shears.

They slid out of the car into the weak moonlight. "Put on your outfit," Chief ordered.

"Are we doing a Kung Fu movie?"

"General Nguyen walks his dogs at night."

Mordecai's face felt hot. "Big dogs?"

He shrugged. "Never seen the dogs, but some Apaches swear the Dobermans are the dogs of the Devil." He spat. "We should kill them for fouling our sacred mountain."

"We should leave before we run into them." His voice climbed to a higher pitch.

"You sound frightened."

"Dogs don't like me."

Chief shined the flashlight on his face. "You look paler than a white man."

He swallowed his fear. "What are the shears for?"

"The short curved thorns of the Devil's Claw grab you and if you try to pull away, they'll tear you up."

Chief's boots crackled on the gravel until it stopped where there was no more path, just endless desert. He halted. "The holy National Resources Conservation Service was supposed to fund a nature conservancy, but instead the Federal bastards gave us a shit house." Rubbing his chin, he began to walk, looking at the moon.

Mordecai double timed to keep up with Chief's long strides. As the moon ducked behind a cloud, Chief evaporated into the darkness. Mordecai's heart fluttered, feeling deserted until the moon cleared the clouds. He trotted to catch up. "Slow down," he said, exasperated. "I could get lost in this freakin' wilderness."

Chief never slowed down. "You outa your league. You get lost and only the coyotes will find you."

Mordecai followed Chief more closely, never more than two steps behind, climbing over outcroppings of boulders and rocks. He aimed his Maglite at his expensive loafers, badly scuffed - ruined.

As they climbed, Mordecai's legs felt sore. His breathing was rapid and raspy. Drops of sweat dripped into his eyes and burned. "How much longer?"

"Another few minutes. Just beyond the outhouse."

Mordecai peered ahead. Off to his left, the outhouse, a squat stone structure, materialized out of the darkness.

"Listen," Chief said, his deep voice gone. "Turn off your light."

Mordecai stood still, hearing the barking of dogs.

Chief tapped him on the shoulder and pointed to the top of a rim and whispered, "General Nguyen is out for an evening stroll."

A figure with two dogs moved slowly along the ridge and the animals occasionally disappeared behind the shrubs. The General was about a football field away. Glancing at his barely visible hands, Mordecai doubted the General could spot them.

Chief grabbed Mordecai's arm and pulled him over to the edge of a gully.

"Shit," Mordecai yelped. A thorn bit into his flesh. Gritting his teeth, he pulled away, but the twig held fast to the branch and the thorn dug deeper into his wrist. He was stuck.

Chief cut the twig close to Mordecai's flesh, but the thorn was hooked tight. Chief looked at the ridge where the General stood. The dogs were moving down the hill.

Mordecai said, "Let's get out of here."

"Don't be chicken."

"You're gonna kill the dogs," Mordecai said.

He shook his head. "Are ya crazy? I just want to get a glimpse of the dogs."

The barking sounded close. "Let's move," Chief said. "The fucking dogs are almost on us." Chief sat on the rim of the gully, crossed his arm on his chest and slid, like on a water slide, to the sandy bottom.

There was no reason to ruin his good slacks. Crouching, Mordecai duck walked down the slope. Three small steps and he tumbled. He banged into a tree stump and for a few moments, gasped for air. Then he turned onto his stomach. The barking dogs were in striking distance. Where were the pruning shears? Shit, lost them in the fall. Defenseless. Run, but where? His hand swept across the sandy slope, touching nothing. Don't panic. He took a deep breath. Something poked his stomach. It was the handle of the pruning shears partially buried in the sand. He unsnapped the latch. The blades clicked open. Were two blades more lethal than one?

Mordecai glanced at the gully rim. The dogs stood close to each other, their heads swiveling back and forth like bobble-head dolls. This was his last stand like Custer's, except Custer had better odds.

Chief crawled up next to him and whispered, "We stab them and push them down the slope. Make them charge uphill."

The moon came out from behind a cloud. The smaller, black-and-tan Doberman never looked down at them, focusing on something in the distance. The larger one, a red Doberman, ducked its head, staring at them. Something resembling twigs protruded from their skulls. "We're dog meat," Mordecai muttered.

Both dogs turned in a circle and swiveled their heads toward the rim. The next time the dogs circled twice in unison like precision dancers.

After Chief gestured with his big hand to retreat, they slid to the riverbed and walked backwards away from the dogs. On the rim, the dogs were repeating their ritual of two circles.

Chief's jaw dropped. "What are they doing, ballroom dancing?"

Abruptly the dogs barked and ran off.

"This is," Chief said, "the closest I want to come to those dogs. Thank the Spirit of the Apache for saving us."

"Why didn't they attack?" Mordecai's bladder was about to burst.

"Did you see those things growing out of their heads?" There was disbelief in Chief's voice.

"Holy Moses, why put a twig on its head?" asked Mordecai.

They climbed back up the slope, which was steeper than Mordecai had realized. There were no signs of the General or the dogs. He hustled toward the outhouse, pulling off his blazer and tossing it toward a twig on a nearby plant.

Chief called, "What's wrong?"

"Weak bladder." He quickly opened the door. Standing at the toilet, he recalled the joke that Big Bertha told him about the two cowboys in an outhouse. Once outside, he asked, "Where's the cave? My legs are killing me."

Chief shined his Maglite at two trees about twenty feet away. "Behind the mesquites. Watch out for needles."

Mordecai sighed.

Chief didn't move. His flashlight was aimed at the ground. Two parallel tracks wiggled toward the mesquite trees. "Well, super sleuth, so what happened here?"

Dropping to his knees, Mordecai examined the tracks. Finally he said, "A body was dragged by the shoulders, shoe heals making these tracks. The narrow width meant a small foot."

Nodding, Chief said softly, "Poor Pedro, things don't look good." He walked toward the trees and crouched under the branches.

Shuddering at the inch-and-half needles, Mordecai duck walked into the cave.

The dampness of the cave made him shiver and once inside, a putrid odor hit him and his stomach clenched. He switched on his Maglite and swept the ground. Bones everywhere. He picked up a bone with teeth marks. Maybe a hungry coyote was chewing on it. It wasn't a human bone, most likely a dog. Next to the wall was a decomposing Doberman with antennae protruding from its skull and infested with maggots.

Chief's beam caught something far back in the cave, resembling a human figure. "Come here," he insisted.

No way was he going to look at Pedro's corpse. It'd remind him of seeing his mom's drug-overdosed dead body, a bitter memory of his mother better forgotten.

"Ya better see this," Chief yelled.

"Pedro isn't going to tell me anything now." Mordecai thought the rotting corpse must smell stomach-heaving.

Chief exhaled loudly.

Mordecai shuffled over to the corpse; his hand shook embarrassingly. The Maglite beam touched the corpse. The belly was ripped open as if by a wild animal and flies were everywhere. He imagined that it would soon be full of maggots.

Chief muttered, "It ain't Pedro. Too small. Pedro was six feet tall."

Mordecai didn't want to go near the body, but a professional detective couldn't walk away, could he? Holding the Maglite with two shaking hands, he shined the beam on the right side of the corpse's face, but it was too mangled and bloody to identify.

"Chief, why don't you lift his head, so we can see the rest of his face?"

"An Apache can't touch the dead until a cleansing ceremony is performed."

Mordecai stepped to the other side of the body, careful that his shoes never came close to the victim. The left side of his face was flat on the ground. He lifted the head with a leg bone. With two quivering hands, it took a few seconds to pinpoint the light on the facial features. He gulped. It was Hans!

TWENTY FIVE

Mordecai stared at Hans' mangled and bloody face. What the hell was happening? Chief promised him Pedro; instead, he got Hans. It was the classic bait-and-switch but who did the switching?

"The spirit of the dead bring police," Chief said breathing heavy.

Mordecai took a deep breath and held it. Leaning forward, he aimed the light toward Hans' face. Strips of skin were hanging from his forehead as if a giant cat had used Hans' head as a scratching post. The sight turned Mordecai's stomach. "He's been scalped."

"Don't look at me 'cause I'm an Indian."

Although his mouth tasted bitter, Mordecai continued the exam, his beam sliding down to the neck which looked as if it had been crushed by a vise. "He's been mangled bad." Mordecai muttered, disbelieving what he saw. "Hard to recognize Hans."

"No coyote chomps on a head when there's a soft belly," Chief said. He grabbed Mordecai's sleeve, pulling him weakly toward the cave opening and saying, "We gotta get out of here."

He shrugged off the loose grip. No way was he leaving. The case was a jackpot, not the dull, chicken-shit jobs Uncle Julius assigned him. The dead body was creepy, but it was the murder that got his juices flowing.

"Nah. We'll wait for sunrise - enough light to give this place a thorough inspection."

Chief snorted. "Stop playing detective. Hans was a mean prick. Who cares who killed him? Nobody is going to weep at his burial. If the cops get involved, then it's big trouble for ARC and Shakespeare."

He glanced at the corpse, so many questions unanswered. Who carried off the rotting, larvae-infested Pedro?

"When did you last talk to Pedro?"

"Four and a half weeks ago."

"Who substituted Hans' corpse for Pedro's?" Mordecai asked.

Chief shrugged and gave a short, sharp laugh. "Half the town could've done it." He paused. "I'll tell you what frightens me: the cops discover us here and charge you with murder and me as an accomplice."

"We're not killers," Mordecai protested.

"Hans kicking your ass is proof enough to hang you."

"Nobody gonna see us in the cave," Mordecai said confidently.

"I ain't stupid." Chief repeated his warning: "The killer returns, where do we run, Mister Smart Guy?"

"Can't you wait for ten minutes? The sun will be up soon."

"Christ, don't you know anything about the outdoors? Even at midday the mesquites will block the sunlight. The cave won't be much brighter than now."

"You can be the lookout," Mordecai said. "I'll finish quickly."

Standing by the mouth of the cave, Chief turned toward Mordecai. "Trouble, I'm gone."

This was the time for Mordecai to be a detective. Hans had been killed between 10 p.m. when Mordecai had seen him leave the Apache Bar and about 4 a.m. when they arrived at the cave. Bending over, Mordecai scanned the dark earth from the corpse to the cave entrance. He saw in the dirt short drag marks and shoe prints. The large ones must be Chief's boots. His shoe fit exactly over a clearly defined small shoe print. Nearby was a blurry footprint and he placed his loafer next to it. The blurry print was slightly larger. It must belong to the killer.

Returning to the corpse, he pulled Hans' pockets inside out. There was nothing in them. "Why don't you cut off some branches so I have more light?" he shouted.

Chief didn't reply but Mordecai heard the snipping of pruning shears.

To finish his search he had to explore the back of the cave, which was about twenty feet deep. He focused his Maglite on the back wall, where a mound of dirt was piled. To get to the dirt, he had to stoop to avoid hitting his head. No sunlight penetrated here. The surrounding darkness gave him the creeps.

His beam caught what looked like a dark wooden stick protruding from the mound. When he touched it, it felt flaky. In the flashlight beam, the substance on his fingers was black. He pulled the object out of the dirt. It was a long burnt bone.

Shoveling with the bone, he uncovered a dog's skull. There was a blackened rod sticking up from the skull. He pulled it out of the burnt brain and, without thinking, wiped it off on his shirt. He turned the thing over in his hand. It wasn't a twig.

Insisting on exploring the cave had paid off. He was holding the antenna that ARC inserted into the dogs' skulls. Mordecai put his finger in the hole someone had drilled in the top of the Doberman's skull. He shoved his shirt back into his pants. There was no reason to worry about being clean now that the shirt was filthy.

Shoveling again, he discovered the partial remains of three more dogs - all with burnt skeletons - which resembled those of Dobermans.

"Holy cow. This place is a dog crematorium."

After a while he tired of finding more bones and stopped digging. He was covered in a fine mist of dust, fatigued, and sweating. He glanced at Hans. His gut feeling was that ARC was involved in his death. But there was no evidence to support his feeling.

In the silence of the cave, he heard the massive man stomping about outside. Tonight Chief had made it clear he didn't give a crap about the homicide. Mordecai would give odds that townsfolk also felt the dead bastard was unworthy of burial. The only murder that worried Chief and townsfolk was that of their cash cow, ARC.

As Mordecai left the cave, Chief began to plug the entrance again with mesquite.

Suddenly he whispered, "Someone is watching us."

TWENTY SIX

Mordecai ducked under the tree, avoiding the mesquite needles lying on the ground which could easily pierce his shoe, and his foot. Crap, there were all kinds of unknown things here that could do him in.

Chief pointed to the ridge of a nearby hill. Standing there was a lone man staring at them. The rising sun highlighted his bushy brown hair, making him look angelic.

The sunlight made Mordecai blink. He shaded his eyes to watch the man retreat and disappear. "Is that General Nguyen?"

"Doesn't look like him." Chief picked up mesquite branches and carefully piled them in front of the opening. "Never heard he walks during the daylight."

"Maybe the killer?"

"Not the killer unless he's stupid."

"Then who the hell is he?" Mordecai asked.

"He's gone."

Standing in the morning sunshine near the cave, Mordecai scanned the barren earth, which looked as if a giant oven had dried it out. Weird plants dotted the landscape. One cactus was shaped like a ping pong racket with long needles; another looked like a creature with tentacles swaying in the breeze. He'd never seen such weird things before, not even in the Forest Park Botanical Gardens. These plants looked ready to attack, like a mad dog, if he came too close.

Crawling near his shoe was a nasty-looking tiny creeper with a stinger curved over its back.

"Is that a scorpion?"

Chief smiled. "If they sting you, put ice on it unless you're allergic."

He asked, "If I'm allergic, what then?"

"You die."

"How do you know if you're allergic?"

"You die," and he laughed, his massive chest shaking. "Let's get out of here," Chief said.

Mordecai took a few steps and stopped to look at a shrub with hooked thorns curved like tiny box cutters. It must be the dreaded Devil's Claw. In the sunlight the plant was easily avoided but at night you were at its mercy.

"Come on," Chief said loudly as he bounded up the path as if walking on a city street.

It was the path that Mordecai had stumbled along going to the cave. It was strewn with boulders, shale and jagged rocks, worthy of an endurance contest. Mordecai did his best to stay upright, but it was a struggle and several times he jammed his foot in the crevices between the boulders.

Chief never slackened his pace, increasing the distance between them. Mordecai wasn't worried about losing sight of his companion because he had the car key. As he passed the outhouse, he spotted his blazer at the top of the gully. It was still hanging on the twig of a Devil's Claw. He had a hard time believing something so small could hold up a jacket.

He kept his fingers away from the thorns and snapped off the twig with his pruning shears. When he held the blazer up to the sun, light shined through small holes. He'd pick out the thorns later. At least he'd saved one piece of clothing.

Chief, sitting on a smooth rock, stood when Mordecai reached his side.

"I can hardly walk on this stuff." Mordecai inhaled deeply, catching his breath. He wiped his forehead with the back of his hand. The sweat felt cool.

"What do you expect the way you're dressed?"

"I'm not a hick."

"You're out of your element."

"Why didn't you tell me where we were going?"

"See what you're up against; don't you get it?" Chief grabbed his shoulder and looked him in the eye. "You could end up joining Hans."

Mordecai ignored Chief's warning. There were worse ways to die. Top of his list was dying of boredom at his dad's shoe store. For a moment, he remembered that life - tilting the shoe under the halogen beam so the leather sparkled, and telling the woman customer that this style flattered her. Repeating the sales pitch over and over had got old quick. "I can handle myself."

"Someone's on the warpath and you think you're cavalry," Chief said. "This is the Little Big Horn, Custer." He stormed off.

Mordecai trudged after him, bone-tired. It dawned on him that if Hans' murder was connected to the ARC, people there might wonder who the hell they were interviewing this morning. Glancing at his watch, he had less than three hours to shower and change clothes before the interview.

The air horn of a truck scattered four birds with dull-colored black wings from a barren, dying tree. They must be near the highway and near where his car was parked. Moments later, he heard the howl of an eighteen-wheeler. He sighed in relief, knowing that below the ridge line was his air conditioned Pontiac. He was battered but unharmed, and never again would he climb these hills and struggle over these boulders.

Chief fell to the ground.

For a moment, Mordecai stood frozen. The shot didn't echo, not even a pop.

Chief motioned for Mordecai to get down and then waved Mordecai toward him.

His pants and blazer would be in shreds by the time this case was over. Mordecai wriggled on his stomach slowly, using his hands and knees to propel himself. Finally he drew even with Chief, who had remained still. Mordecai whispered, "Are you hurt?"

Chief looked at him, his eyebrows raised into a question. "Why would I be hurt?"

"You dropped like you were shot."

"Did you hear a shot?"

"No, but . . ."

"There was no shot." He pointed down to where the Pontiac was parked. Sitting on the hood was a lone figure, his legs crossed. Sunlight anointed his bushy brown hair and from the top of the hill, he looked like an ornamental Buddha.

"The guy who was watching us," he said, shaking his head. "Why's the idiot on the hood?"

Hugging the ground, Mordecai spat trying to remove the taste of grit, but it didn't help much with his dry mouth. Recognizing the figure, he stood, saying, "He's harmless."

"Who is he?"

"Lennie Tarr, a protest leader."

"What's he doing out here?" Chief asked.

Mordecai shrugged. Last night Tarr was going to scout the back way into the ARC for the sit-in and had called Mordecai a chicken shit for not joining him. "Let's ask the jerk"

It took less than a minute to tramp down the hill to the car.

"You fat shit," Mordecai shouted, "get off the hood."

Tarr screamed back, the corner of his mouth foaming with saliva bubbles. "You son of a bitch, you bastard, you Judas goat -- you betrayed me."

"A friend of yours?" Chief asked.

"A good friend," he whispered to Chief and then to Tarr, he said, "I warned you last night to forget the sit-in."

"You squealed," Tarr replied.

"You deserved what you got," Mordecai said. "Next time listen."

Tarr's lips trembled. "You didn't tell me what could happen."

Mordecai studied Tarr, who was shoeless, wearing only black socks. There was gook around his eyes and mouth as if he had decorated himself for Halloween. His lips were bruised and puffy as if he had been hit repeatedly. The sit-in was ill-planned, bound to fail, and now the sit-in would have to be aborted. There would be no Dog Huggers protesting while he interviewed – a big break.

Tarr raised his beefy arms to show them a rope shred hanging from each wrist. Untangling his stubby crossed legs, he stood on the hood. A rope dangled from his left ankle. "You know what the little German prick did to me?"

Mordecai said, "Get off the hood."

Chief placed his work boot on the bumper. "What did Hans do?"

"Hans," Tarr repeated the name three times as if memorizing it. "He kidnaped me, tied my hands and feet, and duck taped my eyes and mouth, and robbed my shoes. Then . . . he said he was going to trade me for a little peace and quiet." His eyes became teary. "If I didn't free myself by the time he returned, he'd kill me. Before he left, he squeezed my nuts until I yelled and prayed someone would save me, but the tape muffled my screams.

"It took me a few minutes to get the duck tape off by rubbing my mouth against a rock. That hurt like hell." Tarr touched his upper lip and winced. "I had to cut the rope on a jagged rock, because the old guy wouldn't help."

"What old guy?" Mordecai asked.

"An Oriental with two mutilated dogs. I asked him to untie the rope. He said that I was a prisoner of war and walked away." He gulped. "I had to work fast before the little prick came back. It took me forever to undo the knots with my fingers losing feeling."

"Hans won't bother you again," Chief said.

"He did his jungle fighter dance on me, too," Mordecai said. "Now get off the fucking hood."

"No, unless you promise to drive me back to the hotel." His legs wobbled and he collapsed. His jaw was slack, his eyes were puffy and his head bowed.

Tarr was an asshole, who belittled Mordecai, but that wasn't a terrible crime. Tarr didn't deserve to be tortured.

Minutes later, Tarr's head leaned against the back of the front seat with his chest heaving. After dropping Tarr off at the Sanctuary Hotel, Chief said, "The pussy didn't do it."

"Who did?" Mordecai pressed him.

"Maybe Pedro."

Mordecai glared at Chief. "First you tell me the killer ain't Pedro; then you tell me the killer is probably Pedro. You son of a bitch, you've been playing me."

Chief smiled. "You can't believe anything you hear."

"Especially from you," Mordecai interrupted, his voice heavy with sarcasm.

"You," Chief continued, ignoring the interruption, "don't have a friend in Shakespeare." He paused. "Someone is going to kill you and that's gonna ruin everything. Your family and the Dog Hugger bitch are going to demand an investigation and ARC is going be ripped apart like Hans. Shakespeare will become a ghost town. So just go home 'cause you won't enjoy your victory in a coffin."

"Afraid the Apache Bar will go under?"

Chief grimaced. "The ARC donates two hundred thousand to the Apache Health Center every year and gives tuition money for any Apache wanting an education. It sent me to ASU for a semester. When I told Sam Houston I wanted to come home, he bought the bar for me."

"Sam Houston was your rich daddy."

"Neah, the Army bankrolls ARC." He shrugged. "Let's go. I'm tired of trying to save your ass."

"Congratulations, you sound like my Uncle Julius."

TWENTY SEVEN

As he pulled up to the gated entrance of the Animal Research Center, Mordecai realized he was twenty minutes early for his job interview. Ahead of him, a pick-up truck idled next to a red brick guard house. With tired eyes, he glanced at the ten foot high fence topped with razor wire as far he could see. The place could pass for a maximum security prison.

Waiting he felt his head snap forward, jerking him awake. His eyelids were heavy from lack of sleep. It was 8:50 a.m., and he'd been up the last twenty-four hours.

The gate slid open, its chain clanging. The truck lumbered onto a black top road.

The gate closed and Mordecai rolled to the guard house. The glass door opened and a thin-faced, youthful guard stepped out, dressed in a black uniform with an automatic pistol holstered on his gun belt. He swallowed the last of a hero sandwich, wiped his hand on his pants and stared at the Pontiac, then its driver.

"Are you sure you're at the right place?" When Mordecai nodded, the guard asked his name. He studied his clipboard and shook his head. "Who are you seeing?"

Mordecai glanced at the slip of paper Hans had given him. "William Travis Cardwell."

A skeptical look crossed his face. "Are you sure, Sir?"

Mordecai nodded again, and the guard went into the guard house. Mordecai looked at the large sign on the closed gate. It read: No Unauthorized Person Allowed. Below this sign was a smaller sign. Patrolled By Attack Dogs. He clenched his jaw. What did he expect? Kitty cats?

The guard strolled out of the guard house, carrying a pole tipped with a polished mirror. "We have to search all visitors' cars. I'm sure you understand, Sir. Protesters." He bent over and shoved the mirrored pole under the car.

Mordecai complied with the request to open the trunk. The guard glanced into it and slammed it closed. He strolled over to the hood and began to lift it.

Suddenly he straightened as if he had touched hot metal. His eyes widened. He muttered, "son of a bitch," and sprinted into the guard house. A siren blared, sounding as if a prison riot had broken out. He stuck his head out of the guard house, looked around with a phone in his hand and screamed into it. "The protesters, they're here." He listened and then asked, "Are you sure, Boss?" He listened again. "Only eleven, twelve of them."

Mordecai turned to see a dozen protesters across the highway. They stood, waving signs, on the ridge of a hill. Behind and off to the side of the protesters was a tall woman. Her strawberry blond hair looked like hay in the early morning sunlight. It was Ana.

The guard hurried back toward Mordecai, carrying a wooden baseball bat. He waved it in the air.

"I wish those assholes would come down here."

The protesters yelled: "Stop the torture," "Free the prisoners," "No experimentation on animals."

The guard touched his automatic pistol. "I'd like to shoot a few of them, but Mr. Cardwell doesn't want trouble."

A rain of eggs and tomatoes fell around them. Some hit the Pontiac's trunk. Some blasted Mordecai's left arm resting on the car's open window and hung dripping from his jacket.

A man with a Santa Claus beard, driving to the guard house on an electric cart, shouted, "Put away the bat." He struggled to get off the cart, yelling, "Open the gate."

As soon as the gate opened wide enough, he squeezed through the opening. "Don't do anything. Don't call the police. We don't want the press. No publicity, understand?"

"But . . ." the guard murmured.

Santa Claus said, "We're getting the dogs out of sight," and smiled, his belly jiggling. The siren went silent. Then he continued, "No matter what, your job is to keep the Dog Huggers from kidnapping our dogs or even taking photos of them."

Mordecai heard distant barking. How could protesters kidnap an attack dog? The beasts would chew them up.

As the electric cart crept away, he pointed at Mordecai, saying, "Let him through. Travis wants to talk to him."

As Mordecai drove along the black top road, the barking grew louder, but it sounded scratchy like a bad recording. Soon it pierced his ears, but where were the roving dogs that could attack him? Stopping he looked around. Then he spotted the loud speaker behind some shrubs. He sighed, relaxing. These attack dogs weren't going to mistake him for a Dog Hugger.

The ARC was a squat, one-story building that had the architectural charm of a warehouse. He watched four electric carts in single file speed from the back of the structure. In the lead was Mai holding a cattle prod on high. The cavalry would arrive in time and give the Dog Huggers a shellacking.

Poor dumb Dog Huggers, he thought.

TWENTY EIGHT

William Travis Cardwell escorted him across his office to a rocking chair. Clutching the videotape Mai gave him, Mordecai sat and looked around. Shadows blanketed most of the windowless office. The track lighting illuminated the heads of a bear, a sheep, a wolf and a mountain cat along the far wall. Travis was a one-man extinction squad. He was a lanky six feet, three or four inches tall. His youthful face glistened as if untouched by the desert sun. His blond hair fell to the nape of his neck with a slight curl. He had the grooming of a model.

Again Mordecai glanced at the trophies. A skilled hunter could take down a jungle fighter like Hans. But did Travis have the nerve to do the kill?

When offered coffee, Mordecai said yes. He watched Travis stroll to a table in the far corner, moving gracefully like a ballroom dancer, with his blond hair flowing gently. He handed Mordecai a cup. "Sorry about the protesters."

Mordecai shrugged. "I needed to clean the jacket anyway."

"No, no, we'll take care of it." Travis lowered himself into an armchair. "Shakespeare hasn't greeted you with open arms. Hans thought you were a spy; said an anonymous caller told him."

He suspected Hans hadn't been lying. "The attack by such a small man surprised me."

"Hans said you were looking for your sister."

He repeated the sad tale of his mother on her death bed asking him to find his stepsister, born out of wed lock, whom he never knew existed until his Mom was dying.

"That's weird. I also had a sister I didn't know about until my father died. Now she's part of my inheritance." Travis leaned forward, staring at him, like a poker player looking for a 'tell'. "What's your mother's maiden name?"

He looked into Travis' eyes. One was blue and the other, green. The mismatch reminded him of someone, but he couldn't think of whom. "Esther, Esther Stein."

"I doubt we're related." Travis laughed. "Hans said you showed him a picture of your stepsister."

"No, the photo wasn't my stepsister."

Travis smiled, but only the corner of his mouth parted. "I was sure that was what Hans told me."

"Hans didn't give me a chance to explain. My mother had no picture of my stepsister. She said my sister looked like her, so I brought along a picture of my Mom."

"You don't seem to know much about your sister."

"My Mom was sometimes delusional. The meds and the brain tumor. I'm not sure if I even have a stepsister or she was ever in Shakespeare."

Mordecai thought his cover story camouflaged his lies. Sometimes you create a perfect bullshit story, one believable fact and the rest of the story, no one can contradict.

"Where are you staying?" Travis asked.

The question surprised him. "The Alamo Hotel."

There was a knock on the door and a plump woman in jeans and a denim shirt entered, pushing a cart of breakfast food. Its rubber wheels squeaked on the pine floor. Stopping next to them, she said, "No one has seen Hans."

Travis dismissed her with a quick thank you, making no effort to introduce Mordecai. "When we need Hans, he always goes missing."

Mordecai looked at the videotape in his lap. "Mai asked me to give this to Hans."

Taking the tape, Travis leaned back and dropped it on the roll top desk behind him. "Let's eat."

Mordecai piled scrambled eggs, hash brown potatoes and a bagel on his plate and poured himself a glass of orange juice.

"The bacon is delicious." Travis tonged two bacon pieces and placed them on top of Mordecai's eggs.

Mordecai pushed the bacon to the side of the plate.

"Your people don't eat pork." He tonged some roast beef onto Mordecai's plate. "Try it. It's special-ordered." He studied Mordecai. His brow was wrinkled as if in deep concentration.

Mordecai forked a piece of roast beef into his mouth. "It's good."

The furrowed brow disappeared. "Protesters tried to infiltrate the ARC, but none of them could eat meat without looking sick." The job is yours . . ." Travis paused, rubbing his forehead. "But you should know that some people are out to get us."

"I understand." Mordecai's passing the test of eating meat had melted away Travis' suspicions, like snow in a spring thaw.

"Can you go undercover?" Travis asked. "You're perfect for the job."

"What? Undercover?"

"Move to the Sanctuary Hotel. Get friendly with protesters. String them along so we know what they're planning to do. He ran his fingers through his wavy hair. "Nobody would believe a regular employee would betray us. ARC supports the town, but a guy passing through, that's another story. Are you willing to help us?" His gaze grew hard and he waited for an answer.

"Undercover is okay, but nothing, absolutely nothing, to do with dogs."

"You're afraid of dogs," Travis said in a mocking tone.

Leaning forward, Mordecai shot out his hand, the bite marks plainly visible. "See that gift from a German Shepherd?"

"No dogs."

"Okay, I'll take the job." Mordecai smiled. This meant double pay for being undercover. He thought he'd call his Uncle Julius and brag. But then he thought about it again. His uncle would protest; it was unethical to double bill. That wasn't Mordecai's problem.

Travis picked up the phone. "Tell Charles he can show Mordecai Glass around."

* * *

Mordecai heard the office door snap shut behind him and looked for the employee who was going to take him on a tour of ARC. The man with the Santa Claus beard scurried down the hall, his hand outstretched though fifteen feet away.

"Sorry I'm late." He shook Mordecai's hand as if it were a pump handle, while saying, "Charlie Abbott, Human Resources." His reddish face was puffy, his hand was soft, and his breath smelled of sweet wine.

Mordecai glanced at his watch. Not yet ten o'clock in the morning.

He steered Mordecai to a door numbered 4032 and punched a few numbers on a key pad. "I need some cafeteria time."

The cafeteria held about twenty tables. Abbott guided him to one as far away as possible from the other employees clustered near a serving counter, where a tall blond woman was pushing a tray along a metal railing. The counter extended the length of the far wall. Two workers were lifting trays, piled high with food, into the counter's serving track. There was no cashier. The food was free, a nice perk. ARC treated its employees first-class, a good reason to keep your mouth shut.

Charlie Abbott returned with pie and coffee for him and Mordecai. "Hans did his number on you?"

Mordecai nodded, his face feeling warm. "Hans caught me by surprise. If I was prepared, the results would have been different."

"You're never prepared for Hans."

"I was an amateur boxer," Mordecai protested.

"Don't feel bad. We hired you to keep Hans out of jail."

"I didn't squeal to the cops."

"We couldn't be sure. A criminal complaint, a trial, might make a nosey reporter curious about what we do." He paused. "Are you a reporter?"

"Me, no. I'm looking for my stepsister."

Abbott opened his mouth wide and pulled back his head laughing. "Sunny Begay, what a piss poor cover story. Only an idiot would use it. Are you an idiot?"

He shook his head vigorously.

"Spies are always trying to sneak in like flies through a screen." He forked a pie slice and greedily shoved it into his mouth. "The last one was a college boy. A lawyer hired him. He was supposed to make sure a Sam Houston heir wasn't cheated out of her inheritance. I caught him."

"You?"

Abbott grinned. "He thought acting dumb made him look like a wetback, but when I used the word elucidate, he understood. I warned him to leave. When he got stubborn, I told Hans and he disappeared like that." He snapped his fingers.

Mordecai wrinkled his forehead. Was Abbott a snitch? Was the wine breath a cover? Like a wine taster, Abbott could have swished it around his mouth and then spit it out leaving enough of an odor to convince Mordecai.

"I'm just a guy looking for his stepsister, and, as it turns out, a job."

"Good." He lowered his voice. "I'm happy you're going to work for us. Nothing dangerous. Just keep your eyes and ears open. Especially, anything about the money. If the Army cancels the contract, Travis can't keep ARC alive with the reserves."

"Must be big money?" Mordecai watched Abbott's mouth clamp shut.

The silence was his answer. "None of my business."

Abbott stroked his bushy beard.

Mordecai took a sip of coffee. Was he being tested? Finally he asked, "What do I get out of it?"

"I put you on the payroll – salaries here are good. I might even be able to double it."

Mordecai nodded. Triple dipping sounded great. "You got a deal."

Abbott smiled and patted Mordecai's arm, obviously pleased. He lowered his head as if talking to the table. He whispered, forcing Mordecai to lean in. "I don't want anyone to hear this. Let me give you some advice: Never criticize the Vietnam War or say the experiments on the dogs are worthless. Slinger, the head of research, would fire you, and Hans would ruin your married life or make you disappear."

"That's good to know."

"If Hans heard this, he'd come after me."

"You don't have to worry, I'll never tell him." That promise was easy to keep.

TWENTY NINE

Mordecai stood as silent as a sniper, hidden in the dimly lit rear of the Sanctuary Hotel lobby, looking for a place to spy on the protesters.

The only light was from the wide-mouth fireplace where red-hot logs crackled. He plopped into a leather chair, his head tilting back. He saw, high on the wall, the mounted heads of a bear, sheep, mountain lion and wolf. The wolf's wide jaws and flaring fangs grabbed his attention. A beast like that could have crushed Hans' windpipe, but would it have left anything of Hans? He scanned the other three heads. Something bothered him. Then it hit him that the animals were the same as those in Travis' office. It was hard to fathom that a dog friendly Sanctuary Hotel and Travis had the same bloodthirsty decorator. Even more puzzling was why the Sanctuary even existed in ARC's hostile turf.

He counted eleven protesters sitting near the hearth, most cross-legged, and smiling. They were too far away for Mordecai to hear if they were planning another piss poor raid. Except for an occasional laugh, all he heard was murmuring. If he wanted to know what they were talking about, he'd have to risk getting closer without being obvious. Under the wolf was a leather armchair, outside their circle but close enough to hear, a good spot for spying. He made his move.

Luckily he'd brought with him a paperback novel he'd found in his room. He ambled toward the chair and sunk into it. It was actually comfortable. Mordecai turned a couple of pages and pretended to read.

A curly-haired female protester smiled at him. It was a welcoming smile, but brief. She had a chubby face that gave her a soft, feminine look. He wanted to invite her to his suite, but he was pretty sure she wouldn't offer herself to anyone but an animal-rights activist.

He sat quietly for about five minutes trying to be unnoticed. Spying on these protesters felt wrong. In fucking fact, five years ago he'd been one of them demonstrating against the CIA's recruiting on the Washington University campus. He'd joined fifty other students to block the hall of the Admissions Building. The leader of the protestors shouted, "we're going to close down this shit house." Mordecai remembered his sarcastic reply, "Good luck."

"What?" The leader's eyebrows arched and he asked, "Why are you here?" Mordecai shrugged and replied, "Nothing good on TV." Just then, the campus and Clayton police entered, banging their nightsticks against their palms. Everyone but Mordecai quickstepped to the exit. For his bravery, he had been suspended, and never returned to Wash. U. – good riddance.

Looking at this motley crew, he wanted to say he was like them, but couldn't. He shook his head. How the hell did he become the protector of these pathetic asshole Dog Huggers?

He turned another page in the book which he was pretty sure was a romance novel from the cover - not his type of literature. He raised the book to just below eye level where he had a good view of the curly-haired protester, her halter top showing her generous breasts. She smiled at him again. Maybe she would be willing to go to his suite. He shook his head to get rid of the thought. He had a job to do.

The protesters had stopped laughing and were now talking in hushed tones. They talked about school, courses to avoid, the food in Shakespeare and beer. Someone spoke excitedly about hiking Mount Lemmon, but was warned that a mountain lion had been spotted in the area. His enthusiasm fled like air leaving a punctured balloon. Everyone fell quiet.

"I didn't find Lennie," yelled a young man bursting into the lobby, his voice quivering. A bandana covered his head, blond hair sprouting from its edges. He was barely tall enough to ride a roller coaster.

"Billie, where did you look?" Someone asked.

"It was freezing." His gaze swept the group.

"Where is he then?" a tall woman with a shrill voice asked.

Mordecai was tempted to tell them Lennie was a chicken shit who hauled ass back to Phoenix.

Billie shrugged. "I got a bad feeling."

The tall woman hugged Billie, her hips pressing against his belt. "Lennie will be okay," she assured him.

The smiling curly-haired woman asked, "How much of Round Mountain did you search?"

"Some, Beth. I saw some of the ARC staff in their electric carts, so I hustled out of there." He sighed.

The tall woman stood and walked a few paces outside the group. A compass, a mini Mag-lite, Swiss army knife and other exotic hiking tools attached to her belt jingled like wind chimes. "We got to be logical. No more wild speculation."

"Liz, what the hell are you saying?"

"Maybe he went home."

A chorus said, "His car is still here."

The curly-haired woman spoke. "He told me last night he was going back to the mountain to find a safe way in."

"Let's go back to Round Mountain and find him," Billie said.

The protesters decided to meet in the lobby again in twenty minutes. When the others left the lobby, the curly-haired protestor walked toward Mordecai with a slow cadence as if in step with music. Her halter top clung to her ample breasts. He couldn't believe his luck. He felt himself swelling. He prayed she wasn't like Rita. He hadn't been laid in over a year.

"What are you reading?"

His thick saliva made it difficult to speak. Finally he croaked, "Trash," and held up the book.

"Lost in Love." She laughed. "You aren't reading it."

"Why would you say that?"

"Real men like you don't read romances."

Was she calling him a liar or flirting? "What would I read?"

"A gory mystery." She looked at his feet. "What happened to your shoes?"

He glanced at his scuffed loafers covered with a fine coat of dust. "They're comfortable."

"While sniffing around Round Mountain?"

"Huh," he muttered

"A source told me that you needed someone to help you dig up dirt on ARC."

He frowned. He'd never seen her before and didn't know what she was talking about. "Who's your source?"

"We should work together." She gave him a wide smile.

He didn't reply. Who the hell did this broad think she was playing? A double dipper, no, a triple dipper wasn't easily conned.

"We got ourselves a gusher – a Pulitzer Prize," she said.

He smiled, "good luck. I ain't a reporter."

"Think about it." She winked and walked away.

THIRTY

Humming, Mordecai rode out of Sky Harbor Airport in a Chevy Cavalier. He decided he needed a change in cars after seeing Mai at the ARC. She hadn't recognized him at the bar, but she remembered the Pontiac.

Heading East on the Superstition Highway, Mordecai passed a few suburban homes until the road narrowed to two lanes bordered on both sides by desert. Off to the left, he could see the Superstition Mountains, where more than a few gold-fevered prospectors had searched for decades for the Lost Dutchman Mine. Poor dumb souls conned by a dream.

He entered Gonzalez Pass and the car started to climb. Darkness began to fall all around him. He felt uneasy driving the narrow winding mountain road on a moonless night, while facing the blinding headlights of oncoming traffic. Off to the side of the road, he could barely make out the wooden crosses, memorials to the Dobermans that had died in ARC experiments. He was pretty sure he counted at least twelve crosses that had been replaced by Dog Huggers after Dutch shattered the previous ones.

Finally back at the hotel in Shakespeare, Mordecai slipped the key card into the slot. Opening the door he smelled a sweet odor of a flickering candle on the coffee table and saw the red light of the phone flashing. The candle shadowed Ana as she seemed to float out of the bedroom.

"I've been waiting for you."

He stood frozen in the doorway, tongue-tied. Finally he sputtered, "Went to Phoenix."

She sashayed over like a model on a runway. Her halter top, bare midriff, and tight skirt slit up the front to above her knees got his attention. Her breasts were small but firm - inviting. She said softly, "close the door."

When the door snapped shut, she exploded with excitement. "You did it. A job at the ARC. I knew you could do it."

He didn't mention his job was to spy on Dog Huggers.

Extending her hand, she led him into the bedroom without saying a word. Her perfume gave off the scent of an exotic plant. He felt out-of-kilter as if walking on uneven ground.

"We can't do anything while you're dressed." She kissed him, her tongue roaming his mouth, and pushed him onto the bed.

While he regained his breath, she unhooked her halter top and slipped out of her skirt. She guided his hand between her legs. She was wet. She pulled at his shirt, ripping off buttons. His clothing became a rumpled pile on the floor.

In bed, she kissed him again and rolled him over onto her stomach. Her legs were spread wide, and she accepted him with ease. She responded in synchrony with his thrusts. If she made any sounds, he didn't hear her. All he heard was his own panting.

Finally, after ten minutes, she whispered, "You can come whenever you want."

He was in no hurry. And then he came.

"I like it when men groan."

He slipped off her, gasping for air.

Immediately she rolled away, resting her head on a pillow. She didn't snuggle like Rita and he missed that.

When his breathing returned to normal, she was all business, saying, "Now we bring down the ARC. We can torch the memorial to Sam Houston Cardwell, so my mother can rest in peace."

"I'm no fire bug."

"I didn't mean a big blaze," she said. "Start a little one in the animal pens so the Shakespeare fire department has to be called."

"Somebody could get hurt."

"Who?" she asked as if only a Martian would challenge her.

"The Dobermans," Mordecai answered.

She rubbed his chest. "Okay, not a fire. We'll free the Dobermans. Let the public see the mutilation."

"Free the dogs? Have you ever seen them? They got things growing out of their heads. I don't trust Dobermans, and I'm not getting near those grotesque monsters."

He felt her body tense.

"Don't get upset," she said in a soothing voice.

"What about the Army investigation?" he asked.

She looked at her watch. "I let my emotions get the best of me. I need to leave soon. But before then . . ." Her hand stroked his penis. "It's shrunk. I can kiss it and make it bigger."

He tried to discern any emotion in her expressionless face. Useless. He saw no smile after she gave him a light kiss on his forehead. He watched her dress quickly and drop an envelope on the bed.

By the door, she felt her ear. She said, "The earring my mother gave me is missing." She looked at her watch again. "I'm late," and continued walking out.

When he heard the door close, he switched on the lamp and ripped open the envelope. Inside was a check drawn on a Bank of America signed by Santa Ana Johnson. Two thousand dollars. He stared at the signature. The significance of Ana with only one 'N' hit him.

"Mordecai," he muttered, "you're a dum-me." The Mexican-American War permeated the whole shebang: Sam Houston, Travis, the Alamo Hotel and Santa Ana. Why did Ana's mother name her after a Mexican General? Why was it important for Ana to lie and say that she was named after her mom's prized Doberman?

THIRTY ONE

The morning sun snuck between the wooden shutters. Mordecai pulled the sheet over his head, hoping to retreat into the darkness of sleep. Under the covers, he took a deep breath, inhaling the sweet perfume of sex. With his eyes closed, the scent brought back last night as if he were watching a movie. He pictured the beginning when she was under him and then over him and when she wrapped her legs around his back like a contortionist. Without being asked, Ana did every sexual act he'd hoped for.

He opened his eyes to stop visualizing the disappointing ending. As soon as he came, Ana had disentangled her limbs and retreated to the other side of the bed as if their business was concluded. Maybe the two thousand dollars and getting laid were his reward for infiltrating the ARC. He hadn't expected true love, but a little snuggling would have sweetened the sex.

He shook the cover off his body and shoved it away with his foot. As it fluttered to the bottom of the bed, he spotted Ana's missing earring, a ruby encircled by tiny diamonds. He fingered it carefully, its post sticking in the sheet. Suddenly his face scrunched up as if he smelled a foul odor.

Holy Moses! Last night he'd been too overheated to see what was going on. Ana hadn't searched for the earring. Instead, Ana casually said that she had an appointment and that it was missing and then she left. How the hell could she not search for it? If it was his mother's heirloom, he wouldn't stop looking until he found it. Her nonchalance didn't make sense. She proclaimed her crusade to rescue Dobermans was to let her mother's soul rest in peace, yet she hadn't shown any distress at the missing gift. Maybe her worship of her mom was an act just like last night's sex.

Minutes later to rid himself of the sexual scent, he plopped into the Jacuzzi and turned on the spigots. Listening to the rush of flowing water, he contemplated that it was costing Ana a fortune for this suite, not that he minded. He was in the lap of luxury, with Ana and Travis thinking each other was paying the bills.

The stream of hot water splashed into the Jacuzzi, a cloud of steam floating up to his waistline. There wasn't enough water in the tub yet to turn on the jets. He picked up the bar of soap and peeled off the wrapper. Idling away the time, he read: ALAMO HOTEL – EAST. Holy Moses, how did a no-pets-allowed Alamo Hotel become the Sanctuary Hotel, a Dog Hugger's haven?

He bathed quickly and jumped out of the Jacuzzi, his mind whirling. It was obvious Ana owned the Dorothea Doberman Sanctuary and the newly named Sanctuary Hotel where she'd booked him, a dead-give-away he was on the side of the Dog Huggers. The bitch kept him in the dark about Pedro. He had learned about his missing predecessor from Chief. Shit! The <u>fuckin'</u> woman had never even asked if Sunny Begay had contacted him.

He wrapped himself in a thick terry cloth robe and picked up his ringing cell phone. He should answer it, but he didn't. The ID showed it was a call from Uncle Julius, who would quiz him, something he couldn't tolerate. If he mentioned Hans' murder, his uncle would lecture him about immediately walking away.

His damp robe clinging to his back, he collapsed into a tufted chair by the picture window, looking across Highway 60 toward the nearby hills that hid ARC and its secrets. His client, too, was hiding secrets.

What did he know about her? Just that she was twisting his balls.

After resting, he phoned his uncle, took a deep breath, and waited for Julius to answer. He started the conversation, "I'm cutting out of Shakespeare in a week or two."

Uncle Julius snorted. "Why are you leaving?"

"It doesn't feel right."

"I can stop worrying when you get your butt back to St. Louis."

"What's happening with the South Side Dragons?" Mordecai asked.

"You're lucky Elizabeth wasn't Elizabeth. It was another runaway named Betsy. She couldn't lead the bikers to you."

Mordecai took a deep breath and released it quickly. "I need a favor. Could you check out what Russell Parker said to my client?"

"That's on my agenda. I have an appointment to see him day after tomorrow. I will probably have to apologize."

"Not to that pompous asshole?"

"Mordecai, I'm in the investigative business. Scraping and bowing doesn't cost me anything."

His face felt flushed. How can Uncle Julius suck up to Parker and then dismiss his ass kissing as if swatting away a fly? "Doesn't it bother you?"

"If you let your pride get in the way, you'll make awful decisions. For what? Hurt feelings? You have to walk away from your ego."

His uncle's chicken shit talk disappointed him - picking money over being a man - and he wasn't in the mood to hear a lecture, but Mordecai had to admit a practical person would do the same thing as his uncle.

"You don't believe I'm a patsy?"

"Forget about Parker, and let me find out. Investigate your client," his uncle insisted, "to make sure she's not playing you."

THIRTY TWO

Mordecai sped east on Highway 60 through the canyon, heading toward Ana's Doberman Sanctuary. The tires moaned as he whipped around a twisting curve. On his previous trip, his fingers had cramped as he tightly gripped the steering wheel, but not today. When he hit the flats, he was doing eighty-five. It felt like he was flying, the tires barely touching the road. He turned off at Apache Junction and headed down Superstition Boulevard.

The town looked like it had never seen better days. Non-descript storefronts sprouted like weeds along the road. The only department store he saw was a Salvation Army outlet. One storefront window had chalked on it 'holiday discounts'. Didn't the bozo owner know it was March? Nothing pretentious in Apache Junction, just a working-class town.

He rolled into the Sanctuary Plaza's sprawling U-shaped parking lot. He looked around for a space until he spotted a teenage girl backing up and waited for her to leave. Half-way out, she stopped, blocking the lane while she talked on her cell phone. He drummed on his steering wheel, muttering, "asshole." Breathing heavily, he resisted a blast on his horn. Instead he gave her the middle finger, his hand below the dash. When she finally backed out, he gave her a big smile.

He drove into the space, parked, grabbed his cell phone and called information. Given the number, he shoved two Kleenex into his mouth and dialed. He asked for Ona Jansen. He repeated the name three times before the woman said Ana wasn't in. He asked when she'd return and he was told she was out for the day.

Moments later he entered the Doberman Sanctuary. The smell of leather couches and chairs permeated the air in the waiting room. A coffee dispenser on the reception counter offered the choice of hazelnut, French roast, or French vanilla.

The decor was like those highfalutin hair salons in Clayton, where the barbers called themselves hair stylists and expected a tip bigger than what regular barbers charged. Behind the Sanctuary counter, a smiling receptionist in her forties wore a T-shirt embossed with the head of a black-and-tan Doberman. She introduced herself as Alice.

"Julius Stein," he replied.

"How can I help?"

"My mother passed away recently."

"I'm so sorry."

Mordecai continued: "She loved dogs but couldn't have one because, sadly, I'm allergic. She bequeathed a gift to a no-kill animal shelter." He paused. "Could I speak to Dorothea?"

"She passed away," Alice said, her words catching in her throat. "Let me give you our brochure."

Mordecai looked around, spotting in the corner a white board on which was printed:

DOROTHEA DOBERMAN SANCTUARY
Goal $2,121,031
Shortfall $1,253, 921

"It must be," Mordecai said, "costly to maintain an animal rescue?"

"We've generous donors. Without them, we would have had to shut our doors long ago."

As she reached behind the counter and retrieved a brochure, a persistent bark came from a door behind her. "Excuse me." She turned and walked to the door, muttering, "Rudy is lonely, Rudy is lonely."

Moments later a black-and-tan Doberman pup with a sleek body galloped around the counter, its eyes locked on Mordecai.

He said loudly, "I'm" – but he didn't get out 'allergic' before Rudy sideswiped him, almost knocking him off his feet. When Mordecai regained his balance, Rudy leaned against him like he was a fire hydrant and then rolled over on his back.

"Could you remove him?" His insides quivered.

"Scratch his belly, and he'll calm down," said Alice. Rudy looked up at him with pleading eyes.

He stepped around the pup, staying two feet away. His back was to Alice, and his quivering hands were hidden from the receptionist's view. He whipped his hand across the pup's belly barely touching Rudy's fur. The Doberman raised its head and licked his hand.

Mordecai looked down at the supine dog wagging his tail. How could a puppy make him quiver? Rudy wasn't his stepmother's Nazi dog. If he'd touched Fritz's belly, the canine would have tattooed a concentration number on his arm.

He sighed.

"Too bad you're allergic," she said, "you could have adopted Rudy."

"It's too bad," he said.

Alice called to Rudy, then looked up at Mordecai. "Do you mind if I just take him into the back and put him in his cage? It will only take a minute."

"Not at all. Take your time."

Alice slipped a leash over Rudy's head and took him through the door to the kennels. Mordecai used this opportunity to examine the papers that were on the counter - letters inquiring about Doberman's, bills from dog food dealers, and a list of donors to the rescue center. His eyes ran down the list to the last entry. He almost gasped. The Sam Houston Foundation had donated a yearly annuity of two hundred thousand, five hundred dollars. He heard the door knob turn and stepped back.

"Thanks for waiting," Alice said as she entered. "Ana Johnson, our Director, will be here tomorrow." She handed him a business card.

"S. Ana Johnson, CEO," he read. "What does the S stand for?"

"Santa Ana," she replied. "Don't forget your brochure."

* * *

Before leaving town, Mordecai bought a croissant and coffee from a small bakery a few doors away from the Sanctuary. He sat in the Chevy munching on the pastry while he thumbed through the expensive-looking brochure. The pages were high gloss paper with a lot of colored photos. Who was Ana trying to impress? The big donors? And why was the Sam Houston Foundation a donor - a big donor? Mordecai was baffled.

On the cover Dorothea looked like an older Ana, except her short blond hair was swept straight back, highlighting her sad eyes. The center piece featured a memorial to Dorothea Johnson. He read the article quickly. She'd dedicated her life to breeding Dobermans and fighting for the humane treatment of all animals. It was a heroic struggle, often futile, against animal behaviorists who were using Dobermans for cruel experiments. The effort wore her out. Her doctor said she died of a blood disorder, but her friends knew better. She'd died of exhaustion and a broken heart, losing too many battles trying to save her beloved Dobermans. The final sentence was 'Long live the struggle' - what bullshit. It sounded like a revolutionary slogan calling the faithful to the picket line.

For whom would Mordecai sacrifice his health? Certainly not a dog.

He thought about the donation from the Sam Houston Foundation. God help him, there was a conspiracy between the ARC and the Dorothea Doberman Sanctuary, supposedly bitter enemies. He was hired to bring down the ARC and Ana never told him there was a truce between the two.

In Ana's and the Foundation's chess game, he was the pawn.

THIRTY THREE

Mordecai strolled into the Apache Bar; his stomach growled just as the thin afternoon crowd stopped chattering. The patrons at the three tables stared as if he had a contagious disease. He swept his hand across his mouth and nose. There was nothing to wipe off.

He strode to a rear table. The bar maid brought over two beer bottles. When he sat, he protested, "I didn't order a beer."

"The guys over there paid for it." She pointed at the three tables. "You can drink for free all day and night."

"What's goin' on?" he asked.

She shrugged.

Mordecai held up his beer bottle to acknowledge the free drinks and in response, the patrons raised their bottles high.

He asked the bar maid where Chief was, and she directed him to the kitchen. Grease hung heavy in the air and cheeseburgers sizzled on the grill. "Why are the drunks buying me drinks?"

"Let me finish grilling the cheeseburgers."

He watched Chief slop cheese, tomatoes and onions on the patties and, when finished, plop the paper plates on the kitchen window with half the condiments falling off the buns. He rang the bell. Turning toward Mordecai, Chief said, "there's a rumor, you made Hans disappear."

"Who started that crazy bullshit?" Mordecai bellowed.

Chief wiped off the grease-encrusted spatula with a paper towel and balanced it on the edge of the grill. "I did. Saved your ass."

"You bastard, you screwed me."

"I saved your ass. Your reputation will keep the ARC cowboys from popping you, or you could be another Pedro."

"I don't think so." Mordecai muttered.

"Why not? He was an undercover agent just like you. If he was lucky, he's probably rotting at the bottom of a mining pit."

"When the State of Arizona straps me on a gurney and jabs a needle in my vein, I can thank you."

"Don't worry, I can tell the cops what happened." Chief had a smug look on his moon face.

The smell of grease and onions turned Mordecai's stomach queasy. There had to be a better place to eat than the Apache. He walked out without returning the patrons' smiles. A killer wasn't supposed to be friendly.

As he strutted down the middle of Derringer Street, pedestrians veered away from him. He scared the shit out of the Shakespeare folk, except he knew Hans' real killer would have no such fear.

His stomach growled again as he entered the Aperitif, dreaming of a veggie omelet with hash brown potatoes drowning in ketchup. The muted décor conveyed the quiet of a library. Crystal decanters, holding red, white and yellow flowers, stood on embroidered tablecloths. Dark paneling climbed halfway up the wall to meet the cerulean wallpaper. The Aperitif could hold its head high among the plush restaurants of Clayton. It didn't belong in a land of mining and ranching.

The waiter stood silent, a petulant look on his smooth-skinned face. He wore a blue polka dot bowtie, a ruffled white shirt and black pants, the standard uniform of an upscale restaurant. He eyed Mordecai strolling to a corner table like he was a homeless man about to ask to use the bathroom.

Mordecai, in his labor outfit - a denim shirt, Levis and working boots - waved to the waiter who responded with his name, Henry. When Mordecai asked for a breakfast menu, Henry tapped his watch. "I'm sorry but you are too late. Breakfast ended at 11:30."

Mordecai clenched his fists and bit his lower lip. "Can't you extend it? I'm hungry for an omelet."

Henry stiffened. "We're preparing for lunch."

The waiter tossed a luncheon menu on the table.

Mordecai stared hard. "Do you know who I am?"

He twisted his lips into a sneer. "Why should I?"

His voice rang out. "Mordecai Glass."

Henry's face turned ghostly white. "Mr. Glass," he stammered, "Would you like champagne with your order?"

"No," he replied crisply.

Charles Abbott, who must have been eavesdropping, appeared from the patio, saying, "Henry, bring us champagne." Sitting at the table, he looked like a hung over Santa Claus with his unkempt bushy white beard.

Mordecai studied the poor slob. "You must have had a tough day."

"I'm celebrating Hans' disappearance."

Mordecai nodded. So was he.

After ten minutes of silence, the waiter arrived carrying the veggie omelet. Mordecai reached for the ketchup bottle. No fancy meals for him.

Henry rattled the dish on the table and, with a tremor, poured a cup of coffee, some of which splashed into the saucer. "Sorry, Mr. Glass."

Mordecai suppressed a smile. "Don't worry about it."

Abbott leaned over and took Mordecai's untouched flute.

"That's Mr. Glass' drink," the waiter said. "Mr. Glass would you like another champagne?"

"Bring him one," Abbott demanded.

Henry lowered his gaze to the floor, his lips twitching. He waited for Mordecai's answer. Finally, the waiter raised his head with lines of worry crossing his face. "Mr. Glass, is that okay?"

When Mordecai nodded, Henry frowned at Abbott and marched off to the kitchen.

"Henry is scared shitless, afraid you'll make him disappear like Hans, if he annoys you."

Mordecai wanted to enjoy his meal and didn't want to talk about Hans. "Henry doesn't have to worry."

Abbott tilted his head back and directed his words to the ceiling. "Have you heard any rumors yet?"

Mordecai laughed, choking on the omelet. It was obvious the guy was delirious from drinking. "I just started the job. What do you expect from me?" He shoveled a hefty omelet slice into his mouth.

For a long moment, Abbott studied him. Finally, he said, "I might be able to up your salary - off the books, of course."

"If you're bullshitting me . . ."

Abbott interjected: "Don't threaten me. You'll get your money tomorrow." He took a lengthy sip, a few champagne drops dripping from his bushy beard. "I want you to listen for something besides the money."

"Yeah? What?" Mordecai asked.

"For anything suspicious - like someone talking incessantly about the Pharmaceutical Consortium." He paused and stared at Mordecai. "Then you report back to me."

Mordecai nodded. "It doesn't sound too hard."

"Whatever you hear, keep it quiet." Abbott gulped the last of his champagne. "Now we have to finish your tour."

"Can we skip the Dobermans?"

Abbott laughed. "Are you scared?"

"I don't trust big dogs." Mordecai thrust out his hand. "These scars are the teeth marks of a German Shepherd."

He could have added that he didn't trust Abbott, either.

THIRTY FOUR

Following Abbott, Mordecai stumbled along the dimly lit passageway of the ARC, its walls, floors and ceiling painted black. He started to feel agitated. Was he bumbling into his nightmare? A firing squad of Dobermans.

Wheezing, Abbott halted and informed him that General Nguyen would be working with the killer Dobermans. "Travis wants you to make sure that the General doesn't do anything crazy. The bastard is dangerous. Don't upset him or he'll sic the dogs on you."

Mordecai figured the Dobermans were caged or he wouldn't even be here.

"I told Sam Houston we should ship the Gook back to Vietnam. The General knows too much. The bastard's heroin financed us before the Army funding." He wiped the sweat from his brow. "Sam Houston believed we should be loyal," Abbott said.

"I heard he's senile."

"Maybe crazy. The bastard wants to invade Vietnam and start an insurrection with a troop of killer Dobermans. If you weren't here, he'd probably sic the damned dogs on me."

Mordecai decided to try to get Abbott to turn around. "Let's skip the dogs. I hate to see you hurt."

Looking exasperated, Abbott exhaled loudly, his breath smelling of alcohol. "If the upcoming Army visit is a failure because the implants miss the hot spot or the Dobies go into convulsions, ARC is down the toilet. I'll have to attend AA meetings again, trim my beard and start searching for another job."

Hot spot. What was the fat bag of wind talking about? It sounded like the name of a strip joint. "What the hell is the hot spot?"

"You don't know?"

"No."

Abbott puffed out his cheeks. "Good. If someone gives you an intracranial stimulation journal article, don't read it. Give it to me."

"You like me ignorant."

He nodded. "Do you know anything about these dogs?"

"Never even seen them, thank God." If Abbott accused him of lying, it meant Chief squealed.

Abbott spit out, "Knowing too much can get you killed."

Mordecai smiled and fell farther behind Abbott, in case he decided to turn around and run to safety.

Abruptly, the dim overhead lights clicked on bright for a fraction of a second and then off as they walked. Dim emergency lights flicked on. His breath caught in his throat. Mordecai imagined killer Dobermans in the shadows.

"Damn place is making my asthma act up," Mordecai said to cover his erratic breathing.

"Your asthma, my fat ass." Abbott laughed.

The tunnel dead ended. Abbott walked to the wall and poked his finger on a keypad. A door sprung open. They entered a passageway, well lit, with a translucent roof. They walked another thirty feet to where Abbott opened an unlocked door revealing fenced-in kennels dug out of a hillside.

Standing in front of one of these kennels was an Asian-looking man holding two Dobermans with antennas sticking through orange plastic caps on their skulls. He was also holding a strange looking gun. Mordecai wasn't sure if he was protecting himself from the killer dogs or about to shoot the intruders.

As he approached the first cage, a massive black-and-tan male Doberman with a smooth skull loped to the fence. It must weigh well over a hundred pounds, Mordecai calculated. He moved behind Abbott. The fat man stuck his stubby fingers through the chain link fence and wiggled them. Wagging its tail, the dog slobbered over his fingers.

"Mordecai, this is General Nguyen, and over here," Abbott pointed to the kennel, "is number 1-4-3. Go ahead and pet the dog."

"I hope the big boy isn't hungry," Mordecai said.

He stepped toward the cage and pressed his palm against the wire, making it look like he extended his fingers through the gap. 143 stuck out his tongue and licked his palm furiously.

"143 loves you," Abbott said.

Mordecai shrugged. "I forgot to wash my hands after lunch."

"What do here?" Nguyen screeched. "Go away."

"Travis wants Mr. Glass to see the dogs in action," Abbott said loudly.

Nguyen said nothing, but returned the two dogs he was holding to their respective kennels. He stared at the men and then raised his gun. Mordecai backed away. The gun wasn't pointed at him, thank God, but he didn't trust this senile - or crazy - old bastard.

Up close, the gun no longer looked like a gun. It was a large, black box that Nguyen held sideways with a thumb underneath and four fingers on top.

Nguyen's fingers danced across the top of the box as if playing a musical instrument. He smiled broadly as the red dog turned in circles and pranced.

The gadget must be a remote control device, Mordecai figured.

"Stop," Abbott ordered. "You're going to give him a seizure."

Nguyen's face hardened as he pressed the keys. The red dog charged toward them, smashing into the metal fence and biting the metal strands. Nguyen opened the gate. The red Doberman (131) charged out, free to attack them.

Mordecai was already running toward the door with Abbott following close behind. "Crazy Gook," he yelled. Suddenly, Abbott tripped and hit the floor hard. Nguyen laughed like a mad man.

With his hand on the door knob, Mordecai halted. There was no way he could save Abbott.

The dog nipped Abbott and then whirled in a strange dance. Abruptly, Doberman 131 froze, frothing at the mouth. Thick white saliva bombarded Abbott's chest.

Nguyen was screaming and pressing the remote fanatically.

Abbott was trying to push himself up but his arms were unable to lift his heavy body.

Mordecai, seeing the Doberman was having a convulsion, ran toward Abbott lying prostrate on the floor. Half dragging and half supporting the fat man, they made it through the exit door and into the tunnel where they both collapsed.

Abbott sputtered, "What took you so long?"

"A big fucking dog."

THIRTY FIVE

In the ARC passageway, Abbott glared at Mordecai. "You didn't try to rescue me. You ran off. Where are your guts?"

"What the hell are you saying to me? I was paid to protect the dogs, not you." Mordecai's face felt hot.

"You could have attacked the Gook."

As Abbott spoke he expelled a fine spray of saliva. He took a few deep breaths and snorted, struggling to stand.

"You let the Doberman nip me."

He thrust his arm under Mordecai's chin. Blood spots dotted his jacket sleeves.

"I'm not blind," Mordecai said. "You don't have to shove your sleeve in my face."

"Next time, if you don't protect me, I'll tell Hans you're a spy and order him to take care of you. You know what that means."

It was an empty threat unless a dead Hans came back to life. "You don't believe my reputation," Mordecai said without hesitating.

He combed his bushy beard and straightened his bloody zippered jacket. "You're lucky that Hans is probably in Southeast Asia working a heroin deal."

Mordecai said, "You're willing to chance that Hans is alive. If you're wrong, then . . ."

Abbott shrugged. "Okay, let's finish the tour."

"No. I'm done."

Abbott's right eye twitched.

"Last time I felt pity for a kid like you, a University of Arizona student, it cost me. I got a Pentagon ass-whipping by General Jensen for not eliminating Pedro Lopez."

* * *

It took two hours to reach Pedro Lopez's office at the Family and Consumer Science building. On the way, he drove through the small town of Winkelman where he slowed to watch a dump truck pour steaming red hot gel down a hill covered in black mounds. Just like Copper City - it looked like another demonic ceremony.

He knocked on Pedro Lopez's office door where a plaque read teaching assistant. Mordecai heard a lock turn and a strained voice said, "Wait a minute."

A young man opened the door. His features were well-proportioned and his smooth brown skin had the luster of someone who pampered himself.

Mordecai was surprised he wasn't a theater major. "Pedro Lopez?"

Nodding, the young man asked, "What's the problem?"

"I'm Mordecai Glass."

"You're in Family Research 201?" he asked, frowning. "Sorry, I don't remember your name."

The sweet mist of marijuana hung in the air, which Mordecai wanted to swat away as if it was a swarm of tiny insects.

"I'm not a student," Mordecai said softly.

Pedro glanced at his watch. His face hardened.

"You're the new football advisor and fifty minutes late. You tell the football players they betta show up to class. No more free passes. Why the football staff shoves them into Family Studies, when guys don't even come to class, I'll never understand."

"Sorry. I'm a private detective, investigating ARC."

"Does smoke bother you?"

"I'm a smoker," he lied.

Pedro pulled an ashtray from a drawer and a can of Glade air freshener. "Thank God, I go crazy without a joint."

Mordecai shook his head. "Ana Johnson was worried that you were killed or Hans ran you off." He lied.

Pedro shook his head. "My Uncle Tomas was her lawyer and my protection."

"How 'bout Hans?" Mordecai asked.

"Hans and his crazy daughter don't frighten me."

"Hans did a number on lots of people," Mordecai added.

"He was a sneaky bastard. He'd kick you in the balls when you weren't looking. I was an all-state catcher with inquiries from the big league until my knee injury. Hans wouldn't mess with me." Pedro rolled up the sleeve of his denim shirt and placed his hand on the desk extending his fingers. His hand was bigger than Mordecai expected. Slowly he curled his hand into a fist, his forearm muscles rippled.

"Why was she worried you were in danger?"

"She's playing with your mind," Pedro replied. "Maybe, playing with your balls like she did with my uncle?"

"What does she want?" Mordecai asked.

"Whatever it is, she's a treacherous bitch. It wasn't what she asked you for, it was always something else she wanted you to do."

"What did your uncle want?" Mordecai asked.

"He was interested in the financials - whether the institute was tightening expenses, giving some staff raises, siphoning off money."

"He never asked about the dogs?"

Mordecai was feeling a little nauseous and definitely woozy from the smoke.

Pedro shook his head. "When I mentioned the Dobermans occasionally, he told me. 'Forget that crap.' "

"Travis has me spying on the protesters, thank God," Mordecai said. "I'd hate to go near those grotesque creatures. Just thinking of them knots my stomach."

"You look pale," Pedro said.

"It's the smoke."

Pedro pushed on the window behind his desk. It didn't move. He banged on the frame with his fist. The window rattled, and he raised it. "Feeling better?"

A breeze wafted in, washing away the sweat from Mordecai's brow.

"Wouldn't spilling the beans upset your uncle?"

"He hates her. He discovered she was screwing a fat-ass protester. When he confronted her, she told him to stuff it or she'd tell his wife. Did she do you?"

"No."

Mordecai almost forgot to ask. "What did Chief know about your spying?"

"Who?"

"The Apache Bar."

"Oh him. I don't waste my time in bars. Gross, overweight women hang there." He inhaled deeply, holding in the smoke for a few seconds and then let it explode out of his youthful mouth. "I was sure you'd ask about Sunny Begay. My Uncle Tomas asked me to write a fictitious letter, wild shit, in the name of Sunny Begay and mail it from Tucson to the bitch."

Mordecai's jaw dropped. Everything she told him was a lie. He was a patsy.

THIRTY SIX

On his way back to Shakespeare, Mordecai decided to stop in Winkelman for gas. He didn't want to stop in this weird town, but he had little choice with his car's gas gauge flirting with the red zone.

He pulled into the station and asked the attendant about the devilish stuff flowing down the hill.

"It's sludge from the copper refinery." He grinned as if Mordecai was an idiot.

"What kind of town dumps its garbage on a hill?"

The attendant's voice dripped with sarcasm. "Where have you been, partner? That garbage is the life of Winkelman."

"You think I'm stupid?" Mordecai asked, balling his hand into a fist. He wasn't gonna take any more shit after what Pedro had told him, not from this asshole or Ana.

The attendant stepped back. "No offense, mister."

He drove off in anger. Chief and Ana were lying sludge. But how could he call himself a detective when he was played for a patsy?

* * *

Just before the junction of I-77 and I-70, he drove into a pull-off to think. His choice was either return to Shakespeare or drive straight through to Phoenix and fly back to St. Louis.

On his way to Sky Harbor Airport, he spotted a sign for a Bank of America branch in Apache Junction and exited into town. He could use some cash for his flight home.

As he parked, he looked at his watch and realized the bank was about to close. The inside was nondescript, a low paneled ceiling shopping center bank. There should be no fuss about such a puny withdrawal of $200.

He halted a few feet away from the bank counter. That amount of dough wasn't enough to cool his anger. Ana had set him up as a Dog Hugger. If he was lucky, an irate miner or an ARC employee would only bash in his skull. If unlucky, he would have been killed by Hans. What was his life worth? More than a lousy two hundred bucks.

His heart thumping, Mordecai stuck his hand in his pocket and fingered the Dorothea Doberman Sanctuary credit card. As he dropped it on the counter, he said to the teller, "Five thousand dollars, please."

The front door lock clicked closed. He was the last customer. God help him.

The teller grabbed the card and guided him to the assistant manager, Manuel.

"Dorothy was a regular client." Manuel went on talking about his dog Chico who misbehaved, tearing up slippers, dumping garage. Why did he get a talkative assistant manager who thought every little thing Chico did was interesting?

Manuel asked to see his driver's license. Studying the license, he said he had never been to St. Louis. He told Mordecai that growing up in Apache Junction, he hardly traveled beyond Phoenix. Once when he was seven years old, his mother took him to the San Diego Zoo.

Manuel's review of his childhood made Mordecai uneasy. He glanced at his watch. The manager got the hint. "Twenty-five hundred is the limit unless you have a Bank of America account."

"Twenty-five, fine."

Ten minutes later, the rays of the sun hit the Chevy's hood at a narrow angle. He wasn't done using the credit card. There were other cows to milk - spying on the ARC for Ana, and infiltrating the Dog Huggers for Travis, and snitching on ARC employees for Abbott.

He wasn't going home poor, thank God.

THIRTY SEVEN

Travis filled half of his glass with vodka and gulped it down in three swallows.

The door flew open, shuttering on its hinges. "Where's my dad?" Mai shouted.

Travis had a hard time imagining anyone calling the Neanderthal Hans, dad? Hans was a madman, seduced by Sam Houston's dream; and he had turned his daughter into a carbon copy of himself.

"You're going to break the door."

"The imposter killed my dad," Mai said.

She advanced to within inches of him. Her eyes were dark with fury.

He backed up, bumping against the roll top desk. "I told your dad to disappear."

"Why would you do that?"

"We can't afford any bad publicity with the DoD contract in jeopardy? Your father was threatening to kill Dog Huggers - that's big trouble."

She smiled. Her mouth loosened as if a relaxing fluid surged through her veins. Her pupils changed from a dark hue to a purple one.

"Aren't you pleased that we scared the chicken-shit Dog Huggers?" she asked.

"No. This place is hanging by a thread."

"It's J.B. stirring up trouble." She stroked his arm. "I'll take care of him."

"Who?" He knew she meant the new hire, but he feigned ignorance.

"Jew Boy." She paused. "And if you were a real man, you'd do something."

Travis felt a knot in his stomach tighten. She was a pain in the ass, but in two months she'd be the Pharmaceutical Consortium's problem. "Your father hired him." He smiled, pleased with his reply, but then realized it was a mistake. He turned away from her.

"What are you smirking about?" Her eyes exploded with rage. She rose on her toes and slapped him. "If you were a real man, you'd kill him."

"Not now." He knew where this was going; violence was her aphrodisiac.

Her face was lava red. She slapped him again. This time it stung.

He grabbed her by her hair and dragged her to the roll top desk and pushed her face down onto the work surface. She slipped her palm under her face as a cushion and then stuck out her thin sexless ass and spread her legs wide.

He felt the top of her jeans. She had unbuttoned her fly. He pulled down her jeans and her panties. He was hardly in the mood for this game.

She squirmed and pressed her rump against him. She wanted him to enter her from the rear like a dog.

"Maybe I should kill you, instead," he whispered. Soon the madness would be over. For now he had to satisfy her. He unzipped his fly.

Damn, his penis was flaccid. This was just a test of his acting skills, no more difficult than portraying fear or greed. Dig into your memory for the emotion, his acting teachers taught him. Theresa, the actress who initiated him when he was a summer stock intern, popped into his mind. She was the fantasy he'd masturbated to as a young man. He closed his eyes.

"What's keeping you?" she protested.

Roughly, he jammed his hand between her legs. She was moist.

A moment later he was hard. He slipped his penis between her unshaved legs, which he hated. She thrust her rump farther back and removed her arm from under her face, which was now squished sidewise on the desk.

She squealed, her body writhing. "Make it rough." Her voice hissed.

With his eyes closed, Travis manhandled his imaginary Theresa. He thrust, his hips banging against her thin rump.

"It hurts," she moaned.

He rammed her harder, hoping this didn't last long. A few minutes later Mai's breathing quickened, and she exhaled a long moan. "You didn't come," she said between deep breaths.

Quickly, he zipped up his fly and pulled away from her. He doubted Theresa would have enjoyed the rough sex. He heard she lived in the Midwest with her accountant husband and three kids -what a waste of talent. "Mai, I've got a lot of things on my mind."

Pulling up her clothing, she said, "I'm ready to find the Jew Boy."

He was irritated that his effort to calm her down had failed. She could ruin the pharmaceutical deal.

"Don't." He paused. "It's over. This was Sam Houston's dream. I would like that dream to live on peacefully after his death."

"No," she protested. "I'll get rid of that Mordecai and the protesters."

"It's more than protesters. Everything is out of control."

"I let you, only you, have me that way," her voice cracked, "because you used to be my warrior."

"That's more of Hans' jungle-fighting bullshit," he blurted out.

"Sam Houston didn't mean anything to you," Mai said.

"We're not teenagers anymore."

She threw a punch at him, but he deflected with his right arm. "Mai, no violence, no strong-arming the Dog Huggers or the Sight and Kill contract could be flushed down the toilet."

"A chicken! Have you become one of those New York fag actors?"

Sighing, he feared he was part of her mad dream.

"Please don't do anything crazy," Travis said.

She wiped her nose with her sleeve.

"I'm a jungle fighter like my father."

"Do it for me. I could take you to New York with me," Travis lied.

She looked at him and her expression softened. "I don't know if I can be with a fag who couldn't come." But she wasn't yelling anymore.

THIRTY EIGHT

Mordecai parked on Derringer Street, and headed toward the Apache Bar. Passing the corner of Mesquite and Derringer, he spotted the back of a limping man who looked like Sam Watkins. Quickly, he crossed to the west side of the street. The gimp stopped at the bar and glanced through the window. The blinking Budweiser sign gave the top of his head a bluish tint. The man shaded his eyes with his hand and peered inside. It was Sam Watkins.

Mordecai ducked into the alcove of Louise's Dress Shop, which was diagonally across from the Apache Bar. He stared at Watkins, who seemed to be waiting for someone.

Suddenly, a dark-skinned woman in a sari opened the dress shop's door and asked, "Can I help you?"

He shook his head.

"This is a woman's store," the owner said.

He glanced at the bar and at Watkins, not sure how long he could delay being spotted. He smiled. "Just getting out of the rain."

Her black eyes widened with fear. "No rain."

Why was he such a wiseass? "Sorry," he muttered but it was too late. The door slammed in his face and the lock bolted shut. Watkins looked over.

As he crossed the road toward the bar, Mordecai saw a cigarillo dangling from Watkins' mouth. "Are you looking for someone?" he asked.

"Where have you been?" Watkins demanded. He pushed off the wall. "We need to talk – right now. Let's find a bench. My leg is killing me."

"Why don't we go into the bar," Mordecai asked, "if you want to talk?"

"I'm a recovering alcoholic." He rubbed his leg. "I like to play it safe."

"You think I'm a schmuck."

Watkins trudged, limping noticeably, to a sidewalk bench and carefully sat and massaged his leg. "I stepped on a poisonous wooden spike."

Mordecai stood over him.

"You got rid of Hans - that's good enough for me." Watkins said grounding out his cigarillo with his shoe.

Mordecai paused for effect. "You left your cigarillo in the hotel ashtray back in St. Louis."

Watkins shrugged. "It took you awhile to figure it out." He lit another cigarillo, inhaling deeply and letting the smoke slowly curl upward. "General Jensen arrives soon for a test trial and we have them over a barrel. Your job, until the test, is to watch over the dog."

Mordecai shook his head. "What do you do?"

Watkins grinned. "There're millions of dollars out there in the Sight and Kill contract and the sale of ARC to the Pharmaceutical Consortium. Travis gets his, Ana gets hers and General Jensen gets his. We get the crumbs. I worked as an infiltrator for them. I know how to squeeze them."

"So who are you working for now?"

"I work for myself."

"How much do I get?" Mordecai demanded

"Sixty to a hundred thousand."

He didn't reply. Let Watkins sweat his answer. It was a lot of money. Unfortunately, he'd probably never see any of it.

Watkins tapped his foot. "So what is your decision?" Standing, he trudged toward the end of the block.

Mordecai yelled, "I'm with you."

Watkins turned and gave him a thumbs up.

As the church bells of the Methodist Church pealed, announcing noon, Mordecai smiled as Watkins veered onto Acacia Street and out of sight.

Mordecai was about to confront another liar.

* * *

Alone at a back table, nursing a beer, he waited for Chief to finish serving three loud-talking customers lamenting how the Arizona Cardinals were the worst NFL team, each one selecting a grievous sin. He could have added that the draft choices of the St. Louis Cardinals were incomprehensible before the team moved to Phoenix, but he had other things on his mind.

Ana didn't care if he was injured or killed. He was tempted to adopt Watkins' attitude - forget the bitch and play the game for himself like Pete Rose. That made no difference in baseball, but for a private investigator it was a denial of his own code of conduct. Physicians and lawyers abided by their ethics even if they despised their clients. Could a private investigator do less than a physician or a lawyer? If he didn't terminate the contract, he was obliged to put his ass on the line for her. It was a dilemma that turned his stomach.

He inhaled the smell of beer and ammonia lingering on the cement floor. He'd walked in hungry but the odor nauseated him, killing his appetite.

He should resign but what did he have going in St. Louis? He couldn't afford to quit because in the small world of investigative agencies, the word would spread fast. But working for his uncle was only slightly more exciting than selling shoes.

Chief brought over a beer that he held high and with his free hand pointed to the coaster.

Mordecai nodded. "Carelessness can ruin a Goodwill antique."

"No lip," Chief said, placing the beer on the coaster. "We'll talk."

Mordecai looked at circular stains on the wooden table. The few ARC employees he recognized never glanced at their watches. "They don't seem to be in a hurry."

"They get to work at 9:30, leave at 4 - a gift from Sam Houston."

Mordecai kept tapping his foot. "So we'll talk at 4?"

"They go back around 1:30."

It was 1:15, and most of the drinkers were at the bar. Someone shouted, "We're ready for another round."

Mordecai watched them chugging their drinks, chatting and patting each other on the back. There was an easy comradeship among these guys. He missed that.

An empty feeling descended on him. Since he dropped out of college, his friends from Clayton High School and Washington University had steadily drifted away as if they were erased from his life. They had gone on to become doctors, lawyers, accountants, Ph.D.'s or to take over their family businesses, while he was a marginal detective.

But he didn't regret leaving college. Although only recently licensed as a detective after nine months of Uncle Julius' supervision, he knew from the first day he was born he would be a detective. Well, maybe not the first day. It was time to act like one. Loneliness was a cheap price to pay.

While he sipped his fifth beer (or was it his sixth?), his mind fuzzy, he realized he'd rarely thought of Hans' death. A detective couldn't ignore a murder even if he despised the victim. Who had a motive? He doubted a pack of coyotes hated Hans. Given the chance to slowly and carefully examine the body, he was sure it would reveal a gun shot or stab wound.

It was almost three o'clock when the chef came out of the kitchen and said a few words to Chief. Calling her a chef was an exaggeration since the menu consisted of a melted cheese sandwich and a hamburger, accompanied by greasy French fries. None of the luncheon crowd, now gone, complained about the menu. Mordecai suspected drinking on an empty stomach was worse than eating the Bar's food.

When Chief lumbered over to the table, he carried a beer and hamburger, which he set in front of Mordecai.

Mordecai drummed his fingers on the table, making a hollow sound.

"The guys were celebrating," Chief said. "A rumor is spreading around the ARC that it is being sold to a pharmaceutical company."

"They don't sound worried."

"They believe Abbott started it to get even with Hans."

The rumor wasn't his concern. "I talked to Pedro yesterday," Mordecai said casually.

"What did he say?" Sitting, Chief yawned.

"He hardly knew you." He studied the face of Chief, who kept smiling, as if amused. "I called him a liar."

"That was foolish." He stared at Mordecai. "Jews are supposed to be smart." He pushed the plate closer. "Eat, you look pale." He waved at a customer walking through the door.

"To you guys, we all look pale." Mordecai felt light-headed. He picked up the hamburger and chomped down. Food wouldn't mollify his anger. "Why did you bullshit me?"

"I wanted to save my bar. Sam Houston made my down payment, and the Institute holds my mortgage. If Hans had killed you (he was threatening to murder all the spies he caught) there would have been a murder investigation that could destroy ARC. If you leave town, the bar is safe."

"You put my life on the line to save your bar."

Chief picked up a French fry. "I saved your life."

Mordecai raised his eyebrows. "How did you do that?"

"Hans knew you were a spy."

"Who told him?" His voice was sharp.

"Nobody told him. A cross-eyed mule could see through your cover - Begay, step sister." He laughed. "He said you were dead meat. I convinced him an ass whipping would drive you out of town."

He believed Chief. His cover story of a stepsister, a gift from Ana, was guaranteed to get him into trouble. He shrugged. "I should be grateful."

Chief picked up two more French fries and chewed them slowly. "We have one industry and we're going to protect it." He shook his head as if Mordecai didn't understand the gravity of what he was saying. "Ten years ago," he licked his lips, "you saw nothing but For Sale signs on Derringer. The price of copper was in free fall and the mines were laying off workers before Christmas and moving their operations to Chile. Do you understand?"

Was he supposed to cry? "Who called you that night we found the body? A man or a woman?"

"No one called me. I planned to lose you in the hills so you'd realize you were out of your league."

"Saving my life again? So who killed Hans?" Waiting for an answer Mordecai sipped his beer.

Chief shrugged.

"Don't tell me the coyotes."

"I don't care who killed him."

"How could you not?" He stopped, realizing until an hour ago he'd felt the same way.

Chief frowned. "Forget about the killer. Are you looking for trouble?"

"Lots of people tell me that."

He leaned forward, resting his large forearms on the table. "If the police find the body, you'll be the number one suspect. Hans kicked your ass. You were on Round Mountain that night. Your friend, Larry, can testify to that."

"You mean Lennie." He paused. "Why couldn't he have done it?"

"Forget about Hans. Nobody cares who did it."

THIRTY NINE

He left the Apache Bar, his steps unsteady, his shirt feeling damp where the condensation from the beer glass had dripped. Vehicles crawled by, their occupants seemingly uninterested in him. Lennie Tarr's story that Hans had kidnapped him sounded true at that moment in the hills of Round Mountain. Now doubt crept into his mind. Could he have killed Hans?

Ten feet ahead was a full grown, battle-ship gray mastiff, its jowls swinging like a pendulum and saliva hanging from its lips. For a second, his mind froze. Where had the dog come from? It had materialized from the blurriness of ten beers. His breath froze. His legs were lead weights. The mastiff was poised to charge and knock him to ground. He saw it in his cold eyes. It could crush his throat in its massive jaws.

A prepubescent girl, not much bigger than the mastiff, held the leash. She was oblivious to the danger, showing no intention of reining in her blood-thirsty canine. Like all owners of a killer, he was sure she would tell the newspaper reporter that the dog had always been a gentle giant. It wouldn't harm a flea.

Well, he wasn't a flea.

He had to escape. He tried to run, but his muscular legs had melted and were wobbly, hardly able to support his body. He sucked in air but little of it seemed to reach his lungs as though he'd just surfaced from underwater. What could he do? Hanging Tree alley was less than five feet away. He could disappear in a few steps from the mastiff's sight. It was a gamble. If the dog followed him, the alley was a dead end, a death trap. He dragged his body to the entrance, frightened to look behind him. He cursed the sour sweat on his brow, praying the mastiff couldn't smell his fear.

Halfway down the alley, he stopped to listen. There was no jingling of a dog chain. He turned to look - nothing there. He'd been smart to walk to safety. Running would have been a signal to the wild animal that the prey was fleeing. But why did he let that dog scare him? He'd been an amateur boxer who knew that if you were intimidated, you had lost the bout before the bell sounded.

He looked around. Trash was scattered everywhere. Rotting leaves, cigarette butts, soda cans and paper scraps gave off a stench of decay. The odor reminded him of the street in south St. Louis, where the San Remo Bar was located.

Sitting on a bench by the Hanging Tree, was an old man hunched over, his head and neck bent like a question mark. His white hair flowed down his back side, which gave him the look of a biblical patriarch Mordecai had seen in his Hebrew school book. He said something, which Mordecai thought was hello.

He was ready to leave; he figured the mastiff was well past the entrance. But then, turning and leaving felt rude so he decided to show some interest. He nodded and struggled to smile, which he did briefly.

"You looked flushed," the old man said.

"Allergies." His answer ended the probing.

He took a few deep breaths to relieve the last of his tension. The panic was over. He remembered a dog owner telling him mastiffs were affectionate, lick you to death. But his fear had barred any rational thought. It was a curse from his stepmother's German Shepherd.

He walked over to the tree to read a note enclosed in a plastic sleeve and tacked to a branch. 'Sunny Begay shot and killed her married lover, the bank manager of the First National Bank of Shakespeare. Her two male companions, when captured by the vigilantes, were hung from the Hanging Tree, while she was forced to watch. The vigilantes refused to hang a woman. A jury, moved by her defense as a jilted woman, acquitted Sunny of bank robbery.'

"They couldn't hang a woman?" Mordecai asked.

"Ain't true," the old man said.

"Really?"

"Folks here don't have big hearts - hang you easily as swatting flies." He spat. "The jury was all male." He pointed his cane at the street. "And she had slept with all of them, my father included."

"She got around, I guess." Mordecai chuckled.

The old man's lips clamped shut. His dark eyes glared at Mordecai. "Sunny Begay was my birth mother. When my father's wife was angry, she would say I was the son of that whore. One day my father told me the whole story, even stuff I didn't want to hear. This is her memorial."

He pointed to the withering tree. Glancing at his watch, he pushed himself up, using the cane.

"Time to go to the senior center. Special meal tonight."

Although he rested two hands on the cane, his legs wobbled. He bowed his head with his lips moving and then crossed himself. "I'm Alberto Gomez. I hope to see you here again, my friend. I'll tell you more about Shakespeare."

Mordecai watched the old man shuffle down the alley. Was his story a strange family history, or was it a tall tale? Mordecai had no idea, but he was certain everybody in Shakespeare knew the truth: Sunny Begay wasn't his stepsister.

Before leaving the alley, he halted at the entrance and peeked to make sure the mastiff was gone.

When he neared his car, he saw Bertha leaning against the hood. She was dressed in a black skirt falling below her knees and a ruffled blouse. Her attire gave her a gentle appearance. She must be going to a funeral.

"My God, Bertha, it's the first time I've seen you in a dress."

"We have to talk." She looked around. "Not here. Drive me home."

He unlocked the door. She slid her big body into the passenger seat gracefully, amazing for a woman of her size.

"How did you find my car?"

"The rental logo."

Everybody was a detective. He should peel it off the bumper.

"What's up?"

"Drive."

Following her instructions, he U-turned, swung under the railroad trestle to the Superstition Highway, went west for two blocks, turned onto Hackney Hill Road, and ascended a steep hill. Near the top was a parking slab, barely big enough for the Chevy.

She lived in what the locals called a miner's shack. It was a ramshackle cabin with its back resting on the hill and its front on stilts. He sunk into a battered couch while she kept the door cracked open and peeked outside. Sighing, she closed it, apparently assured no one followed them.

"Want a beer?"

He nodded, looking down. Where the rug wasn't covering the floor, the sloping ground was visible between the floor boards. Moments later she handed him a Coors and settled into a stuffed chair with rug tape covering the tears on the armrest.

"Shit is going on," Bertha said. "Travis wants you to stay at ARC."

"No way."

Bertha swallowed hard. "It's an excuse. Mai is gunning for you."

Mordecai exhaled. "An ant doesn't scare an elephant."

"You can stay here until you leave town, but no sex until I'm slim."

His cheeks felt hot. He gulped his beer to cover his embarrassment.

"It ain't you. I don't want any man to feel he's doing a fat girl a favor when we have sex."

He grinned. "How long before you're slim?"

"After my gastric bypass."

"I'll wait."

"Leave town while you can. Mai is dangerous just like Hans."

FORTY

The next morning Mordecai drove to the ARC, braking at the window of the guard house, his bumper almost touching the sliding gate. Marching out was a tall guard, dressed in a crisp blue shirt with an insignia of the Animal Research Center and khaki cargo pants with a sharp crease, carrying a metal mirror on a long pole. He asked Mordecai his name and looked at his clipboard.

"You're the guy who screwed the protesters - good job."

"I guess there are no secrets."

"Still have to check out the car."

He shoved the pole under the Chevy, glancing at the mirror.

"Good to go."

***

Minutes later Mordecai walked through the open door of Travis' office and was greeted by silence.

Sitting on a cushioned chair with his head bowed as if in prayer, Travis was manicuring his fingernails. Straightening, he lifted his hand and eyed the manicure. Clearly pleased with his workmanship, he leaned back and dropped the nail file on the roll top desk behind him.

"Good intel, old boy," Travis said adopting a British accent. "Christ, that was a terrible imitation. If I stay here, all my acting talent will erode."

"From one of your plays?" Mordecai let sarcasm creep into his voice.

He nodded in response, clearly unaware of Mordecai's tone. "From Lost Brigade, a comedy. My brilliant defense plan was a copy straight from the third act. We staked a few illuminated signs on Round Mountain: Trespassers Shot on Sight - which stood out on a dark night like the ones on the stage. Put a little fear in the Huggers. Then we blockaded them on three sides and the guards fired their weapons into the air. The Huggers scattered like stampeding cattle; a few of them are probably still trying to find their way back to the Sanctuary Hotel."

"It seems to have gone well."

Travis laughed. "I thought I was directing <u>Lost Brigade</u>. Better than the play: the hero was accidently shot in the butt. Thank God, no protesters were hurt. We couldn't afford any investigations of ARC, not now."

"Weren't you worried the police would be called about the gunshots?" Mordecai asked.

"Yes and no, this is a federal reservation. The police have no jurisdiction. And now we have another problem. I wanted you to get involved with the Huggers, but Mai thinks you're involved in Hans' disappearance. She and her friends want to kidnap you. To torture you until you tell her what you did to Hans. Then kill you. She's crazy like her father. You need to live at the ARC until the site visit."

Mordecai grinned. "I ain't afraid of a five foot tall girl."

"I've been trying to get ahold of you, to warn you. Where were you?"

"I was doing a surveillance of the Dorothea Doberman Sanctuary."

Travis' jaw dropped. "What did you find out?"

"No protesters there."

Travis nodded. "They're all here."

"But there were plenty of Dobermans - for adoption. The woman at the front desk even offered me one."

"You took it."

"No. I told you, I don't like dogs."

"Christ, we could use a few dogs."

He slumped in the chair, his body seeming to deflate. He ran his fingers through his wavy neck-length blonde hair.

"The woman said the Sanctuary made sure the dogs weren't used for experiments. Is that us?" he asked, sounding innocent.

His voice shrill, Travis said, "We have only one dog for the site visit and Nguyen hunts coyotes with it in the middle of the night. If the dog stumbles down a mining pit, we're screwed. Now the Sanctuary is offering twenty-thousand for kidnapping the Doberman."

"That's a lot of money to snatch a dog."

"If that happens, no test run."

Travis furrowed his brow. Suddenly his face brightened. "I've a brilliant idea. Instead of spying on those loud-mouth Huggers, a waste of your time, you guard the Doberman."

"I ain't going near those killers."

Travis shook his head, his neck-length hair flowing side-to-side.

"You can be the understudy - never appear on stage. Just watch General Nguyen to make sure the senile old bastard doesn't do anything crazy with the dog."

Travis licked his lips and inhaled deeply. "Extra money for babysitting Nguyen and thirty thousand when we pass the site visit."

"That's big money," Mordecai responded. He wanted to reject the smug Travis' offer, but the money was powerful. How difficult could it be to help the dog escape - leave a gate open. If he was successful, twenty thousand from Ana. If he failed, thirty thousand from Travis.

"It'll give me something to do while I'm hanging around."

"You got over your hatred quickly," Travis said.

"Money does that." His reprieve had ended, his stomach started churning again.

FORTY ONE

Travis handed Mordecai an instrument resembling the one General Nguyen had used to attack Charles Abbott.

"Guard it with your life," Travis said forcefully.

"It's a pretty big remote."

"Yeah," Travis said loudly. "It's a remote control device, our SK gun. It's broken so check it out with Mike. He'll show you how to use it."

God forbid, the remote meant he was caged with the Dobermans. His stomach went into overdrive. What he needed was a bathroom, quick. Over his shoulder, Mordecai said that it sounded good and double stepped out of the office and down the hall.

He crashed the bathroom door against the tiled wall and banged open a stall door. Jerking up the lid, he launched his head over the bowl and waited for the upheaval. He belched. Nothing came up. Then his stomach quieted. A false alarm - thank God. He lowered the lid and sat. Suddenly his lunch was rising in his throat. Flinging up the lid, he heaved.

* * *

Exhausted, Mordecai walked slowly to the cafeteria to drink something to wash away the sour taste. The kitchen was quiet now and he filled his cup with tea. He chose a rear table, a good spot to observe, with his back to the wall to avoid a sneak attack. As he sipped his hot tea, he stole glances around the room, although he was the only occupant in the antiseptic cafeteria with its hospital-white walls and stainless steel tables glistening under fluorescent lights and no windows. The cafeteria had the charm of a hospital emergency room. Why was nothing done to jazz up the place? It dawned on him that the drabness helped disguise the ARC from the fact that it was a place of deadly experiments.

A tall, wide-shouldered man entered. He belonged in the western frontier with his thick mustache curving downward, hiding his upper lip. He wore a metal buttoned western shirt and a big belt buckle featuring an insignia of crossed dueling pistols. He poured himself a coffee, grabbed a piece of pie and ambled over to Mordecai's table. Smiling he settled into the chair across from him, saying, "You must be Mordecai Glass, the guy who drove Hans into permanent hiding. Welcome aboard."

"What do you mean by permanent?"

"He isn't coming back."

Mordecai protested. "I did nothing to him. The opposite is true. He kicked my ass."

The mustached man extended his hand. His fingers were thick and calloused. "Harley Fuller, Chief Behavioral Scientist, but everybody calls me Slinger - short for gunslinger. We owe you our gratitude."

"For what?" Mordecai knew what Slinger meant, a crime that could send Mordecai to prison for life.

"Hans was part of the old guard. He and Sam Houston wanted our research to be a secret. Sam Houston is dead and Hans is out of the way. Some of us - you met Charles Abbott - want to tell the public what we do here. Otherwise, our mistakes are never corrected. Implanted dogs keep convulsing. Why?" He paused to smooth his moustache, staring at Mordecai as if he expected a response.

Mordecai remained silent. He wasn't gonna look stupid answering.

"Nobody inside the ARC had enough nerve to contradict Sam Houston and because of secrecy no one outside the center knew enough to challenge him."

Forcing a smile, Mordecai felt Slinger had handed him a canned speech. "The public might consider the surgery torture." He hoped his remark popped Fuller's balloon.

Slinger slammed his fist on the steel table. The metal rang like a bell. "Torture is Hugger propaganda because they believe that dogs are equal to humans."

"Not equal in my book," Mordecai said.

"When the public hears our Dobermans could be our guerilla Army, well-controlled killers so we don't have to sacrifice the blood of our boys, they'll not protest but support our research." He grinned. "I just had a brilliant insight. The police would love these dogs for control of an unruly crowd or an inner city riot."

Mordecai was certain this jerk had nurtured his idea too long. "Will the public believe these killer dogs won't attack innocent bystanders?"

"Easy to convince them."

He reached across the table and patted the back of Mordecai's hand. "Let them read the journal article." Abruptly he said, "I'll be right back."

Mordecai watched Slinger, the arrogant bastard, strutting out the exit. He never asked Mordecai his opinion, not even something as simple as 'what do you think.' Slinger belonged to a breed of creatures that he disliked. Even when he sort of agreed with these opinionated assholes, their arrogance raised his blood pressure.

Slinger strutted back into the cafeteria and dropped a Xeroxed journal article on the table. "Good reading," he said and left.

He was gonna study every damn detail of the article to make sure he wasn't conned. He wasn't gonna believe research published by the Institute of Metaphysics or scientists graduating from mail-order universities.

It took Mordecai three cups of coffee, two trips to the bathroom and two and a half hours to check out the article. The 'Journal of Comparative and Physiological Psychology' looked okay. The authors were two guys affiliated with 'Walter Reed Institute of Research.' That fit with the Army sponsoring the project.

The hard part was the gist of the article. He had to read it three freaken times until he figured out what the researchers were doing to a bunch of white rats. The rats would press a lever to electrically stimulate a spot deep in their brains, receiving a powerful reward. The rodents, choosing between electrical jolts and food, preferred the subcortical reward and would starve to death. Damn.

He pondered why the Army was lavishing big money on the ARC. As he trudged to see Mike about the remote control device, the intelligence he gathered was fitting together like a jigsaw puzzle and the picture was terrifying, a mad man's dream. These dogs were the rats, only bigger and meaner and with great sense of smell and hearing and very powerful teeth.

FORTY TWO

As Mordecai entered the hall, he flipped the remote control device, what Travis called the SK gun, back and forth between his hands as if it were burning his fingers. It was a funny looking weapon, a cross between a snub-nose and a TV remote with pushbuttons on its grip. Why it was designed this way was beyond his comprehension. But sanity wasn't prized at ARC, certainly not by Slinger. The Chief Behaviorist wanted to turn the Dobermans into storm troopers patrolling urban streets and herding unruly urban civilians into barb-wired camps.

Mordecai passed the kennel door beyond which the passage narrowed into a dimly lit tunnel. Farther down was visitor room #3, his sleeping quarters, on the left. He halted at a door stenciled Electronic Workshop, Mike Flynn, Engineer. Above the stencil was a cardboard sign: 'Press Buzzer and Wait for Permission to Enter'. Below the stencil was another cardboard sign: 'Trespassers Shot'. 'Shot' was underlined twice.

Who could he trust around here, with at least half the people crazy and the other half torturers? Maybe his fear of dogs should be the least of his worries. He pressed the buzzer. No one responded. Trying again with his ear pressed against the metal door, he detected what sounded like a clicking clock and someone coughing. He didn't hear a buzzer, which must be broken. He knocked vigorously. No answer. Why stand here like an idiot?

He shoved open the door.

The workshop was a handyman's delight. Various kinds of pliers, wrenches, screwdrivers and hammers and mallets hung from pegboards, arranged in an orderly fashion. A dozen clicking oscilloscopes and meters were arranged on a workbench. Mike was studying a blueprint, ignoring him.

While waiting to be acknowledged, Mordecai became hypnotized by the oscillating waves jitterbugging across the screens. Minutes passed; Mike still ignored him. Maybe Mordecai should kick him in the ass. A difficult task while Mike was sitting. He tapped Mike on the shoulder.

Turning, Mike glared. He picked up a hearing aid and fiddled it into his right ear and then repeated the process for his left ear. "You pressed the buzzer?"

When Mordecai nodded, Mike Flynn stood. "I didn't give you permission to enter," Mike said in the guttural voice of the hard of hearing.

"Asshole," Mordecai looked down and muttered.

"Look at me. I need to see your face."

"Are you a lip reader?"

"I can hear a little." Sighing loudly he folded the diagram with all the edges even. He asked in an annoyed tone, "Why are you here?" When Mordecai tossed the device toward him, Mike jumped from his swivel chair and lunged. It hit the tip of his fingers and he fumbled it for a few moments before grabbing it. He held it gingerly like it was a precious piece of glass. Breathing rapidly, his face red, he hollered, "You dumb bastard."

"Don't wet your pants. It's just some kind of remote."

"This is an SK gun. This remote control gun, dummy, took three years of me and the Army to develop. Without it, the dogs couldn't lick their ass." And then he added, "The rat-faced Gook was too chicken shit to face me so he sent an errand boy, a dumb shit like you."

Mordecai smiled. "Travis told me you'd repair the gun."

"Not the General?" He smiled.

He shook his head. "Travis."

Unscrewing the gun's grip Mike peered into the interior, holding it at different angles like a jeweler examining a watch. "General Nguyen has no respect for craftsmanship," he said, more to himself than Mordecai. He selected a volt meter from the end of the bench. He fell silent as he turned on the meter. His gaze narrowed to the connections, and he moved two testing wands from one connection to another. He twisted the dials and when satisfied, moved on. Something told Mordecai this guy knew what he was doing.

Mike selected needle-nose pliers and two pair of tweezers from the peg board. He worked systemically from left to right, tugging on the wire with the tweezers and tightening with the pliers. Sometimes he soldered.

"Done, good as new." He waved Mordecai to the workbench, saying, "The gun is color coded. If a wire comes loose, you solder it back to the same colored terminal. It's a simple fix. That's the Army way. Even an idiot can do it."

"Of course I understand."

He handed Mordecai a repair kit with a soldering gun, solder, a jeweler's screwdriver and tweezers.

"Now you won't have to bother me with repairs. That rat-faced Gook pounded the gun if it didn't respond immediately. Don't be an idiot like him."

"Travis said you're supposed to show me how the instrument works?"

Mike rubbed his chin. "Sam Houston said never to give out that secret without his okay."

"I heard he's dead. Travis said it was okay."

The skin around Mike's eyes tightened. "Sam Houston can't argue with that. Tell anyone who questions you, you figured it out on your own."

"My lips are sealed."

Mike placed the gun on the counter and said, "The gun design is mine and the Army's, mainly me. See the capital letters in the grip's pushbuttons on the top row: F is move forward; B move back; L move left; R move right; H halt. In the middle row: R is reward; W is the night light; OO is on/off. In the bottom row: G is nip; K is kill. And never get confused." He picked up the gun. "This is the weapon of the future. The Army loves it 'cause it looks like a pistol."

Mordecai asked, "How can a remote be better than a real gun?"

Mike grinned. "The dogs can kill any target as long as you can see it."

"Sounds like a space age weapon." Then he whispered, "In a comic book."

"You're going to work with the dogs?" Mike asked.

"No, General Nguyen."

"Not that crazy Gook."

"You don't like him."

Mike's thick lips twisted as if tasting something awful. "He tried to set the dogs on me 'cause he said I was a traitor. Had to climb a tree to escape. Nguyen might do the same to General Jensen. And the site visit is down the toilet - just like that. As quick as . . ." he snapped his fingers. "Then our annual bonus will be us in the street with a tin cup."

"That bad?"

He handed the SK gun to Mordecai. "Go test the gun to make sure it works."

"In the cage?"

"Where else?"

Staring at Mordecai, Mike went silent, his face darkening.

After about twenty seconds, the gaze made Mordecai uncomfortable. "Something wrong?"

"Yes," Mike replied. "Travis telephoned yesterday. Said he needs a backup in case the Army handler doesn't show up."

"No way!"

"All you have to do is practice controlling the dog without looking at the keys, so you can guide it like a show horse. If you do that, the visiting General will come in his pants."

"I ain't going near those killers."

"Don't be silly. You're the Dobermans' brains. Your thoughts are their thoughts."

"What if the killers have a mind of their own?"

FORTY THREE

Mordecai took a deep breath and exhaled slowly, as he quivered in front of the kennel door. He checked his cell phone. Ana had left a message. Another five thousand for kidnapping the test dog, with a warning not to harm the Doberman. The bitch should worry about him, not the damn dog. Screw her, screw Travis, screw Shakespeare.

Pushing open the kennel door, he stared at the massive black-and-tan Doberman, 143, the test animal, such a majestic-looking creature. Poor baby, they're gonna drill holes in your head and ram electrodes into your brain. He should feel pity. It was only natural. But how could he? He shook his head. The Dobermans were born to crush his bones.

He proceeded toward the implanted Doberman, when 143, alone in the first kennel eyed him, wagging its tail furiously and pressing its muzzle against the fence. The massive size of the black-and-tan male made him thankful for the fence between them. He halted. Just like on the previous visit with Charles Abbott, he barely extended his index finger through the mesh and scratched 143's skull. "Okay, I'll be your buddy, but don't get used to it."

While being petted, the Doberman sometimes snorted or made what sounded like a string of deep throated 'grrr's'. It was unbelievable, but this must be the dog version of 'purring'. When he stopped petting, 143 stopped purring. The Doberman raised his head, his pudding brown eyes pleading for Mordecai to continue, his tail still wagging. 143 was so different from Fritz. When Fritz, the Nazi, wagged his tail, it was a warning of an impending attack.

He glanced at the empty food and water dishes beyond his reach. "I'll feed you later, but remember I ain't your afternoon snack, sweetheart."

He continued to the end kennel to test the SK gun. It felt heavy in his pants pocket, with one end protruding out the slit. He was afraid it was too heavy and would tear the fabric.

The black-and-tan female had hardly moved since his entrance. Its glassy eyes looked as if they had been anesthetized. According to the metal signs attached to the chain-link fence, the dog in the cage was numbered 119. There were no numbers between 119 and 143 which suggested most animals succumbed to the brain operations.

The gun in his hand, he recalled Mike Flynn's instructions about the key functions. He was stumped by a translucent switch that Mike never explained. The nasty bastard probably forgot it on purpose.

He pressed OO and F. The dog didn't move. Finally after hitting the keys haphazardly, he stroked the translucent switch, then OO and B. The black-and-tan female stepped back and Mordecai quickly pressed R. Her head snapped up as if the electrical jolt had given the female a burst of energy. He saw he could make the female do all kind of movements. He moved her to the metal fence and pressing G, she nipped the fence. He directed her away from the fence and pressed K. Her teeth made a snapping sound until he hit OO.

He noticed on the underside of the gun was the number 119. So his gun worked only for this female.

Even if he was close enough to feel her breath on his face, 119 wouldn't attack him. The SK gun did her thinking. He walked into her kennel and circled around the dog, even petting her. A miracle had happened: The sight of a big dog didn't make him piss in his pants. The Pope should sanctify him, the first ever Jewish saint of dry underwear.

He shoved the SK gun into his waistband. He had promised to feed 143. He looked around for an implement to retrieve the dishes. Where the hell were the tools and the dog food?

As he walked toward the shed at the end of the compound, it struck him how Hans must have been killed. Shit, 131 had been trying to tell him the answer. He should have seen the connection.

* * *

He jiggled the shed handle. Shit, locked. Annoyed, he made his arm into a V and slammed his elbow into the handle. It now dangled at a forty-five degree angle.

He entered the shed, the smell of manure choking him. He pinched his nose. A swarm of insects hovered over three garbage bags, obviously brimming with dog shit. He flicked on a light switch. The bulb immediately attracted the flies. He had to get out of there before the odor or the flies overwhelmed him. He scanned the shed and spotted a bag of dog food near the door. Also, three shovels, a garbage can, a rake, a cord of heavy rope, a water hose, three pails, a trowel, a spade, a pooper scooper, clippers, shears, a push lawn mower, and a wheelbarrow.

While two flies buzzed around his face, he quickly dumped food into the pail. He grabbed a second pail and a rake and carried the items outside. He filled the second pail from the faucet, then struggled to carry everything to the first kennel.

He saw 143 lolling on the grass. It really was a shame Slinger was planning to turn him into a robot. Once implanted the dog would dance to whatever key was pressed. But what was it like without the implant? Docile or aggressive? If he stepped into the cage, could he trust his life to this creature? He had no idea how 143 felt about him. Sure, it licked his hand, but how about the rest of him?

"Here's your dinner." He opened the gate just far enough to shove the two pails into the cage and then crouched on the grass. The SK gun pressed against his ribs. He pulled it from his waistband. Such a strange weapon, whose bullets were killer dogs. The Dobermans were likely the assassins of the wily jungle fighter, Mordecai remembered all the torn flesh. But Dobermans didn't hide his body? Maybe the General did? He didn't seem smart enough to plan the attack or follow through. Unless he had orders.

Was Mordecai also a target? How the hell do you protect yourself when you're in the dark? Suspect everyone.

God protect him, he could no longer deny how deadly the situation was.

He heard the door slam against the stair railing.

FORTY FOUR

General Nguyen scurried down the hall toward Mordecai and yelled, "One-fur-three … min dog … you steal … you VC."

He stared at the rat-faced general. "I'm no VC," he protested.

"Lou tell me, you spy." Rat-faced general smiled with crooked lips. He pulled an electric prod from his waist. "I learn dog."

"The dog doesn't understand pidgin talk, you dumb shit," Mordecai yelled.

Nguyen thrust his tube at Mordecai who backed away. "What the hell are you doing?" he bellowed.

Travis ran into the compound, shouting, "Mike called and said, 'Nguyen went ballistic over you handling the dogs.' Did the crazy bastard hurt our field-test dog?"

"No, not the dog. Rat face wants to fry me, thinks I'm Viet Cong," Mordecai said, breathing rapidly, watching Rat-Face's every twitch.

Travis studied 143 for a minute and then turned to Nguyen, "No VC," Travis shouted, pointing at Mordecai.

General Nguyen muttered, "Lou say, 'Vietnam we go.' "

"We go soon." Travis responded.

"Vietnam - go twenty dogs. Lou say General Nguyen must learn dogs. Lou say dogs must protect General." Cracking a crooked smile, Nguyen entered the cage. The Doberman's fur on his withers stood up and his cropped ears pulled back.

Travis asked, "Who the fuck is Lou?"

When Mordecai shook his head, Travis gulped.

"Sez down," Rat-Face yelled at the dog. He waved the prod in the air.

The dog growled, displaying its canines and advanced. Nguyen jammed the prod into the dog's flank. The Doberman squealed and retreated a few steps.

"Dog bad." Spit rained on his chin.

Travis looked stunned but didn't move.

When the Doberman advanced again, Rat-Face slammed the prod into the poor dog over and over again. The dog gave forth a cry from hell.

Squealing made Mordecai shiver.

Travis shouted at him, "Do something."

Mordecai froze. He wasn't going into the cage of a killer Doberman and a crazy General.

Travis laid his palm on his shoulder blade and shoved him toward the fence. Mordecai halted two feet from the gate, turned and slapped away Travis' arm, saying, "No way."

"Another five thousand," Travis said.

Not for five thousand, not for a million, he thought.

143 scrambled away from Nguyen and stopped by the gate quivering. Its eyes pleaded.

"Stop," Mordecai shouted at Nguyen, "You fucking old fart, I ought to use the prod on you!"

Rat-Face drove the dog into a corner where 143 couldn't escape the shocks. He emitted a high pitched shriek.

Mordecai felt his face turn red. He banged open the gate, rushed in and slammed Rat-Face to the ground. 143 scuttled behind Mordecai.

Lying on the ground, the old man aimed the prod at the dog, but missed.

Nguyen pulled the prod back and aimed it toward Mordecai's balls whose hand shot to his groin as he sidestepped. The prod hit his calf. His leg muscles twisted into knots, worse than any cramp he'd ever felt. He crumbled. On the ground, he was eye-to-eye with the fallen Nguyen.

Mordecai with a wobbly right leg could only squat while Nguyen struggled to his feet. Nguyen's mouth twisted into a grin. He stumbled toward Mordecai. His weapon pointed at Mordecai's torso. "You VC."

When the prod neared his chest, he gritted his teeth preparing for the impending shock. 143 growled and leaped, and hit Nguyen in the midsection.

Mordecai quickly got to his feet, staggering away from Nguyen who hobbled toward him.

The Doberman advanced to attack. Rat-Face swung around to face the snarling dog, giving Mordecai time to sneak forward and bounce a right fist off the rear of Nguyen's head. The old man dropped the weapon and sunk to the ground.

Mordecai picked up the prod. "You're dead meat."

Nguyen stared at him with his eyes burning hatred. "You commie like Hans. Lou say, 'Kill all VC.' "

Mordecai shocked Rat-Face's right leg and then his left leg. Tears rolled down his face.

"How does it feel, you piece of shit?"

143 rubbed against Mordecai, its tail wagging fiercely. As Mordecai limped to the gate, the Doberman circled around him.

Travis had stood motionless during the entire confrontation. Finding his voice, he cried out to the General, "get out now!" As Nguyen staggered out the door, Travis yelled at Mordecai, "Christ, never leave the dog alone, never."

FORTY FIVE

Mordecai glanced down at the Doberman staring at him with dark brown eyes glittering with affection. The dog brushed against his leg. Too close for Mordecai's comfort. Panting, his large canines showed below his drooping upper lip. He refused to pet the dog.

But what to do with the Doberman? He couldn't leave 143 here because Nguyen would surely return and torture it more. He sighed. He didn't want to be the dog's protector, but 143 had protected him - saving him from a prod in his face.

"Okay, you win." He tapped 143 on the head, a mistake. The dog brushed against his leg as if suffering from a bad itch. Mordecai looked through the fence mesh at Travis' beet red face.

Travis spoke in hushed tones, "General Nguyen will kill you and the dog. Murdering you I can tolerate. The dog, no. This is my seizure-free Doberman for General Jensen."

"It's good to know my worth," Mordecai replied.

"We have to house it someplace else." Travis went to a shed and returned with a leather collar and a leather muzzle. He tried to put the collar around its neck, but the dog skirted away, hiding behind Mordecai.

After several failures, he handed the collar to Mordecai. "The dog loves you."

"It's unrequited love," Mordecai said.

"Don't be a chicken."

Crouching, Mordecai dangled the collar in front of the Doberman. He was glad that his slight tremor was hidden from Travis. The dog moved forward as if it knew what Mordecai wanted. Its hot breath rained on his face.

Travis said, "He'll stay with you."

Mordecai's protest died on his lips. How could he turn his back on the Doberman who saved his ass? But could he stay in the ARC lodging with his nightmare, a hundred pounds of fury? Maybe the dog was friendly because they had been partners-in-battle. But if he annoyed the Doberman, could 143 turn against him? If he guarded 143 for a few days, Travis promised him thirty thousand dollars more than Ana offered, but ARC would drill into the poor dog's brain. On the other hand, Ana would save 143. Screw it, he'd decide later.

When he stepped into visitor room #3, his ARC lodging, he immediately leashed the muzzled Doberman to a leg of the small desk. The nylon leash was frayed, pieces hanging off, obviously torn by chewing dogs. The nylon didn't inspire Mordecai to trust that the material could restrain 143, but it was the only leash Travis had given him. For the money promised, Mordecai didn't want to let on he was afraid of dogs and lose the job.

His room was claustrophobic. There was scarcely space for the desk, a chair and a bed. The bathroom was a tiny cubicle where the shower rained on the toilet. Through two narrow windows, the sun rays heated the stale air. He opened the rear door that looked out at desert plants and rolling hills. He sighed, feeling relieved.

Tired he collapsed onto the bed which was so small that he had to rest his forearm on his chest or it would drop off the mattress. He heard stirring and opened his eyes to watch 143 walk to the water dish, its tongue protruding and waiting. He couldn't let his partner suffer from thirst. He filled the bowl from the bathroom faucet and removed the muzzle. Quickly he scurried back to bed, far enough away so 143 couldn't reach him.

The Doberman sauntered toward him. Only a worn nylon leash kept Mordecai from becoming a doggie treat. Abruptly, the Doberman tugged and jerked the leash.

His stomach quivered. Think! There was no getting to either the front or back door. Crap, he always prayed he'd die in his sleep. That was one prayer that wasn't gonna be granted.

143 stopped at the bed frame and nosed his leg.

"Forget it, I ain't gonna pet ya." He shuffled his body to the far edge of the bed, out of reach.

With its back legs planted on the floor, the dog put its front paws on the blanket and lifted its front torso onto the bed, poking Mordecai's thigh with his nose.

Mordecai grabbed the pillow and placed it in front of his thigh. "You can't outsmart me. I have my shield."

143 grabbed the pillow with its teeth, wrestled it away from Mordecai, shook it vigorously and dropped it on the floor. Again the Doberman poked his thigh.

Mordecai couldn't stop the nosing. He finally shoved the Doberman away so the front paws slid off the bed. 143 continued to set his front paws on the blanket and Mordecai kept shoving them off. Then the dog picked up the pillow and placed it back on the bed.

The Doberman thought they were playing a game, but how long before the dog became enraged over losing. Mordecai laid awkwardly on his side, with his arm beginning to cramp. Resistance was futile. He took a deep breath and gently stroked the dog's rump. The dog emitted 'grrr', a noise he was sure was like purring. No need to get his hand close to 143's jaw.

His stomach had stopped quaking. No fear. He had to tell someone about his bravery, but he didn't want to admit that a hard-nosed detective had been afraid.

Opening his wallet he placed his mom's photo on the bed and said: "Mom, you can call it a miracle. I'm free of my shackles. No more quaking when a dog comes near me. I thought it'd never happen."

The Doberman stood erect as if posing.

"I wish you could see this beautiful black-and-tan Doberman. I trust this dog, because we fought together, because it saved my 'tochis'. When I return home, I'm planning to get a dog, a small one, of course. It'll be a female so I can name her Esther after you."

At the mention of the name, the dog's ears became erect. "The dog likes the name Esther, too." He continued: "Did you hear that? He perked up when I said your name. Let me repeat it to see what the dog does. Esther, Esther, Esther. Believe it or not, the dog's wagging its tail."

A knock on the door startled him. Quickly he kissed the photo and hid it in his wallet.

Travis entered pushing a cart filled with supplies. He unloaded a 50lb bag of dog food, a flash light, poop bags, a food bowl and an alarm clock. With a quizzical look, he stared at Mordecai. "Who is Esther?"

"The dog. I named her after my dead mother, Esther. We were having a conversation." He smiled as if he knew his behavior was weird.

"You're telling me, you're developing a close relationship with this dog? A guy who hates dogs?" Travis tore open a bag of dog food and filled the bowl again.

"Of course," Mordecai protested. "It's my constant companion for a while - right?"

It was obvious Travis was suspicious of how quickly he'd bonded with the Doberman. Mordecai brushed his hand across the dog's back. When the Doberman turned his head slightly to see Mordecai, he pulled his hand away. He picked up the muzzle and dangled it in the air.

Travis grinned. "I thought you were afraid of the dog but it was General Nguyen. I was worried I'd have to find a new dog handler."

"Me? Scared?"

"Give him a cup and a half twice a day, plus treats every once in a while. Walk him at least three times a day: at sunrise, at noon, at night. Leave by the back door. No Dog Huggers will see you." He picked up the alarm clock. "No sleeping in."

"You'd have made a great kindergarten teacher."

"I don't want the dog to become upset."

"How about me?"

He clasped his hands together. "Finally, we solved the Big Problem. None of the dogs will have seizures, thank God." He cleared his throat. "But Santa Ana is on the warpath."

"Who?"

"The bitch is the owner of the Dorothea Doberman Sanctuary." He massaged his earlobe. "She bribed Sam Watkins to destroy ARC."

Mordecai felt his face becoming hot. "Why are you telling me?"

"You can make Watkins disappear."

He shrugged. "I'm not a magician."

Travis' forehead wrinkled. "Additional ten thousand might change your mind."

"Why do you think I'd do it?"

"You made Hans disappear."

Mordecai shrugged.

"How about thirty thousand?" Travis asked. "It's best if you make it look like an accident."

His answer was a big smile.

As Travis was about to leave, he handed Mordecai an envelope. "This should keep you smiling."

FORTY SIX

After Travis left, Mordecai closed the door and lay on the paper-thin mattress, the coils poking into his back whenever he moved. These coils would help keep his attention on his predicament. Rat Face was dangerous, but he didn't make his own decisions. Mordecai worried that this Lou had ordered Rat Face to eliminate him. If Lou stuck to his pattern, he'd tell Nguyen to direct an implanted Doberman to crush Mordecai's throat. He had to neutralize Rat Face. In fact, he needed a bodyguard to watch his back, but there was no one he trusted.

Mordecai heard Esther stirring, shaking his head and torso and grunting. Raising his head from the pillow, he saw Esther scooting on his belly across the floor as if unsure about Mordecai's greeting. The black-and-tan was inches from the bed. Mordecai reached down and brushed his hand across his back. He just kept thinking that if the Dog Huggers failed to rescue the dog, the ARC behaviorists would implant electrodes in his brain and turn him into a robot!

With his dark eyes locked on Mordecai, Esther hopped onto the bottom of the bed. Mordecai bolted upright. How could he sleep with the dog on the bed? He trusted the dog but he wasn't stupid. Asleep he'd be defenseless. Hadn't he learned a lesson with Elizabeth who hit him with a beer bottle; Esther could kill him.

Going over to the dresser, he picked up the muzzle where Travis had left it. He sat on the bed next to Esther and dangled the muzzle in front of the Doberman like it was doggy toy. The Doberman glared. Mordecai slowly inched closer, without making any sudden moves. His hands were steady, which shocked him.

The dog watched him. As soon as the muzzle touched Esther's face, the dog twisted its head to the side. He wasn't going to cooperate.

After his tenth attempt, he had to do something drastic. He grabbed 143 by the collar and tried to force the muzzle over his mouth. Ducking, the dog pulled back his lips, displaying his teeth. Continuing might be dangerous, Mordecai thought. Dropping the muzzle on the floor, he said, "Esther, you win."

He settled on the bed, with Esther curled near his stomach. "Don't move. Understand?"

The Doberman cuddled against him. He stroked Esther's skull, and the dog vocalized his pleasure with grrrs and snorts. He felt connected to Esther, so unlike his feelings for his stepmother's German Shepherd. Why couldn't Fritz be as loving as Esther? If that had been the case, he wouldn't be suffering from a dog phobia today. Anyway, what kind of Jew gets a German dog and names it Fritz?

He fluffed up the pillow, his eyelids heavy. His body felt drained of energy. He'd close his eyes. He promised himself, only for a few minutes.

* * *

He was floating through a warm puffy cloud when he felt something heavy on his shoulder. Was the weight part of a dream? He must have drifted off. He blinked a few times to orient himself. Esther was sleeping on his shoulder, snoring softly.

143's foul breath tickled his neck; his jaw was inches from Mordecai's jugular vein. He waited for his panic to explode. Nothing.

Instead, the dog resting on him gave him a warm feeling. He could never abandon anyone who saved his butt from the senile General - even a dog. He was done deciding what to do. "Don't worry sweet boy. I'd never betray a buddy."

He stroked his coat with his free hand, his fingers gliding across the dog's neck to its back. He was aware as he petted his smooth coat, how peaceful he felt.

He whispered into Esther's cropped ear, "You'd make a good partner." He was sure the dog understood when he grunted in response.

As the sunshine streaming through the narrow window began heating up the stale air, a thin layer of sweat formed on Mordecai's forehead. He could crack open the back door to the hillside to let in fresh air, but that was risky with Nguyen and his chum Lou at large, who could sneak in and kill him.

How good a guard dog was Esther? The sunshine was highlighting his brilliant black-and-tan coat. It'd be a crime to mutilate such a beautiful animal.

There was a knock on the back door. He gently moved Esther's head from his chest. The dog yawned and closed his eyes.

"What kind of guard dog are you?" he whispered.

Shaking off the grogginess, he rose from the bed and shuffled to the door. Esther followed him. Peering through the peephole, he opened it, and Chief pushed past him, banging against his shoulder. A low growl came from behind Mordecai. A second later, the big guy retreated outside, his dark eyes wide.

He had to smile that Esther intimidated the mammoth man. "It's okay, Esther." Mordecai stepped back and tapped the bed spread, and Esther leaped onto the bed, making the tired springs squeak loudly.

"Can I trust the dog?" asked Chief.

Mordecai shrugged. "As long as I'm safe."

"Can I believe you?" Chief stepped hesitantly into the room, his gaze fixated on the dog. There was a noticeable tremor in his deep voice. "I've come to save you."

"Save me?" Mordecai paused. "Be serious. You're a lying bastard. Pedro isn't dead. How'd you get in here, anyway?"

"I know this country better than anyone," Chief smiled. "Fences can't keep me out." He lowered himself carefully onto the wooden chair, his bottom flowing over the seat. "Someone with half-a-brain would have left town when they were told about Pedro. Too arrogant, because you think you're a great detective, too smart for us yokels."

"I can take care of myself."

"Five thousand – I'll tell you something and if you don't think it's worth five thou, don't pay me." Chief said dryly. "Mai and her boyfriend Dutch want to kill you for killing Hans."

"Old news. That's why I'm living here. Besides you know I didn't do it."

"Maybe I could tell the cops that, maybe not. But five thousand dollars buys your innocence."

Mordecai sunk onto the bed and petted Esther, who crouched next to him and stared at their visitor.

Chief wiggled, causing the chair to creak. The noise irritated Mordecai.

"How do you know this garbage?"

Chief pushed back his thick black hair. "You don't know shit, Pale Face."

"Really!"

"You believe Ana paid you to save the Doberman. This is all 'bout revenge. In the beginning of ARC, Sam Houston needed Dobermans for his project. He charmed Dorothea, Ana's mother. She discovered what the bastard was up to and stopped the shipment of dogs. But he had knocked up Dorothea and when the shipments stopped, he dumped her. She threatened to sue for child support. His lawyer convinced her to drop her law suit in exchange for Ana becoming an heir. The rumor spread in Apache Junction that she committed suicide. Who knows why? Because of her love for Sam Houston or because of the sacrificing of her beloved Dobermans."

Mordecai shrugged. "Stopping the field trials to save the Dobermans or revenge - what's the difference?"

Chief grinned. "Listen, Pale Face, you don't get it. It's not enough to burn down ARC. The name of Sam Houston should be poison on the tongue of anyone who mentions him."

"It's a soap opera - big deal," Mordecai replied.

"She's planning to have a Weeper martyred, so the investigation will reveal how evil the ARC is."

"Who's the victim?"

The big man stood and stretched. He raised his immense arms above his head. Esther sprung upright, the hair on his back erected.

"You're sure that dog isn't dangerous?" Chief asked.

Mordecai replied, "You never know."

He lowered himself back on the chair. "You'll need the protection of that dog."

"What are you saying?"

"You're the chosen Weeper to be martyred," Chief said, smiling, satisfied with his answer.

Mordecai shrugged. "How is the bitch going to do that?"

He rubbed his chin. "General Custer, no way is your scalp worth less than ten thousand."

"Thanks for the increased valuation."

Chief snickered. "She put a bounty on you."

Mordecai contemplated if Chief could be the mysterious Lou. He shook his head. Chief had always been friendly but he was also a liar. He was sure he couldn't be trusted. But a killer?

"Remember," Mordecai said, "You get a partial payment only if I'm alive."

"You travel to the Spirit Land, bad for ARC, bad for Shakespeare. Police will be crawling all over the town and its pile of dirty secrets. My bar will die, too. I just want you to leave town. I'm goin' now. You should go, too."

He walked out the door, looking back at Mordecai who kicked it shut behind the big man.

.

FORTY SEVEN

Mordecai yawned and rubbed his eyes to stay alert. The cramped room felt like a tightening vise. Pushing open the back door, Mordecai carried the chair outside. The porch light penetrated about six or seven feet and then disappeared in the blackness. He learned while finding Hans' corpse that the flat land extended to the distant hills and eventually climbed to Round Mountain. Somewhere out there Chief was sneaking his way to Shakespeare. And somewhere out there was the route to smuggle Esther to freedom. To pull this off required a moonless night, but in the hostile darkness the Devil's Claw could put a strangle hold on your clothing, while the cactus with the six-inch sharp spines would penetrate deep into your body. Worse, out there waiting in the darkness were vipers: General Nguyen and his killer Dobermans, the unknown Lou, Mai and Dutch, Watkins, Ana and the Dog Huggers, Lennie, Travis and Slinger. He forced himself to stop thinking about all his possible enemies before he got so scared he'd decide to leave town just like Chief wanted him to. How do you defend yourself against so many unknowns? It didn't inspire confidence that Hans, a jungle fighter, was rotting in a cave.

"Crap," he said to Esther, "how can I put my ass on the line for you? I wanna but you're asking too much."

Esther strolled past him, peed and then began to paw the earth. "Give it up, Esther." The Dobie stopped digging and turned to face him. He continued his conversation: "Chief told me, the ground is caliche, hard as concrete. For once, Chief ain't lying."

The Doberman strolled over to the chair, leaned against his leg and settled next to him. A flock of birds with dark brown bodies and long tails, nesting in a tree, emitted a tinny clicking sound. The dog cocked its head. The Dobie looked ready to spring into action until Mordecai said, "Stay." With that command, his head dropped to his chest. The birds flew off, and the desert went silent.

* * *

An hour later, the chair's seat uncomfortable, he wiggled and the folded envelope deep in his pocket poked against his thigh. It held three beautiful checks. The first check was his salary that he and Travis had never discussed. From the dates on his pay stub, he earned $1,100 per week and accrued 8 hours of sick leave. The expense check for his lodging was $1700, which was his to pocket, because Ana was comping the room. Unlike the first two ARC checks, the last one was marked "bonus" in the notation space. It was for three thousand dollars. It dawned on him that the money was bait, tempting him to get rid of Watkins.

He pulled the checks carefully from the envelope and fanned them. "You girls are beautiful."

Before this case, his own agency was a distant dream. Uncle Julius, when he retired in ten years or so, promised the agency would be his. But that verbal contract was iffy - if he was exiled to the shoe store, the promise bounced like a bad check.

His own agency would make him a 'mensch.' No more would his father lend him money to cover his bills; no more would Witch bitch he was bleeding his father dry; no more would his uncle remind him of his mistakes and sentence him to limbo. No more lecturing him to play it safe, to remember the bottom line. He'd run his agency like a detective, not a bookkeeper.

If he made a mistake, he would decide, not Uncle Julius, not his father. "Soon," he said to Esther, "I'll be free, my own man."

Letting Esther be mutilated disturbed him. Reporting Hans' death would bring down ARC and save the dog. Should he call the police or tell the location of the burial site to Ana? Would it look like a murder, or that he'd been attacked by wild animals? He had to examine the corpse to decide.

Mordecai looked over the landscape, trying to figure out the direction of the cave where they had found Hans' body. The location was somewhere to the northeast. He plotted his course across the barren ground which stretched for a quarter of a mile to a charcoal-colored hillside. But when to begin? If he climbed the hill at night, the ARC's light would disappear and he'd lose his sense of direction. God forbid, the only thing he'd recognize on a moonless night, if the wind was blowing into his face, was the outhouse.

Maybe Ana had commanded one of the Dog Huggers like Tarr to murder Hans. She hated Sam Houston and everything he stood for - no better motive than that. If he had killed him, it would have been with a gun or a knife. Ana was also connected to ARC, a double agent. Mordecai remembered the huge donations from the Sam Houston Foundation. Maybe she was working with somebody who then sent Nguyen to sic the dogs on Hans.

He should have examined the corpse better. Instead of tramping through the hills, he could call and ask Chief what he'd seen. But Chief would invent something to induce Mordecai to leave Shakespeare.

It was possible that Chief was the killer, but he dismissed this idea again. His gut told him that Nguyen and the mysterious Lou (whom he had no idea how to identify) were the main suspects.

Esther rose and his ears perked up. Moments later a faint howling rolled down from a distant hill. Esther had smelled or heard the coyotes before he did. The dog's senses would let him navigate easily in the night. Mordecai would have to rely on Esther to guide him. He prayed that Coyotes didn't like the taste of human meat. His stomach was growling. He'd need energy to tramp around the woods. This place was too small and the bed too uncomfortable.

"Esther, the coyotes ain't feasting on us tonight."

FORTY EIGHT

Mordecai shoved a couch against the Sanctuary Hotel suite's door, which was latched with a metal chain. Not much of a barricade. Could he defend against an intruder? The Dobie was at the far end of the couch, snoring softly. Lying at the other end, he ran his finger across the blade of the pruning shears, thinking about Hans.

The killer must have been petrified that someone would stumble onto the corpse. He must have dumped Hans' body where he thought that it wouldn't be found by man or beast.

He rubbed Esther's stomach with his foot. The dog's eyes flickered open for a second, then closed. "Who would protect you if I were killed?"

He needed a plan to save Esther. This time it'd be a well thought out scheme of a hard-nosed detective willing to lie and maybe, if necessary, to kill. But first a massage in the Jacuzzi to relieve his aching body. He placed the pruning shears on the tub edge.

For the next twenty minutes he soaked in the cooling water. As the fatigue dissipated, his mind cleared. The phone rang. It was Julius.

"I had to call you," his uncle said. His voice was excited. "This lovely girl Rita called. I didn't know you had a nice Jewish girlfriend. She would like you to come home."

"Forget that. She ain't my girlfriend. Tell me what Russell Parker told Ana about me."

There was a long pause and then the sound of a squeaking door. Uncle Julius had gone into his private office, and had closed the door because there was something he didn't want the secretary to hear.

"He told her you were a loose cannon and not very bright."

"Not a great recommendation," Mordecai chuckled.

"He was getting even for the fight over the parking space. He even told her, a shrimp like you challenged him to a fight, then chickened out."

He felt his neck muscle pulsate. "That lying bastard was crapping in his pants."

"I wouldn't trust her. The more the lawyer badmouthed you, the more she wanted to hire you. He said she was looking for someone who would stir the pot - reckless."

"Did you apologize?"

"I did. Business is slow." He paused. "If you apologize, Parker will forget the matter."

Mordecai swallowed hard. Apologizing wasn't in his vocabulary, especially to an asshole lawyer.

"By the way, a General Jack Jensen called the office to do a background check on you. Something about a secret canine project. What kind of general does background checks?"

"I don't know and don't give a shit."

"Okay." His uncle's breathing was rapid. "Call her. She's a nice Jewish girl. I know her father."

"I ticked her off."

"She was talking of going to Shakespeare."

"That's hard to believe."

"You should come home. There are a couple of jobs pending that I think will interest you."

"Oh, yeh. What are they?"

"I'll tell you when you get here."

Mordecai wondered if Julius was making up the possibility of new jobs. "I'll be back soon."

Esther, who had wandered over to the tub, barked when Mordecai stopped petting him.

"Is that a dog?"

"Yup. It's Esther, my male Doberman."

"A male – Sometimes I wonder about you." His uncle exhaled loudly, obviously exasperated. "Call her."

FORTY NINE

Lying on the king-size bed, he eyed Esther stretched out next to him. He shook his head.

Mordecai pulled out his wallet and removed his mom's picture. "Mom, I haven't talked to you for a while. Here's the problem: If I'm discovered sabotaging the field trials, who knows what Travis or Thumper or General Nguyen would do? . . . You're right. I need to be careful. . . But ARC is going to turn this sweet dog into a vegetable. That's not right. He loves me as you loved your cat. I never told you this. After your passing, I used to pillow my face into Muffin's thick coat to relieve my grief. Then Dad abducted Muffin and despite my pleas, dumped her at the Humane Society to please Witch. I can't let the same thing happen again, but it's crazy to risk my life." He kissed the picture and put it back in his wallet.

He turned to the Dobie. "Esther, you're not going to be a test animal, if I can help it. God willing, I'll have more backbone than my father."

Hearing his name, the dog wiggled over and rested his head on Mordecai's lap. The warmth of his coat matched the warm feeling seeping through Mordecai's body.

* * *

In the morning light, he picked up Ana's earring and shoved it into his pocket. He drove to the Dorothea Doberman Sanctuary with Esther curled up in the passenger seat. Stroking his back, Mordecai felt calm.

Twice he'd driven onto pull-offs to check if anyone was following him. Nothing suspicious.

His body stiffened when a flock of bikers, wearing blue scarves, roared alongside him on Goldfield Road. For a second he felt paralyzed. He thought the South Side Dragons had caught up with him.

As he slowed to let them pass, Esther, now standing on the passenger seat, emitted a low growl at a sweet-faced teenage girl clinging to a skuzzy biker. She threw her arms in the air and screeched as if on a roller coaster. In a few years this kid was going to be another Elizabeth, a biker groupie - if she wasn't already.

Soon he'd meet up with Ana, who wanted to conduct their business over the phone. He refused. He wanted to see her reaction when he confronted her.

Pulling into Sanctuary Plaza he noticed the parking lot was nearly deserted. He stopped near the coffee shop, facing the entrance, letting his motor run. If a car entered the plaza, he'd spot it. He drummed his fingers on the dashboard, time ticking slowly. No cars drove into the plaza. Feeling safe, he leashed Esther and they walked to the Dorothea Doberman Sanctuary.

The leather smells were still there, but no Doberman puppy jumped on him. Instead of a receptionist behind the counter, Ana stood there.

She had applied coloring to her eyelids and cheeks and her hair flowed like a graceful wave, befitting a seductress. He wasn't going to succumb to temptation again.

She placed a sign on the counter, which read: Please Wait. Adoption in Progress. Will Be With You Soon. She waved for him to follow her behind the counter and through an office door.

As she offered him a cup of coffee, she exclaimed, "You brought me the test Doberman." When he shook his head, she let out a short disappointing sigh and sat behind an oversized oak desk as if she were a CEO.

Esther stood at his side, his body pressed tight against Mordecai's thigh. His stare focused on Ana, never once did his gaze waver. He moved two feet in front of Mordecai, looking ready for action. Esther must sense Mordecai's mistrust of Ana.

Mordecai moved his chair back from the desk and sat. He didn't want to give the impression he was a flunky waiting for orders. He was signaling this wasn't a friendly meeting.

She sighed. "Why the meeting? I have a business appointment in Phoenix." Her tone was dismissive.

"Let me tell you what you got for five thousand: the answer to what Sight and Kill is."

She shrugged.

He related how a lowly dog trainer for the Army read a psych journal which described how an electrode, when implanted in a spot deep in the rat's subcortical brain and then buzzed (that is, stimulated), could give the world's greatest high, better than food, sex and morphine. The rodent would rather starve to death than miss the buzz. "Like the rats, the Dobermans Sam Houston trained had the hot spot, too. That would allow him to turn the Dobermans into attack dogs and give him absolute control over them. Dogs of war were literally true," Mordecai said.

He noticed her eyes fluttered a few times as if she was about to fall asleep. She peeked at her watch.

"That's the secret," she said, her eyebrows rising. "Amazing." She started to stand. When he continued to speak, she collapsed back down.

"I had to read a damn journal article three times before it became clear how Sight and Kill worked. You're lucky you hired a guy who went to college. The average detective can't get beyond 'Dick and Jane'."

"I knew you were smart enough to handle the job." She stifled a yawn.

He began to tell her about the remote control device when she interrupted. "I'm satisfied you did great uncover work, but I've an appointment with a Pharmaceutical Consortium that's interested in sponsoring the Dorothea Doberman Sanctuary." She straightened her dress.

It was obvious she already knew what he told her and would tell her. She didn't hire him to be a detective. She hired him to be a fall guy. "Maybe I should send you a written report."

She said. "There's still the site visit."

"I'm resigning."

Her eyes shuttered twice like a camera. "Haven't I done right by you?"

He stared hard. "You cut off my balls and served them to me for breakfast."

"No," she screeched.

He paused to gather his breath. "You met Russell Parker at an animal fund raiser where rich folk boast how they help the unfortunate."

"It's called the annual Animal Protection League charity ball. And of course I know him. I told you I did. We're both on the Board." She finished with a triumphant grin.

"Parker tells you about this wild man, Mordecai Glass."

Her grin faded. "I wanted a man with guts. What's wrong with that?"

"You balloon my ego with money until I think I'm the top of the line. Money is no object for you. Twenty G's, a hundred G's - your promise is a bad check. You thought I was the perfect patsy."

She slammed her palm against the table. "You're talking crazy."

Esther jumped to his feet, his fur bristled. When Ana froze, the Dobie settled to a crouch.

"You expect I'll be killed. That wipes out the debt. The murder investigation shatters ARC and terminates Sight and Kill. It's a perfect plan, costs you nothing."

"How dare you?" She picked up her coffee cup with a slight tremor. "Russell is an asshole. I saw the truth - you stood up for the pizza-delivery boy, so I thought you would also fight for tortured dogs."

"You didn't warn me about Hans." A few drops of saliva exploded from his mouth. "You only care about the Dobermans and destroying the ARC. How about my welfare - did that matter?"

Her lips trembled. "I never wanted you hurt."

"You wanted me to risk my life for a lousy twenty thousand. I can blow up ARC, but it's going to cost not five thousand, but another 20G's up front."

Her voice boomed. "Everything is mortgaged: hotel, plaza."

"I don't give a shit where you get the money, so don't screw with me."

"Don't you see the empty stores?" Ana whined, tears making a rivulet in her rouge.

For a moment, he was stymied. How could he squeeze money out of a crying woman? He took a sip of his coffee. "Nothing for nothing."

Her shoulders slumped. "Okay." She wiped her tears. "A Pharmaceutical Consortium wants to buy my share of ARC." She looked at her watch. "I'm meeting with my lawyer to discuss it. When I close the deal, I'll have the money to pay you and then you can destroy ARC a thousand times."

"Why did you lie to me about your name, saying your mother named you after a Doberman?"

"She named me after a Mexican General. She just had to get in another jab at Sam Houston. They're both gone now."

"What about your brother?"

"I don't have a brother," she spit out the words.

"So it's all money to you."

"Alright. It's all money. And I will be able to pay you lots of money when this is over."

"No, it isn't good enough," he insisted. "General Jensen arrives in just days and then they'll be hunting for Esther."

She stared at Esther. "You're not thinking of letting the ARC have the Dobie because I can't pay you immediately." She balled her fist.

"A sob doesn't cut it."

Her face brightened. "If you do it before my deal closes, the consortium will renege and Lennie will tell the police you and that Indian were in the hills when Hans went missing."

"So was Lennie. And besides, no corpse has been discovered."

"Can't you do something to postpone the test a week or two?"

He shook his head. "A shipment of ten Dobermans is due soon and when that happens, this Dobie is just another test animal."

Her mouth quivered. "Please don't."

Maybe he was a Dog Hugger, maybe not, but whatever he was, there was no way he'd hand over Esther to Ana or ARC. "So long, Ana."

When he reached the door, she said, "Wait. I can offer you another ten thousand."

"Twenty up front," he insisted.

"But my lawyer," she poured herself more coffee, "says we can get double the offer if we hold out. Then I can give you fifty thousand."

"I trust cash."

"You would really bomb ARC?"

"The best bomb is where Hans' corpse is hidden. An anonymous call to the police, just before General Jensen's plane lands in Phoenix and the cops will be crawling all over ARC. Maybe a call to a reporter I know. Jensen will deny he ever heard of the place. The Army contract goes up in smoke."

"You murdered Hans?"

He grinned. Sometimes you're blamed for something you didn't do and you complain to high heaven you didn't do it. Murdering Hans wasn't one of those things. "Forty thousand up front," he said without hesitation. "Remember, you're hiring my reputation."

She sighed. "That's outrageous. They'll drill holes in your dog's skull."

"Okay, twenty thousand up front," he said.

She nodded. "I really don't have it. You've got to wait."

Mordecai reached into his pocket and pulled out the earring. "I'll just hang onto this until I see the cash."

Ana caught her breath, but said nothing.

He was no longer a patsy.

FIFTY

Damn, he was in the desert, not his favorite spot after sunset. Soon the rays of sunlight would weaken and disappear. When the sun descended behind the small hills, he could lose his way in the darkness, walking in circles, surrounded by scorpions, Devil's Claw, coyotes, killer Dobermans and deadly humans.

Now in the fading light his gaze swept over the balding desert. He glanced at a plant with a twisted stem like braided twine, resembling an alien creature about to stalk some unwary prey. He took a few steps, his steel-toed boots rubbing his toes. He bent over to loosen his laces. Crawling up the boot tip was a black creature, its tail curled. A scorpion. He jerked back his hand.

Pulling his pruning shears from his tool belt, he gently pushed it away, afraid he might anger it. When it raised its tail to strike, he batted it off his boot. He shook his head. He yearned for green grass and loafers. Only a scorpion and a cowboy could love this God forsaken land.

He looked down at Esther. "Travis warned me not to walk you beyond where you can see ARC's lights. There're coyotes and stray mountain lions out there. Travis might have said that to keep you out of danger or to stop me from marching you off ARC land. Well, you're in this investigation, even though you didn't volunteer." He rubbed Esther's back who wagged his tail and pushed against him.

Mordecai glimpsed a shadow rustling in the darkness - a coyote? Esther slid from his side and planted himself in front. His ears pulled back and his tail lowered. His head thrust forward and his body taut, ready to explode into action. The coyote moved to Mordecai's right and Esther stepped to the right, blocking the coyote if it attacked. The coyote slinked off. Mordecai petted the dog while saying, "You got balls. You're a mensch."

He glanced around to make sure the coyote didn't have any dinner companions. Off to his right, a security cart was raising a cloud of dirt. He was pretty sure he'd gone unnoticed by the guard.

Walking farther, he made out in the dim moonlight seven or eight stationary security carts. He could tell by the narrow separation of their headlights they were off in the distance. Suddenly the carts crisscrossed each other, their lights slowly sweeping a wide area near the highway, where the Dog Huggers had previously launched their invasion. Shit, the carts began to crisscross an adjacent area. He had to haul ass before they were spotted.

Esther at his side matched his quick pace. He scurried without looking back, a man without an ulterior motive, except to exercise his dog. The boots were rubbing his toes. There was no need to break them in, because he was going to leave them in Shakespeare. He promised himself once he left he'd never wear work boots again.

They scurried uphill, sweat dripping from his brow and Esther panting heavily. He unhooked a small canteen, unscrewed its cap and poured water into a tin cup attached to the canteen bottom and offered the Doberman a drink. Esther lapped up the water, his tongue flicking as quickly as a frog catching a fly.

He picked up the cup and saw a few drops remained. His throat was parched. It was his turn. He refilled the cup and tipped over the canteen. It was empty. Esther stared with sad eyes. He shoved the dog away with his foot and raised the water to his lips but hesitated. The Dobie's panting grew more rapid. He was an asshole to treat a friend so badly, who took the same risks as he did. "Here," he mumbled and lowered the cup.

When Esther finished drinking, Mordecai looked at the remaining water. There was a discolored liquid floating on it. It must be disgusting dog spit. He could get a dog disease. Had he become a chicken-shit afraid of a little spit?

He took a swallow of water into his mouth and held it a few seconds; then gulped down the rest. If he got sick, he'd see a vet.

The terrain was flat, and he quickly recognized the path he'd taken with Chief. He spotted the gully paralleling the path and remembered passing the outhouse. He spotted the clearing in front of the cave.

The worst was over. He tickled the dog under its chin. "You're gonna be free of ARC soon."

He studied the mesquite, the camouflage that Chief used to hide the cave entrance. It looked undisturbed.

He cleared away the covering carefully, cutting long branches into small pieces with his pruning shears, so the thorns didn't puncture his gloves or catch his clothing. As he pulled away the mesquite, Esther remained calm as he sniffed the immediate area - no sign of danger.

Off in the distance, he heard the howling of coyotes, and Esther began to whirl in circles. Esther's presence, he was sure, would keep away these predators. Abruptly, the Dobie stopped whirling, facing north, his body rigid, his cropped ears erect ready to detect any footsteps, any breaking twigs, any coyote sneaking up on them, any noise breaking the low hum of the desert.

As he started to step into the cave, Mordecai pulled on the leash but Esther refused to move. After a few tugs he realized Esther's instinct to protect him had kicked in. While they were in the cave, they were trapped, prey to a sneak attack. Esther wasn't stupid.

He unfastened the leash, wondering if Esther would be spooked and run off. He doubted the dog would abandon him.

After putting on his work gloves and stepping into the cave, he snapped on a mini Mag Lite that knifed through the darkness. He flicked the narrow beam across the ground, capturing piles of what? His jaw dropped. "My God," he uttered. There were more bones than before. There were leg bones, ribs, skulls and some he didn't recognize. What the hell was going on?

He knew this was a burial chamber. The odor of decay, of death filled his nostrils. His stomach churned. Breathing rapidly, he felt dizzy.

He crouched to steady himself, breathing through his mouth to keep out the smell, as he wondered what poisonous bugs floated in the air. Damn, he was a detective, not a hypochondriac.

His dizziness fading, Mordecai stood and slowly walked over to a pile of bones. He'd need both hands to quickly do the job of sorting through them. He held the Mag Lite in his mouth, the metallic taste coating his tongue while forcing him to breathe through his nose. They were all skeletons of Dobermans. The ARC was dumping more failed experiments. Focusing the light he saw the tear-bites on the ribs, where animals had ripped away the flesh. He had no interest in dead dogs. His heart accelerated when he realized these carnivores might return and he might be in their dining area. Why worry? He had Esther to protect him.

To be thorough, in his mind he divided the cave into four quadrants and picked up random bones in each section and meticulously examined them, except for rotting corpses with crawling vermin. After a half hour, he found no human bones. Where was Hans? Maybe he was in the wrong cave. No, this, he was sure, was the right cave.

Exhausted he started to leave. Near the entrance, he spotted two parallel drag marks. Inside the drag marks were shoe prints pointing outside. Someone had dragged a stretcher out of the cave. Where was the body? He shrugged. He was sure he'd find the corpse in the cave. Well, he was wrong. The missing corpse had screwed up his plan. What could he tell the police? "Gee, officer, there was a corpse in the cave and now the body vanished." The cops would tell him he could be arrested for the crank call and hang up. Without a body, how could he bring ARC to its knees and save Esther and the other Dobermans who were arriving soon.

Outside, Esther bounded in the dim light to greet him.

"Don't worry, we'll find the body." As he continued to explain his new plan to the dog, an ironic thought hit him, leading to a smile. His only confidants were his dead mother and a dog - maybe the only two who listened to him.

FIFTY ONE

Mordecai froze in his tracks. Something strange was happening. Initially, he saw six pair of headlights in a semicircle formation, moving slowly. The guards were searching for him and Esther. Then the headlights of the two outside carts went dark. After a minute, the lights of the two darkened carts turned back on. They must have sped wide and ahead of the other carts. He heard someone yell, "Squeeze the Dog Huggers." A chorus of voices replied, "Bust them."

The patrol sped up, heading toward him and Esther. If the guards caught him it would raise suspicion about what he was up to.

He began to jog, with Esther at his side, along the path in the cold desert air. His breathing was rapid and he felt out of shape. When he'd boxed in the Golden Gloves, he'd trained by running 10 miles in Forest Park – never breathing hard. When he got back to Clayton, for damn sure, he was heading straight to the gym.

They passed the outhouse on the right and were on the path that leads to his ARC lodging. With the security patrol nearby he couldn't use his flashlight and the dim moonlight hardly provided enough illumination to make sure he didn't wander off his route.

Esther began to limp and then halted and held his right paw off the ground. Mordecai lifted Esther's front paw and dragged the Dobie behind a shrub lowering him to the ground. Mordecai crouched with his legs tucked under his rump and rested the dog's head on his lap. In the feint moon light, he saw a spiny cactus, the size and the shape of a cocktail tomato, embedded in the dog's pad. Esther whimpered as he pulled out the needle-pointed spines.

During the extraction, Mordecai bit his lip when a few cactus slivers pierced his skin, some breaking off in the finger tips of his right hand. Although the splinters were stinging like a paper cut, he checked Esther's pad to make sure he hadn't missed any spines. Finding none, he rubbed the Doberman's leg to soothe the dog. Esther swiveled his head and licked his hand.

He tried to remove the slivers from his fingers, but discovered they were too small, barely protruding above his flesh, to pull out with his left hand. Raising his fingers to his mouth, he used his teeth as a tweezer to extract the spines. While removing the slivers, he prayed he didn't swallow one. As he finished he spat, hoping they'd all been expelled.

The lights of the carts were coming closer. He was sure the head lights were unable to pick out the black-and-tan Doberman in the dark, but he wasn't so sure about his white skin. He grabbed a handful of dirt and rubbed it over his face.

The carts stopped fifty feet away, short of the path and only one cart rolled forward. The driver stood and faced the guard. It was Sam Watkins. "In the next few days," Thumper shouted, "the slimy Dog Huggers will try to blow up General Jensen's visit. Our informant tells us there'll be about fifty invaders and we'll be about eight defenders. How do we stop them?"

"Discipline," the guards shouted.

"When we attack the protesters," Watkins continued, "our shock sticks should be held high and our yells should be loud."

Mordecai saw the guards raise their electric prods high and scream.

"That will scare the piss out of them," Thumper said. "We've only days to prepare for the General."

Mordecai could hear the smugness in his voice.

Watkins' cart began to roll down the path and the guards followed, parading in a tight formation with their shock sticks held high.

When the carts faded in the dim moonlight, Mordecai sighed, his anxiety dissipating, but his sense of relief didn't last. Thumper wasn't a petty hustler. He was a formidable military leader, capable of capturing Esther.

Time was running out, with General Jack Jensen about to arrive for the test trial. He looked at Esther trotting next to him. If this Dobie was captured, he'd never forgive himself.

FIFTY TWO

The smell of the beer and cooking oil filled the hallway. The narrow wooden steps creaked as Mordecai and Esther climbed to Chief's apartment over the bar. The cook, now tending bar, told him Chief was upstairs resting.

Standing before the scarred door, he reminded himself that he had to be careful what he told Chief. The Indian's prosperity was tied to ARC. He wanted Chief to tell him where Hans was most likely buried. To do that, he had to invent a story about his interest in Hans' corpse without making Chief suspicious of his motive.

He knocked on the scarred door and a deep voice said, "Enter." Chief rested in a recliner, his massive arms swamping the armrests and his naked feet on a hassock.

Esther crouched on the wooden floor, his dark eyes focused on Chief.

Chief opened his eyes wide, obviously wide-awake now, and gestured toward the dog. "You took my advice. The dog is your protector."

Mordecai looked around the apartment. On the wall were hung arrows, tomahawks and spears. The eagle feathers of a war bonnet on a stand glistened even in the dim light. Scattered around the large room were Indian baskets and pots. "You collect Apache art," Mordecai said, surprise in his voice.

"No. The Apache are warriors, not artists."

Mordecai nodded. "You have enough weapons to attack an Army fort."

Chief didn't laugh. "I was hoping to see you."

"Why?"

"To say goodbye." He leaned forward and the hassock retracted into the recliner. "You're leaving town."

"Is that a subtle warning?" Mordecai asked. "I've heard it before."

"There's a rumor you pissed off some people."

"It's a talent I have."

"You haven't been around lately," Chief said

Tired of banter, Mordecai said, "The corpse is missing."

Chief shrugged. "Why do you care? Hans is dead."

"I don't have a clue who the killer is. Whether this guy wants to kill Esther, too? Examining the body might tell me something." He paused and added for emphasis, "To keep Esther safe." He gazed at the linoleum floor, dropped his jaw, to appear anxious about the dog.

"Perhaps Hans was carried off by a mountain lion," said the Indian.

"I doubt it unless the mountain lion removed the bushes from the cave entrance and, after dragging off the corpse, replaced them like they were before." He stared hard. "Who did you tell?"

Chief grinned, "Christ, you sound like a Dog Hugger, protecting your precious dog, the way you're quizzing me."

"Dog Hugger! Are you out of your mind?" He ran his hand across the Dobie's back. "This puppy is worth forty thousand dollars." He lowered his voice. "That's what Travis is going to pay me if I deliver the dog for the field trial."

"What's my share for helping you?"

"Always the money with you," Mordecai said.

Chief expanded his arms wide like a bird in flight, rolled back his head and grunted. "Exactly what do you want?" he asked in a harsh tone.

Mordecai slumped onto a squeaky wooden chair and exhaled loudly. "You watch my back."

His lips twisted into a sneer. "You can't figure where the body could be hidden, you ain't much of a detective." Chief smiled. "I can't stop someone from putting a slug in your skull. Half the town would gladly do it to save ARC. I hate to see that happen. So why don't you leave before you're killed?"

"Ten thousand for being my partner."

"Not enough money," Chief said, "to risk my life."

"You, afraid? I can't believe it." The son of a bitch wasn't going to tell him where Hans might be buried.

Chief walked over to a crouching Esther. Staring at the dog, he asked Mordecai, "Is he friendly because soon he's going to be an orphan?"

"You worry too much." He exhaled loudly. "I ain't leaving town."

Grinning, Chief petted Esther on his head. "Then you have to make the killer disappear."

"Don't be crazy. I ain't killing anybody." He paused to gather his thoughts and wondered if he really could kill someone. Maybe if they were after him. Or after Esther. Definitely for Esther.

"Sight and Kill is our pot of gold." He came back to reality. "As long as we have the corpse, ARC can't mess with us."

"But you said the body is missing."

"Yeh. That's why I have to find it. Then we can say to Travis, 'Loose lips can tell the police or the free Phoenix newspaper rag where Hans is buried.' "

"That's extortion."

Mordecai grinned. "Of course. Would you expect less of me?"

"What's my share?" He stopped slouching in his chair and sat ramrod straight.

"Twenty thousand, half of my bonus."

Chief said, "I ain't going into the woods. ARC could shoot me and dump me into a mining pit. Nobody in Shakespeare would care what happens to an Apache and an out-of-town White Man."

"Don't worry, you just keep Esther safe for the next few days."

Chief nodded. "The money seems good. What are you goin' to do?"

"Extort more money."

FIFTY THREE

Continuing to search for Hans' body was pushing his luck, especially with Watkins and his goons patrolling the woods. If Mordecai didn't discover the corpse soon, he was gonna need a new radical plan.

He hid behind the dumpster on an asphalt parking lot. His only company was the humming of lonely, late night vehicles on the city highway. It was, in realty, no more than a two-lane road through Shakespeare. Peeking around the dumpster, he scanned the path across the highway. It looked safe.

The descending darkness added concealment to his camouflage of black pants, black shirt and black leather jacket. He slipped on a black ski mask and hustled across the road. He began to track the route he and Chief had taken the night they stumbled across Hans' corpse. After hiking about a half-mile, he came to a small dirt area, where they had parked. Using his pen light, he found no evidence of recent tire marks. So far, he was on the right path. Still, the desert darkness made him uneasy. He had to avoid stepping on a scorpion whose sting could turn his leg into a bursting red balloon or brushing against the thorns of the mesquites or those of the Devil's Claw. These plants were capable of hooking deeply into his skin. Adding to the risk, a misstep could send him tumbling sixty feet into an abandoned mining pit. Worse, running into the ARC goons could lead to being shot.

The buzz of insects erupted as he walked parallel to the gully. He inhaled the pungent plant odor that wafted through the dry air. After ten minutes plodding in the sandy soil, he began to pant. Off to the left, he was relieved to see the ghostly outline of the outhouse. That meant the cave was nearby.

When the thick clouds drifted away, the moonlight reappeared. He halted. Just in case he was spotted, the goons would think he was a shrub. When it darkened again, he stood and continued toward the cave. In less than five minutes he reached the mesquite guarding the entrance.

He spotted the stretcher marks and followed them for about fifty feet when they petered out. Shaking his head, he had to guess which way the stretcher was pulled.

He heard a pop as the nearby earth erupted. He whirled and hurled himself to the ground. "Shit," he uttered and shoved his fist into his mouth to keep himself from further cursing. The shooter must have seen the feint outline of his moving black clothing.

At the top of the nearby hill was a pair of headlights and then the shooter's cart began to barrel down the slope, followed by a formation of patrol carts. The lead cart braked, turned around and stopped. The shooter stepped out of his cart and limped back toward the formation. It was Thumper, whose voice blasted forth like a drill sergeant. "Men, you're not civilians, you're ARC military."

On his belly, Mordecai studied the flat, wide expanse beyond the outhouse, unbroken by trees, houses or city lights. His stomach knotted. Outrunning the patrol on this terrain was futile. What the hell could he do? He could hide. Where? The shrubs - too small to conceal him. The only chance - the outhouse.

He wiggled forward with his nose almost touching the ground, inhaling dirt. Whenever the clouds slid away from the face of the moon, he halted, spitting out dirt and hearing the guards' mumbling while they examined the nearby bushes.

When the clouds obscured the moonlight, he ran to the side of the outhouse, pressing against the solid stone wall. He caught his breath. The outhouse must have a hiding place. When the cloud cover stalled, he said a quick prayer, took a deep breath and scurried to the front door. The top half of the door was unhinged and he opened it slowly, with each squeak making his heart jump. He made sure the door didn't fall off. When the opening was wide enough, he wiggled through and left the door open. Closing it would attract attention. Once inside, he eyed the logged ceiling, spotting three vents on the wall, just big enough for a snake to crawl through. His only concealment was a toilet in the far corner.

Headlight beams knifed between the wooden door planks, starling Mordecai. Peering through these gaps, he watched a diminutive woman dressed in Army fatigues exit the cart. It was Mai, waving a small pistol. "We're gonna kill the scumbag," she shouted in a manic voice and shot her pistol into the air.

Watkins lectured the guards. "Capture the saboteur. If it's necessary to shoot, shoot to kill."

The threats narrowed Mordecai's options. He could surrender to a guard who might not shoot him in cold blood. He could bargain Esther's whereabouts for his life. He'd never forgive himself. Or he could hide in the toilet.

Mai continued toward the outhouse.

Well, here goes nothing, Mordecai thought. He raced to the far corner and pulled up the wooden seat. He sat on the metal rim, his feet dangling inside the hole. Realizing the shaft was a straight drop downward, he squeezed his legs and waist into the hole. Mordecai hunched his shoulders, closed his eyes and lowered his arms against his side. He fell swiftly into the muck below, dropping his tool belt. Someone was striding toward the toilet.

A flashlight beam played over the room. "No one here. Just a toilet," Mai yelled.

Thumper replied, "Check every inch."

The muck splashed over his face. His feet hit bottom. The thick surface, making a soft plop, reached his chin.

She was standing over the toilet. He ducked into the muck. A light beam shot by his face. What an awful place to die, a shit pit.

"Ain't here," she shouted and shuffled off.

Muck was the perfect camouflage, thank God. Spitting to get rid of the awful taste didn't help much. The smell was turning his stomach and burning his nose, but it was too dangerous to leave yet. They could still be out there.

He shuffled his feet across the concrete floor of the septic tank, hoping to kick his tool belt. He wasn't going to duck under the muck to find it. He had no luck in the front half of the pit. He changed his attention to the rear half. After a few steps, he kicked something that seemed bigger than a tool belt. He rammed his foot under it and lifted it. It was too heavy to rise to the surface on its own. He bent over and grabbed the unknown object.

Turning his face to the side, his ear brushing the muck, he lifted the object waist-high with his foot and pulled it to the surface. It was a body. He gasped. A bloated face missing one eye and little bugs crawling from its nose. It was Hans. He had the ARC by the balls with one call to the police and say bye, bye to this butcher shop. He felt like shouting in victory.

Instead, he was about to puke. He let the body sink to the bottom and strode over to the shaft and raised his arms. His fingers were about five inches from the seat. He bent his leg until the muck touched his chin. He jumped – still short about three inches.

He prayed God would help him. He pushed away an island of feces, closed his eyes tight and took a deep breath. He felt the muck tangle in his hair and squatted, his backside almost touching the concrete floor. He exploded with both legs.

Breaking the surface, he felt the metal seat. Panting, he gripped the edge under the seat. The seat itself was too narrow for him to crawl through so he pushed it up. It fell back on his fingers - stinging. He muffled his curse, fearing Mai and Thumper might be just outside the door. He shoved the seat upward slowly. It wobbled but didn't fall. Three deep breaths and he pulled himself up and through. Stumbling outside, he gasped for fresh air and slumped against the stone wall. He threw up.

FIFTY FOUR

It took Mordecai two hours to trudge from the outhouse to his Chevy parked behind the dumpster. Weary, his sludge-soaked camouflage outfit was like lugging an extra twenty pounds. He wiped his sludge covered hands on the passenger seat carpet, yanked it out and tossed it into the desert. He took off any outer clothing he could and threw it into the dumpster. He started the car and rolled slowly forward. With his headlights off, he braked only when he got to the edge of the dirt lot, just in case the ARC goons were still searching for the intruder.

He watched two long-haul trucks rumble by. No danger there. Turning on his headlights he drove to the Sanctuary Hotel and parked the rental in the darkest part of the lot. He entered through the back door and snuck up the back stairwell. He took off his boots, but his socks still left wet spots on the stone stairs.

Entering the suite, he rushed to the bathroom and immediately undressed. He flung his outfit into a plastic laundry bag, muttering, "Goodbye, Shakespeare." He turned the shower to hot to melt away the sludge. The cascading water was music to his ears. He scrubbed himself, again and again, abrading his skin. He rinsed his mouth with tooth paste. He turned off the shower when the draining water went from dark sludge to clear. He doubted a girl would kiss him for a long time. He dressed quickly, putting on his St. Louis clothing, no longer afraid to wear his tasseled loafers. The assignment would be over soon - not soon enough.

It was time to retrieve Esther.

A banging on the door startled him. He peered through the peephole. Mordecai let out a deep breath and opened the door. Mike Flynn was wearing both hearing aids and held a SK gun in his bony hand.

"What's that smell?" Flynn asked, entering and looking at the laundry bag.

"Smells that bad?"

"Yup."

"I fell in a shit pile," which Flynn seemed to accept.

"Travis is having a fit over the site visit." Flynn shook his head. "Sam Houston had the Army in his pocket and now the Army has their hand in Travis' pocket."

"Even General Jensen?" Mordecai questioned.

Flynn rolled his eyes. "What do you think?"

Mordecai shrugged.

"Travis picked you to run the test, but Jensen anointed Sam Watkins to be the dog handler. Thumper is a nasty piece of work. I wouldn't go within ten feet of him. Travis wants you to make sure the SK works for 119 and train Watkins on how to use it."

"How about you do the training?"

He shook his head and handed Mordecai the SK gun. Now he had a second SK gun.

"Why can't Nguyen do it?"

"They put him in the loony bin. The crazy bastard might have the Doberman attack General Jensen. He's worse than all of them. He uses the dogs to do his dirty work."

"What are you talking about?" Mordecai asked.

"Never mind. I said too much already."

"Who did the dogs attack?"

"You know who they attacked. Don't keep asking me. I'm not supposed to say. I could get attacked next."

"Hans," Mordecai said and watched Flynn turn away. That's gotta be it. Nguyen sicced the dogs on Hans. But somebody else gave the order and dumped the body. Probably Watkins. Mordecai sighed. It just didn't matter anymore. When he called it in, the police could sort it out.

***

Mordecai had to act fast before Watkins realized the born-again invading Dog Hugger was him. He banged on the wooden door and then pressed his ear against the carving of an Apache warrior. Esther began to bark and Chief yelled in a sleepy voice to shut up. He heard Esther whimpering and scratching at the door.

Gigantic feet thumped across the wooden planks. When the door opened, he looked up at Chief, who rubbed his eyes, saying, "What are you doing here? It's three o'clock, Pale Face."

"I miss Esther," Mordecai said. He stiffened, ready for the Apache to explode; instead, his expression was somewhere between a grin and a frown.

Esther pushed past the Indian and leaped against his chest and licked his hand. Mordecai bent over and kissed the Dobie on the forehead.

Chief said, "I thought you hated dogs."

"Esther isn't a dog. He's my best friend."

The Indian stared down at him. "Is it raining?"

"No." Mordecai replied.

"Really! At three o'clock in the morning, you wash your hair." He backed into the apartment and slumped into his recliner. "What are you up to? You're gonna flee with the dog?"

"Not me," Mordecai replied, settling on the couch. Esther jumped up next to him, resting his head on Mordecai's lap.

He laughed. "So relax." After clearing his throat, he continued, "Thumper is now the head of security. He set up road blocks manned by Fort Huachuca Army troops. The staff told me tracking devices are attached to any car whose driver's loyalty they have the slightest doubt about - like you. The only way to save the dog is to make Thumper disappear."

Mordecai's face contorted. "Kill him?"

The Indian nodded.

"Are you crazy?" He leaned back and closed his eyes. "He deserves to die." After a long pause, "but I'm no killer."

Chief said, "You sure? Anybody can kill if it's important enough."

Resting his head on the cushion, Mordecai sighed again. Chief was right.

The Apache said, "You're wearing fancy loafers again."

"I ain't trying to be a townie anymore." He pulled an Afghan off the back of the couch and covered himself and the Dobie. Silence fell over the room. After a while, he heard the Apache snoring gently. Mordecai settled back on the couch and tried to focus on a well-thought out plan, not exactly his style. When he had charged into the biker bar, the only person in danger had been himself. Tonight if he had been captured, Esther would have been sentenced to an implant.

As he descended into sleep, he knew there'd be no more charging into a biker bar ever again.

FIFTY FIVE

After making a partial payment to Chief, Mordecai drove from the Bank of America across Derringer Boulevard to the restaurant. The gravel made a crunching noise when he pulled into the parking lot of the Aperitif. He was looking forward to brunch. This meal might be his last until he could sneak off in the middle of the night to Sky Harbor Airport.

Mordecai looked at the Dobie's sad eyes. What kind of man sacrifices a loving creature for personal gain? If he talked to his mom, she'd figure a way out of his dilemma. He pulled her picture from his wallet and turned on the car radio which was at full blast. The music made his ears ring. Esther crawled into the back seat. He lowered the sound and stared at the photo, knowing what his mom would think. He inserted the picture back into the wallet. Could he do the unthinkable for a dog?

The dog jumped from the car and followed him through the wooden gate onto the patio. He spotted the lone diner, a woman with brownish hair fading to gray, who was holding a toy poodle on her lap. She eyed him suspiciously. He nodded at her; she hugged her poodle to her chest and looked away. He was too hungry to feel slighted.

A few minutes later the waiter, Henry, his face cheery, appeared and handed her a bill that she quickly paid. Henry watched her leave hurriedly through the screen door into the restaurant, and then approached Mordecai.

"Dogs aren't allowed except for you, Mr. Glass."

"How about her?"

"She's Slinger's wife. She adds a big tip to the ARC charge slip."

"I can top her."

Henry smiled. "Will your order be champagne, spinach and mushroom omelet with Swiss cheese, rye toast and coffee, no cream?"

"Henry, you have a good memory."

"And a special treat for your friend." Henry's step had a bounce as he hurried into the restaurant.

Mordecai yawned and stretched his arms wide to embrace the warmth. He was wearing a long-sleeved shirt, but it was comfortable enough to wear shorts, which, in March, would be a shivering mistake in St. Louis. Mordecai felt calm, his body still. He patted Esther's head as the dog stared back at him. "Maybe I should have ordered a special breakfast for you, too."

The door banged open and Watkins limped in. His wry-mouth smile radiated glee. As he headed to the table, Esther pulled his head off Mordecai's lap, stepped in front, blocking Thumper's path and crouched.

Watkins' smile disappeared. "Is your girlfriend dangerous?"

Mordecai stretched his leg under the table and pushed out a chair.

Watkins turned the chair around and sat with his legs spread wide over the cushion, his arms resting on the chair back, and smiled. He'd never seen Thumper smile. "What's with the happy face? Who died?"

"We hit pay dirt."

"That's news to me." Mordecai spoke loudly. He would have told him to piss off, but he was curious about pay dirt.

Thumper shushed him and gazed cautiously around the deserted patio. He whispered, "The test run is in the bag. An out-of-state breeder is bringing us a dozen Dobermans."

"So far, it doesn't sound like I'm part of 'we'."

Watkins ignored the challenge. "The Field Operation is a military plan that Slinger and I have come up with. General Jensen will be here day after tomorrow. It will all be over then."

"So it will be business as usual."

"Better than that – the Pharmaceutical Consortium will be here. Business will double. Money will double. On test day, Jensen will see Slinger implant an electrode straight into the hot spot. Partner, we're gonna to be rich. Big bucks for you, too."

"What happens if any of the Dobermans are duds?"

Watkins glanced at Esther. "The failures are dumped in a mining pit."

"Alive?" Mordecai queried.

"That's classified." Thumper looked gleeful. "Nothing is gonna stop me. I lost my toes following Sam Houston and the mutts around the jungle and having my Army career as a lousy lieutenant shuffled off to a dead-end civilian desk job in the Pentagon. Do you understand? I plan to collect."

Mordecai inhaled deeply. How could Watkins drop a beautiful animal like Esther down a pit to be crushed by the fall and die while convulsing, and be joyful about his cruelty?

"Nothing will go wrong." Watkins continued. "Slinger knows what he's doing. If any of the dogs are determined unfit for electrode implantation, the Pharmaceutical Consortium will use them for testing new drugs. It's a perfect set-up. Travis goes to New York and I am in charge." Watkins smile was huge.

Modecai's stomach felt queasy. How would he be able to walk away, leaving Watkins in charge?

Watkins leaned over the chair back. "Your orders are to show me how to operate the SK gun tomorrow at 17 hundred hours sharp. Second, you parade your mutt around Shakespeare. Third, you make sure your girlfriend isn't kidnapped."

"You're not my boss - yet."

"I'm the head of ARC security - Lieutenant Watkins. Remember that." He spoke with assurance.

"Lieu-ten-ant." Mordecai said loudly as three words and then gave a sloppy salute. "Did anyone tell you Sam Houston is dead?"

"If the Huggers disrupt the field trial, you'll think losing a few toes is nothing compared to what will happen to you. I killed a few Gooks in my time."

Mordecai grinned. "I ain't crying over your toes."

"Seventeen hundred hours sharp." Thumper stormed out of the restaurant.

"Bye Lieu-ten-ant," he yelled.

* * *

As Thumper disappeared through the patio door, Abbott, his white beard stained with red wine, strode over to the table. "I heard you provoking Watkins."

"I thought you were leaving town," Mordecai said.

Abbott shook his head. "Hans retired instead."

Henry entered, carrying a big tray, lowered it on a nearby table and quietly positioned his plates and drinking glass in front of Mordecai in an orderly array. Bending over, Henry placed a water bowl and a dog dish of cooked meat, which Mordecai couldn't identify, on the floor.

Henry asked, "Mr. Glass, what happened? The gentleman rushed out of here, almost knocking me over while I carried a loaded tray. My God, can you imagine the mess? I'd be cleaning up for hours? Not even an apology." He sighed.

Mordecai grinned. "I told him he'd have to pick up the check. Bring us champagne. I need a tranquillizer. The son of a bitch ruined my appetite." Mordecai pushed his plate away.

When Henry returned with the champagne and more treats for Esther, Abbott's face lit up like a Halloween pumpkin. After a big sip, Abbott ran his tongue over his lips. "Did you ask yourself why Watkins threatened you?"

"He did threaten to kill me - I guess."

"No guessing about it. He wasn't frightened of you. Yet everyone in town knows your reputation - the man who got rid of Hans."

Mordecai said, "Lieu-ten-ant Thumper doesn't believe the rumor."

"I like the way you called him Lieu-ten-ant Thumper." He elongated the syllables longer than Mordecai had. "It pissed him off."

"Say it again," Mordecai said.

"What should I repeat?"

"His nickname."

"Lieu-ten-ant Thumper."

The significance was obvious. He'd been mistaken, thinking "Lou" was a first name – it was a first syllable.

He had solved one more mystery; his uncle's advice would be to go back to St. Louis and forget the forty thousand dollars.

Abbott said, "I made a reservation for Watkins at Betty's B&B on Chestnut Hill, in case you want to make him disappear."

"That sounds like movie dialogue."

Esther, who had dipped her snout into the water bowl, pulled up her head and rested it on Abbott's leg.

Mordecai expected Abbott to move his chair away, exasperated by a wet spot on his pant leg. Instead, he stroked the dog's head, saying, "She's a beautiful animal. It'll be a shame to turn her into a zombie. Are you going to free her?"

"That would be putting my life on the line for a dog - insane."

Esther returned to his side, laying his chin on Mordecai's boot. "What happens if the Army contract isn't renewed?" Mordecai asked.

"ARC becomes a distant memory, and Sam Houston's dream is shattered."

Mordecai smiled. "I'd hate to see that happen."

FIFTY SIX

Sitting on the couch at the hotel, he stared at the two SK guns on the coffee table, wondering what to do with them after making the call. As soon as the police flooded ARC, the investigation would expose Sight and Kill as barbarous and Sam Houston's dream would be kaput and Mordecai would claim his twenty-thousand-dollar bonus from Ana.

"Esther, this is our moment." Mordecai pulled the Kleenex from his pocket and slowly stuffed one, two, then three in his mouth. He told Esther, "Free at last, free at last." He shook his head. His voice didn't sound muffled enough. He pushed another two into his mouth and gagged. He pulled out one. Four was enough.

He dialed, saying the number out loud.

A deep voice answered, "Shakespeare Police, Sergeant Duffy."

"I found a corpse."

"Speak clearly. I can hardly hear you."

Mordecai removed a Kleenex. "A dead body."

"Where?"

"The outhouse behind the ARC. In the shit hole."

Duffy laughed. "What were you doing in the shit hole?"

"I swear I looked down and saw a body."

Duffy cleared his throat. "The outhouse is on Tribal land. Call ARC security. It's their jurisdiction." He hung up.

Mordecai pounded the coffee table. "What now?" he yelled.

Wiggling on the couch, unable to relax, he grabbed Thumper's remote control transmitter, which, in reality, was a gun and the Doberman, its bullet. It was foolhardy, no crazy, to let Thumper have a weapon that could kill him, considering yesterday the bastard had threatened to kill him. He could disconnect the SK attack key. Not good enough. Slinger was going to implant Esther. And Watkins would take over. Something had to be done - Watkins could not take over ARC.

He knew what he had to do - sabotage Thumper's 119 SK gun. Then Mordecai's SK gun could orchestrate what 119 did in the cage.

He slid off the couch without disturbing Esther. In the bedroom, he found Mike Flynn's repair kit. Back on the couch, with the Dobie's head resting on his leg, he unscrewed the back cover of Thumper's gun with the tweezers. Colored wires were connected to their corresponding colored terminals. Which wires to disconnect or switch? The choice had to be something he could easily handle - and lethal.

The deception would only work if Watkins never suspected the dirty trick that his bite and crouch/freeze buttons were inoperative; also he must remain unaware that these two responses were controlled by Mordecai.

Finally, he pulled the blue 'bite' wire, the black crouch/freeze wire, and several others from the terminals.

But what if his scheme backfired? He'd end up a corpse on a slab. He tugged on Esther's collar, coaxing the dog to scoot closer. He wrapped his arms around the dog's neck and hugged the Dobie.

"If I screw up, you're a robot."

* * *

"It's seventeen hundred hours sharp," Mordecai said. Thumper, a cigarillo dangling from his lips and staring at Esther as he entered the dog compound, flicked the smoldering stub at the Doberman who darted away. "Keep that killer away from me."

Mordecai crushed the cigarette stub under his loafers. "I don't want the dog harmed before the site visit."

Sneering, Thumper asked. "Are you one of those animal crybabies, more worried about a mutt than national security? Put him into the Goddamn cage."

"Esther, he'll pay for this," Mordecai whispered, leading him into his old cage, the one nearest the door. Shoving his right hand into his coat pocket, he slid his finger gently over the taped bite key of his SK gun. He had spent most of the night learning to finger the gun while in his pocket.

The spotlight burnished the black-and-tan coat of Doberman 119 as Mordecai and Thumper entered the dog's cage. Mordecai felt the blood pulsating in his forehead, the same sensation he'd experienced when he had stepped into the boxing ring. Unlike the Golden Gloves, this was a fight to the death. One of them would be carried out in a body bag.

He spotted a bulge under Thumper's coat - surely a revolver. He handed Thumper the sabotaged 119 SK gun.

"How does the gismo work?" Thumper asked.

He explained in detail how the transmitter sent a signal to an implanted receiver that stimulated the brain's pleasure center. The lecture shoveled fact and fiction, but it seemed to convince Thumper that Mordecai was serious about the training.

"Who cares about all that technical crap?"

Mordecai touched each key, in turn, as he described its function. He explained that after each response, Thumper immediately needed to give an electrical reward, a little buzz in the brain or the dog would stop responding.

"Christ, you're more boring than a fucking college professor. You're putting me to sleep. No more background, no more history."

Turning away from Watkins, Mordecai smiled. Thumper was aggravated, but he wasn't suspicious. It was a good beginning for a lethal accident.

"Remember, if you go too fast, the receiver won't register the signal. So go slow, understand?"

"Enough bullshit."

"These dogs' fried brains make them killers," Mordecai said. "They can turn on you like that." He snapped his fingers. "I want you to be alive to show 119 to General Jensen."

Thumper grinned. He patted the bulge in his coat. "I got this to protect me, so don't get any ideas."

Mordecai looked at 119's sweet face with his blank eyes. He hated what ARC had done to this elegant animal. "Start with movement: side to side, forward and back, until you get the rhythm."

Thumper stared, eyes wide, at the swaying dog. "I'm making it dance," he said, unaware that Mordecai's SK gun was in control of Doberman 119.

Mordecai smiled, barely parting his lips. "The dog is dancing to your tune. You're a natural."

"I hit bite, nothing happened. What's wrong with this brain-damaged dog?" Thumper stared at 119 as if the dog could answer him.

Having missed Thumper's pushing the blue bite key on the SK gun, Mordecai stopped breathing for a second, afraid Thumper would discover his bite key was inoperative. "I told you the receiver is sensitive. Try again, but go slower." He tightly held his SK gun buried in his right coat pocket.

When Thumper punched the bite button, Mordecai pushed the taped attack key. The dog opened its mouth wide, flashed its canines and banged shut its jaw. The cracking noise of its teeth smashing against each other sent a shudder through Mordecai. Thank God, he was in control, not Thumper.

"Look at those teeth." Thumper's sour look disappeared. "They could tear a soldier to pieces in minutes." Thumper laughed. "We could have owned the jungle if we had a company of these dogs. Too bad we don't have a coyote to test the kill button. How 'bout a volunteer? How 'bout your mute?"

"Over my dead body. Not till I get my money."

"How about you being the victim?"

"Can I trust you not to have the dog attack me?" asked Mordecai.

Thumper chuckled. "I need you to show me what to do next."

"Hit the attack key, then the crouch/freeze key. The Dobie will crouch, even in the middle of an attack." Mordecai faced the black-and-tan, knowing the dog would maul the nearest person within three feet. He coaxed Thumper next to him, but they were too far away for the dog to attack them.

"We need to be closer."

"Not me. Just you." Watkins shoved Mordecai down in the dog's striking range and laughed. Watkins pushed the attack button, but Mordecai didn't, slowing the dog down. He crawled backwards rapidly.

"Shit," Thumper yelled. "The damn thing didn't work again."

Facing his enemy, Mordecai yelled back. "You were gonna let him maul me."

"Just a little," Thumper laughed again and pressed the key repeatedly.

This was it - kill or be killed. Mordecai touched the SK gun in his coat pocket, making sure his finger was on the taped attack key. The risk was high but there was no turning back from taking out Thumper.

Mordecai took two quick steps back from the Dobie and, now safe, pushed the attack key.

The Dobie's canines flashed like two ivory daggers. His teeth sunk into the right arm of Thumper, accompanied by a crunching sound. Screaming, Thumper tried to pull away, but Mordecai hit bite repeatedly, and the dog mangled Thumper's limb.

Mordecai pulled out his SK gun from his coat pocket to assure he'd hit the right key. He maneuvered the Dobie to attack Thumper's right leg, splintering it open.

Watkins tumbled to the ground and reached for his twenty-two pistol with his left hand.   The holster was positioned for a right hander which meant he had to twist the revolver around to pull the trigger with his left hand. He couldn't do it, and his right arm with exposed ligaments, tendons, and muscles looking like crimson string, was useless.

Thumper mumbled something that sounded like, "Help me."

"You dirty bastard," Mordecai yelled, "I'm gonna make sure you never hurt another dog."

Thumper's eyes rolled back in their sockets.

Mordecai manipulated the Doberman near the victim's throat and hit bite without hesitation.

The mangled body twitched and then became motionless.

.

FIFTY SEVEN

Two flies buzzed around the dripping blood, slivers of flesh hanging from Thumper's neck like meat on a butcher hook. Mordecai had to act fast to create a cover up. A guard checking on the dog compound too soon would smash his alibi.

Stooping, Mordecai unbuttoned Thumper's leather coat and pulled the twenty-two from his belt and unlatched the cylinder, seeing two chambers were empty. He was positive that night in the desert Thumper had been the one who shot at him. He shoved the hand gun into his waist band.

He watched five flies feasting on the thick blood and muttered, "Enjoy this piece of shit."

Pulling on a pair of latex gloves hidden in his back pocket, he picked up Thumper's sabotaged SK gun. He unscrewed the back panel and squeezed the loose wires onto their terminals with the tweezers. He was surprised that his hands were as steady as a surgeon's. He tested the transmitter - Doberman 119 danced to his pressing the SK key. Bending over, he carefully positioned the transmitter close to Thumper's right hand.

He searched Thumper's pockets for cash, keeping his face turned away from the disease-carrying flies. No money. Mordecai stepped toward 119, small reluctant steps, hesitated and took a few more. The dog's jaw was only three feet away. His legs trembling, Mordecai prayed this was the edge of the dog's bite range, minimizing the damage.

He hit the bite key. The dog lunged. Esther went crazy in his cage, barking and running back and forth. The pain was like a nose-bursting punch. He screamed and felt faint, sinking to his knees. For a few seconds, a dark cloud passed in front of his eyes. He wanted to close his eyes and rest his head on the hard earth.

As he inhaled deeply, his vision cleared. He whipped off his belt and tied it around his bleeding leg as tight as he could and knotted it, praying he didn't pass out. He had things to do to complete his plan.

He told Esther to be calm as he shuffled toward the fence, keeping as much weight on his right leg as was possible, praying his left didn't start to bleed profusely. At the fence he removed his gloves. Kneeling he untied the belt, splashed blood on his hands and the soles of his shoes, and retied his belt.

A minute later the door banged open and Dutch ran in. His sleeves were rolled up displaying a barbwire tattoo on his forearm. From across the compound he shouted, "What happened?"

"The dog went crazy."

Dutch hustled over to Watkins' dead body, then scowled at 119, and said, "What a mess." Before Mordecai could say anything else, Dutch drew his pistol and shot the dog.

Stunned, Mordecai yelled, "What the hell!"

"The dog's a killer," Dutch yelled back.

"And so are you," Mordecai mumbled. He had to get out of there. He hobbled toward Esther's cage, dragging his left foot, grimacing, and opened the gate to release the Doberman.

"Where are you going?"

"To the hospital."

"You can leave, but not the dog."

"What the hell are you talking about?" Mordecai's face felt red hot.

"Mr. Watkins told us, you can't take the dog. The dog belongs to ARC." He squared his broad shoulders.

"Travis made me responsible for him. I'm not to let this dog out of my sight." He could bleed to death while convincing this idiot.

Dutch shook his head. "I've got my orders. 143 has to be here for Sight and Kill."

"Yeah," Mordecai glared at Dutch." What do your orders say about a Doberman who just killed Lieutenant Watkins? And tried to kill me? Shoot him?"

With a scared expression on his face, Dutch looked first at Watkins and then 119. "Watkins is dead, 119 is dead," he mumbled. He looked up at Mordecai. "What will happen to all of us? Without Watkins, there is no Sight and Kill."

There was no reason to explain what would happen to this muscle-bound idiot. Mordecai knew that if he left, Esther would follow. He took a few steps.

"I'm going to the hospital and this Doberman is going with me."

"Stop," Dutch yelled. When Esther didn't, he said, "You ain't going anywhere." He pulled an electric prod from his security belt and shocked Esther who yelped and retreated.

Mordecai rushed toward Dutch, his nose inches from the guard's chest, inhaling his sweet after-shave-lotion. It was the right separation for a punch. "You do that to my dog again, I'll kick your ass."

Dutch's eyes widened, as if surprised that someone so short wasn't intimidated by him. He tightened his forearm muscle. The barbs of the tattoo spread further apart as he slapped the prod against his palm.

"Shorty, you're looking for trouble," he mumbled through barely moving lips. "If you don't step away. . ."

Mordecai hit him with a left hook, the blow landing just below the ear.

Dutch stumbled, looking more startled than hurt. He smiled. "You're just asking for it."

With a bad leg, he couldn't generate enough power to hurt the guard. He shouted, "Attack," but Esther just growled.

Mordecai swung. Dutch easily ducked the punch. In return, Mordecai received a shock on his leg. He cried out.

This was Esther's battle call. He charged, biting into the leg of the guard, who screamed and collapsed.

Picking up the prod, Mordecai shocked Dutch. "That is for my partner."

The guard curled up like a baby. "Please don't."

"One more thing, tell Travis I'm going to sue him. I'm friends with a badass lawyer."

Tossing away the prod, Mordecai turned and said, "Thanks, Esther, you saved my ass. Now it's time to get out of here."

FIFTY EIGHT

On the way to the hospital, Mordecai detoured onto a dirt pull-off and ran over his taped SK gun, smashing it to smithereens. Later he dropped his latex gloves into a medical pail in the ER cubicle.

As he lay on the exam table, a white cloud drifted across his closed eyes. The morphine was capturing his mind. Raising his head, he looked at his torn pants and the compression bandage. It had taken over fifty stitches to close the wound. He shook his head. This injury was a mishap, a risky one, but he knew from this day on, risk-taking was as much a part of him as breathing.

His cell phone beeped, telling him he had a message. He pulled it from his sweatshirt pouch, and retrieved the name of the caller. It was Uncle Julius. If Mordecai told him what happened, Uncle Julius would declare he was crazy. Mordecai knew he'd never be able to explain to his uncle why he did what he did, not after killing Thumper. He owned the killing, which was his alone, and which he held in secret like a silent prayer.

The ER physician parted the curtain, carrying a metal-covered chart. Peering at his handiwork, he uttered "Um, hum," nodding. "Tomorrow, you'll be ready to go home."

"Tomorrow." He sat up. "I'm ready now."

The doctor scratched his chin. "Just to be safe, one overnight."

"I'm okay."

"To make sure there're no infections, no allergic reactions, no leaks."

Mordecai slid off the exam table. "My dog's in the car."

"We'll have an aide take care of it."

"No good. Partners watch out for each other."

The doctor raised his eyebrows. "Who are you talking about?"

"I'm leaving. Just give me my pain script." He balanced on his right leg, his hand on the exam table.

Opening the chart, the doctor grinned as if he was a poker player who was sure he had the winning hand. "There's no prescription if you don't stay the night, and I'll guarantee you'll feel the pain."

"No way I'm staying, Doc."

Handing Mordecai a pen, he said, "You need to sign the 'Against Medical Advice' form."

"You sound like my Uncle Julius. I ain't listening to him, either."

***

Mordecai shuffled to the car and collapsed on the front seat. He looked at the Doberman in the passenger seat and smiled.

"It's time to go home, Esther. Uncle Julius has a big job waiting for us."

Made in the USA
San Bernardino, CA
15 September 2019